PREDATOR&PREY
JUDGE

By Gherbod Fleming

Author	Gherbod Fleming
Cover Artist	William O'Connor
Copy Editor	Melissa Thorpe
Graphic Artist	Pauline Benney
Cover Design	Pauline Benney
Art Director	Richard Thomas

Copyright ©2000 by White Wolf, Inc.
All rights reserved.

No part of this book may reproduced or transmitted in any form or by any means, electronic or mechanical — Including photocopy, recording, internet posting, electronic bulletin board — or any other information storage and retrieval system, except for the purpose of reviews, without permission of the publisher.

White wolf is committed to reducing waste in publishing. For this reason, we do not permit our covers to be "stripped" for returns, but instead require that the whole book be returned, allowing us to resell it.

All persons, places, and organizations in the book — except those clearly in the public domain — Are fictitious, and any resemblance that may seem to exist to actual persons, places, or organizations living, dead, or defunct is purely coincidental. The mention of or reference to any companies or products in these pages is not challenge to the trademarks or copyrights concerned.

White Wolf Publishing
735 Park North Boulevard, Suite 128
Clarkston, GA 30021
www.white-wolf.com

Part One: Adam   7

Part Two: Mr. and Mrs. Kilby   89

Part Three: The Lurker   223

PART ONE:
Adam

CHAPTER 1

The sprawling apartment complex was like a massive, decaying honeycomb, a crumbling hive of the less affluent. Burned-out streetlights stood sentry over tenants' rusting cars. Of the residents who did have jobs, most worked on the assembly line at Iron Rapids Manufacturing. Once, Douglas Sands would have thought that employees of an auto company drove newer automobiles, but now he knew better. The employees did get a good deal on new cars—and then promptly sold them out of town for a tidy profit. They needed the money more than a new vehicle. They favored older, cheaper cars. Instead of collision insurance, they paid rent or bought groceries, bought clothes for the children. That was why the streets of Iron Rapids were littered with abandoned, broken-down heaps of steel, vinyl, and rubber.

Parasites, Sands thought. Parasites living off corporate largesse. If they didn't start having babies before they were fifteen, or if they stayed married—even *got* married—when they did, or if they finished school, they might be able to support a family. *Nobody just hands it to you.* Nobody had ever handed anything to Douglas; he'd gotten where he was through hard work.

He wouldn't have been caught dead in this place if it weren't for Melanie. How many times had he urged her to move, even offered to pay her rent elsewhere? But she was determined to be independent. That was all fine and good in theory, but it aggravated Douglas that she wouldn't get out of this squalor.

The building next to Melanie's was currently vacant. Several months ago, a balcony had collapsed. A few people were injured or killed—Sands didn't remember all of the details. An inspection, apparently overdue, had followed shortly thereafter, and the entire structure condemned. Nothing had happened since—nothing except the tenants being kicked out to find room with relatives, or perhaps to rent some of the dilapidated shacks closer to the river. There was still a blue tarp nailed over the hole where a set of sliding glass doors had pulled away along with the falling balcony. The building's lower windows were boarded up, but vandals had tested their arms—and their trigger fingers—and shattered several of the higher windows. The complex had been the brainchild of the social engineers of the Great Society. Thirty years later, beset by crime and drugs and poverty, the housing project had been privatized—so now the inhabitants, as well as the facilities, foundered and decayed on their own, rather than at the expense of the public dole.

Why in hell does she stay here? Sands wondered.

Finally, he found a parking spot relatively close to a streetlight that actually worked. His shiny, latest-model vehicle stood out among the dented cars with their primer-colored panels. As he stepped out into the night, the grimy, packed snow crunched like small bones beneath his feet. Even wearing his overcoat, Sands felt out of place with his slacks and dress shoes visible. It was next to a miracle that he hadn't been mugged coming here, or had his car vandalized. Not yet, anyway. He glanced around, feeling much like a spotlighted deer beneath the lonely street lamp. A chill ran down the length of his spine; the tiny hairs on the back of his neck stood up. He pulled his overcoat more tightly together at the neck, tucked his scarf in more securely.

The parking lot was a treacherous glaze of ice, melted and refrozen snow compressed to a grey mass beneath countless tires. Sands' shoes were meant for the boardroom and afforded him no traction. He spread his gloved hands wide to help balance and shuffled across the glacial lot; he would have made it unscathed, had it not been for the car.

The headlights whipped around the curve of the parking lot, their path zigging and zagging. Grinding tires tried, and failed, to find purchase on the ice. The car slid toward the outside of the curve, compensated, fishtailed the other way. The engine was gunning, the tires spinning faster than the car was moving—which was still far too fast for the conditions. Sands wasn't sure if the driver saw him sliding unsteadily across the parking lot, but the car didn't slow. It hurtled toward him, a mass of steel, blinding lights, and pounding bass.

Sands moved more quickly and felt his precarious balance desert him. His feet slid from beneath him. He lurched, trying to stop the fall, and felt the familiar twinge in his back. He caught himself against an overflowing dumpster as the car roared past, spinning tires and skittering erratically across the ice.

He stayed there for several seconds, supporting himself against the dumpster, not wanting to lower himself to the ground and dirty the knees of his slacks, but unable to lift himself because of the pain radiating from his lower back. The green metal of the dumpster was cold through his driving gloves. The stench of uncollected garbage, along with the pain in his back, began to churn his stomach.

Trying not to breathe, Sands gripped the metal tightly. He pulled slowly, sliding his feet beneath him. Excruciating barbs of pain shot up his back and down his leg as he re-established his balance. Supporting his weight again, he couldn't help releasing his breath, and when he breathed in again, the greasy, permeating odor of the garbage nearly overwhelmed him. He raised his hand to cover his mouth and nose, only to realize that his gloves were covered with some tacky substance from the side of the dumpster. He stared at his open palms for a moment, then ripped off the gloves and threw them at the dumpster in disgust. More jolts of pain shot through him with the sharp movement. The gloves landed amidst the bags and boxes and tattered mattresses that formed a cascading abutment beneath the opening of the over-filled dumpster.

Cursing under his breath, Sands struggled to the stairwell. He couldn't stand straight, and with each very small step that he took, the pain streaked like lightning along his back. The individual stairs were just tall enough, and he had to raise his foot just high enough, that he wasn't sure he'd be able to overcome the searing agony of each step long enough to reach the third floor. Without his gloves, his hand quickly froze against the metal handrail. After tearing off one patch of skin, he managed to slide the sleeve of his overcoat low enough that he could support himself; he couldn't make it up the stairs otherwise. And still, the stench of decay clung to him, as if it had seeped within him and was now leaking through his pores, actively trying to make him retch.

The breezeway at the top of the stairs was aptly named; the wind whipped through the dark cavity and pushed Douglas ahead more quickly than he could comfortably move. Sanctuary was so close now. He hoped that Melanie realized exactly what he went through on her behalf—he certainly planned to tell her. It wasn't enough that he ventured into this misbegotten pit; now some maniac driver had tried to kill him!

Then, as Sands reached for the faux-brass knocker on Melanie's door, the metal twisted away from his fingers. The crude lion's head, above the engraved numbers "666," stretched open its mouth, like some Dickensian apparition, as if to roar, as if to *bite*. Sands jerked his hand away—

And there was nothing. Nothing unusual. The faux-brass lion waited patiently with the ring of the knocker between its teeth. There was no "666," just the apartment number "3031". Sands stared at the knocker. He forced his rapid breathing to slow, and licked his cold, dry lips. "What the hell…?" he whispered, the steam of his words escaping toward the obscured heavens. His legs felt weak, and his stomach boiled like a vat of hot grease. His back—it was all because of his back, he told himself. He knocked on the door, at last, weakly, and was relieved beyond measure to embrace the warmth and safety within.

CHAPTER 2

She couldn't face the house during the day, so she'd waited until night. Strange, Julia realized, because night was when it had happened.

She stood by the curb for quite a while. Beside the car. As long as the car was only a few feet away, she could jump back in and leave. She fought that impulse the entire time she was standing there.

The house was very much like most of the others in the subdivision: white vinyl siding, with a brick garage facing the street; a basketball goal above the garage door; a few shrubs buried under snow around the base of the porch; hanging baskets, home to dead, shriveled plants. The ivy and flowers in the baskets had probably died well before the snows came, during the summer, maybe even the spring. David wouldn't have thought to have watered them. Only brown stalks and a few withered leaves remained. No lights were on inside the house.

Eventually, Julia Barnes stepped away from her car. She took one step, then a second, up the walk. She stopped. Down the block, a car door slammed. Someone was laughing, talking. A teenager, a parent, home from somewhere. Did they see her? She didn't think so. Or if they did, they didn't notice. A few more seconds passed—less than a minute altogether of the cheerful voices—and then another door closed and they were gone, as if they'd never been there. Julia wished to God that she'd had nosy neighbors, just one—someone with her face pressed against the kitchen window, watching every time anyone came or went. Then Julia might know the truth. But every family was snuggled warmly inside its bunker of vinyl, brick, and insulation, a television set—or multiple sets, one in each room—the sole link to the outside world. But not to reality.

Julia started forward again. She managed to traverse the entire walk this time, to climb all three steps, but she found herself helpless before the front door. Once she stopped moving, inertia seized her body. The key, just in the pocket of her parka, seemed so far away. The coat's hood dangled on her back; her ears and her nose were numb. The police tape that had blocked the door was long since gone.

How could the police have been so sure? How could they be so *wrong*?

She took a deep breath, removed the key from her pocket, unlocked the door, opened it…. She faced the dark entry hall from the porch. A dusting of the lighter, more powdery snow followed the draft through the open door. Hesitantly, Julia followed as well.

The darkness and silence were stifling. This didn't feel like her own house. The tension in her body made her face and fingers and knees hurt. She had to pee. She'd been away for less than a year, yet when she turned on a light, she kept expecting someone to confront her, to decry her intrusion. But there was only the faint hum of the heat, left on by the realtor to keep the pipes from freezing. Julia left the bathroom door open while she urinated. The intense emptiness of the house made her heart ache. This wasn't right, to be so alone in a place that had been so full of laughter and happiness at one time—even if not at the end.

But none of that had been Timothy's fault—hers, and David's some, but never Timothy's. How could the young couple that she and David had been just a few short years ago have known the strain that an infant would place upon their seemingly firm relationship? How could they have known that, once they each truly began living for someone else, for precious Timothy, their love for each other would grow pale and fruitless? A child was supposed to be the fulfillment of a marriage; for most people that was true. That it had not proven the case for them was no fault of Timothy's. In the end, she had been the one to find work elsewhere, back East; she was the one who had left, agreeing to leave her child behind, so he could be close to his grandparents. Such a flimsy excuse. None of Julia's friends had understood— or maybe they'd understood too well, understood better than Julia had. She'd not been able to believe that she could be so callous, that she would choose single life and freedom over motherhood for any but the most unselfish of reasons, for Timothy's welfare. Not until catastrophe had struck, and she'd found herself an empty shell of a person, hundreds of miles from home.

Standing in the empty house, she wondered what could have happened that night. She found it hard enough to believe that David had grown suicidal after their separation; he was not one to internalize, to suffer in silence and grow depressed. Julia winced at that thought, at the implied criticism, but she knew the truth of it; even David would have agreed. If he were alive.

She made her way through the living room. Her movements were hesitant, as if she were peering into someone else's life, a stranger's; the books and the pictures on the shelves seemed foreign. She climbed the steps in darkness, not turning on other lights because of a strange fear that the neighbors would see, and call the police. But the neighbors wouldn't see. They *hadn't* seen.

She looked into the master bedroom, her old bedroom, her and David's, where they had conceived Timothy. This was where it had happened—where David had shot himself. The carpet and the comforter were new; the realtor would have seen to that.

The next doorway was more difficult for her—the nursery, and later Timothy's room when, at some point, it had made that ambiguous transition because he was too old to call it a nursery. As hard as it was to believe that David would take his own life, Julia could not imagine for a second the conclusion that the police had come to—that Timothy had found his father's body and then run away. Timothy had never been a particularly adventuresome or brave child. "Timid" would be a better, more accurate description. When he was a toddler, she had kept him away from the stairs by leaving the vacuum cleaner sitting at the bottom. The machine frightened him so badly that he would run screaming from the mere sight of it. Was this a child that would run away and stay away on his own? With his grandparents living a few blocks away?

The police, too, suspected that the boy had met with foul play after he fled the house; perhaps he'd been snatched off the street. But their inquiries had been limited to the conventional, the mundane. How could Julia have told them about the other dangers, the dangers she knew *must* have conspired to rob her of both her estranged husband and her only child? She would have spent the rest of her days in an institution. As it was, she'd found other people who might be able to help her find Timothy. If it wasn't too late already.

"If only I'd been here…" she said, crumpling to her knees beside the narrow twin bed where Timothy used to sleep. If she'd been here, she might have been able to stop whatever happened, or at the very least, she wouldn't be left behind to wonder and mourn alone. "If only I'd been here…" she said again, and the words unleashed her tears. She sat crying late into the night, alone in the empty house.

CHAPTER 3

It was all Douglas could manage to take his coat off. Undressing would have been an ordeal had Melanie not been so obliging. She eased his suit jacket from his shoulders and laid it neatly over the back of a chair. She had to know, as soon as she opened the door, from his expression and the awkward way he held himself, that something was wrong. If she noticed the stench from the dumpster, she didn't say anything or wrinkle her pert little nose.

"You look like you need a drink," she said, ushering him to the couch.

"A beer would be great." Sands sounded more pitiful than he meant to, he realized by the overly sympathetic look she gave him. He couldn't get out of his mind what he'd seen, what he *couldn't* have seen—the door knocker opening its mouth to bite him. That, and the nausea, and his back, were plenty to make him miserable. Getting off his feet helped his back a little, but sitting was not comfortable either, and every attempt to shift his position generated renewed jolts of pain.

Melanie opened the refrigerator door. "How about a wine cooler?"

"Don't you have anything else?"

"I have…wine coolers."

Douglas sighed loudly. "Good God. All right."

Without him asking, she helped him recline on the couch, lifting his legs for him, and then she carefully removed his shoes and socks. Douglas could not have reached his shoes at this point, much less untied or taken them off, but as she brushed the snow from them and laid them out by the space heater to warm, he was more concerned with the foul, bottled, kiwi-something concoction that she'd handed him. With the first sip, he felt his stomach turning again, and bile rising in his throat. "*Uh.* This is worse than the garbage."

"What?" Melanie sat on the edge of the couch and began to stroke his hair. She liked to seek out the first few strands of grey that were beginning to appear. The fact that he was greying at forty-six was not something Sands liked to be reminded of, and he continually pushed her hand away in irritation.

"What kind of hell do you live in?" Douglas muttered. "Rap music and wine coolers."

"I don't play rap."

"You don't *play* it, but you sure as hell listen to it," he complained. There was, in fact, pounding bass of a neighbor's music vibrating the floor slightly. It was just background noise to her. This was how she chose to live while she paid her way through community college, instead of accepting Sands' offer to put her up somewhere else. He wished she would agree, so he wouldn't have to come to this pit anymore, if for no other reason.

"Is that why you come here?" she asked, loosening his tie. "For the music?"

Sands laughed derisively. "Yeah, right."

Melanie's hand pressed against his chest and then his not-so-tight stomach as she traced the line of his buttons down to his waist. "You're working late tonight." She began to unfasten his belt, but then noticed his hand. "You're *bleeding.*" There was a trickle of blood where his skin had torn away, frozen to the metal handrail.

"Yeah, your door knocker bit me," he said. He felt stupid as soon as he said it. What was he hoping, that she would confirm what he'd seen? *Yeah, it does that sometimes. You have to watch out for it.*

But she just gave him a curious look and left him to ponder his sanity as she hustled away to find a bandage, some hydrogen peroxide, and a bottle of ibuprofen. She ministered to his injuries and got him a glass of water when he refused to take the ibuprofen with the kiwi stuff. Only when that was all taken care of did she finish unfastening his belt. "What were we talking about?" he asked.

"You were saying that I work too hard."

"I think I said *late*, but now that you mention hard…" She slid her hand under the waist of his pants.

Douglas Sands didn't come to this Godforsaken place for the music, nor for conversation, nor even for love or companionship. He came to see Melanie naked. The sex was a nice bonus—tonight, after adroitly helping him undress and then casting away her own clothes, she climbed on top and rode him with an intensity that was worth the slight strain on his back—but even more rewarding was afterward. Sex energized Melanie. She wasn't one for lying with her head on Douglas' chest; she pranced naked around the apartment, getting something to drink, burbling incessantly about her dreams of the future, of the time when the two of them would be together. Sands feigned interest, but mostly he watched her.

Melanie was attractive but unremarkable in street clothes. Nude, however, her small, lithe body took on a luster disproportionate to her size. Her hair hung almost to her shoulder and was constantly in her face. Her shoulders were strong, not bony; her breasts, little more than a handful, were alluring and pert and had a pleasantly firm bounce. Her stomach and legs were tight but not muscled. She had generously curved hips. She had used to speak often of her desire for children; she'd gone as far once as to suggest that she and Douglas should someday begin a family, but his stony silence had cowed her, and there had been no talk of children since.

Similar to the way in which sex invigorated Melanie, Douglas felt twenty years younger watching her. He would lie there and watch as she walked and talked, not flaunting her body but completely at ease with her nakedness. Her total lack of self-consciousness absolved Sands of concern—and regret—about his own aging body. As far as Melanie was concerned, life was a spectrum of myriad possibilities; she had yet to experience the trials that so tenaciously weighted Sands down—and in watching her, he took part in her dreams. Not in the way that she would have thought. He knew he would never be part of her long-term future; they would never have children together, or even marry. But so intense were her dreams that Douglas could lose himself in her *intensity*, if not in the dreams themselves. For a few hours, captured by her effusive ambition, he could be young and alive. His normal, tired life would catch up with him soon enough.

✣   ✣   ✣   ✣   ✣

He awoke to the sound of the shower. That the sound he heard was water running behind the closed bathroom door registered only slowly to his tired mind. His first sleepy sentiment was of mild regret that Melanie would be clothed again when she came out. In the next breath, he fully grasped the fact that he'd fallen asleep—

He jolted awake and jumped up—or halfway up, before his conscious mind remembered that he'd strained his back. It was easy enough to remember—

unavoidable, really—once the jagged lightning shot up his spine and he collapsed to the floor, banging his head against the coffee table on the way down. He lay naked and panting for a minute, his eyes squeezed shut against the pain. By the time he'd struggled up and back onto the couch and then, with great difficulty, dressed himself, the shower had stopped. But he didn't have time to wait for Melanie. Unable to straighten completely from the waist, Sands stalked around the apartment looking for a scrap of paper to leave a note. He found nothing that met his approval readily at hand, so he stomped down the hall to Melanie's bedroom. Heaps of clothes, but no suitable paper. Sands glanced at the clock; it was after midnight. *Good God.*

Thinking that the only other thing that could go wrong would be for someone to steal his car, he went to the window and pried open Melanie's cheap blinds with two fingers. His car looked fine, he was pleased to see, but as he was turning away, something else caught his eye—a figure, not in the parking lot, but on one of the balconies near the blue tarp across the way, the condemned building.

Sands stopped and looked through the blinds again. Nothing. There was snow on the balconies around the tarp, but no shadowy, ominous figure. He stared at the spot for a long time, waiting to see movement of some kind. But the shifting shadows that he did see were merely from snow- and ice-laden trees swaying in the wind. "Must have been a reflection," he told himself. Somebody's headlights, off the snow, or the tarp. But the shape he'd seen, *thought* he'd seen, hadn't been a bright flash. It was dark and somehow, he felt, sinister. He scoffed at the figments of his own tired mind. Over-worked and in pain. That was it. His back pain was almost as bad as a migraine; he saw spots sometimes, and it could make him queasy. "That's all that's happening."

"What are you doing in here mumbling in the dark?"

He started at Melanie's voice behind him. He rattled the blinds and, again, hurt his back as he twisted. He brushed past her attempts to sooth his pain. "You shouldn't have let me fall asleep," he snapped at her. "It's late. I have to go."

"Can't you stay a little longer?"

"No," he said, then added sharply, "I have to get home to my *wife*." He stalked down the hallway, struggled to get on his overcoat, then paused at the door. Melanie hadn't come out of the bedroom. He knew he'd hurt her—but, hell, his wife was reality, not just a girl's childish dreams. "Tell your landlord he needs to put down more salt in the parking lot," Sands said, and then let the door slam behind him.

CHAPTER 4

Douglas sat in the car with his head slumped against the headrest for several minutes after the garage door closed behind him. The clock on the dash read 1:16 AM. He'd come to a tentative understanding with his back: He didn't move, and it only hurt half as much. But now his head was throbbing where he'd struck it against the coffee table. He felt a knot forming a few inches above his right eye.

The heater was blasting—he'd left it on high trying to keep his fingers warm after throwing away his gloves—and the interior of the car was now so stuffy that he could barely breathe. Eventually, he switched off the ignition; he might be exhausted and in pain, but by no means was he suicidal. In a perverse way, he was almost thankful for the pain. Grumbling to himself and dwelling on his own misery served to distract his thoughts from more disturbing topics, impossible sights, there and then not there, the lion and the lurker. The entire night had been a surreal mix of the painful and the base: the driver's reckless disregard in the parking lot, the foulness of the refuse that had, and still, clung tenaciously to Sands (but surely Melanie would have said something if it had been as bad as all that). The familiarity of home would be a reprieve.

Inside, the house was dark. Faye had left no lights on, not that Douglas needed any. The green glare of the microwave clock saw him through the kitchen. The living room and the family room, even with the curtains drawn, received enough ambient light from the street lamps that he made his way without difficulty. He struggled briefly with his coat and then left it over the recliner. The back hallway was very dark, but it was also short and straight. He opened the bedroom door carefully, so as not to wake Faye, but she did wake up. That was always the way of it: He tried to be quiet, to avoid her questions, and she thwarted him and woke up anyway. Always. Just to spite him.

"Working late? What time is it?" She didn't sound *very* awake; her voice was scratchy, thick.

"Go back to sleep." He tried to be calm and soothing, but the words came out flat, emotionless.

"Doesn't anybody at your office answer the phone?" She was starting to roll over. If she sat up and kept talking, Douglas knew he'd have trouble putting off her questions.

"That's what voice mail is for. I'm going to take a shower." He didn't pause but headed straight for the bathroom.

"But you have to *check* your voicemail, or it doesn't do any good," she said as he closed the door and flicked on the light and the fan.

She was right. He *should* have checked his voice mail and let her know that he was going to be late— told her he was working late—before he'd gone to Melanie's. Douglas never could decide if Faye *knew*. She'd never tried to confront him about another woman; her questions, like tonight, always seemed innocent enough. Was the undercurrent of suspicion a product of his imagination? Of his guilty conscience? *She must at least suspect*, he thought. Probably the signs of his affair were things that she saw, but refused to let herself recognize.

The Faye he'd married twenty-five years ago would have known. But then again, the Douglas of twenty-five years ago wouldn't have been sleeping around. They were different people back then. The Faye he'd married had been ambitious, determined. *She's still those things*, he thought as he slowly undressed, favoring his back, and hung his suit on a hanger on the back of the door. *It can't be just me who's changed.* What had happened to them couldn't be solely his fault. She had changed too. Twenty-five-year-ago Faye's eyes had always been open. She would have *known.* She would have cared enough to know. Not that Douglas was sleeping with Melanie hoping to get caught. He wasn't an unruly youth seeking negative attention rather than no attention. That wasn't it at all. Faye *had* changed. Something inside her had died, and for the past ten years the two of them had been following gradually diverging paths, until now the distance between them was greater than Douglas had ever thought it could be. *And she still doesn't know.* Whether she didn't see or didn't let herself see, really didn't matter.

The hot water of the shower was welcome relief. Douglas hadn't fled here purely to avoid Faye's questions. The steam and heat eased the pounding that was growing, like the knot, above his right eye. Warmth seeped back into his fingers, and his back slowly began to loosen. With careful movements and plenty of soap, he scrubbed himself thoroughly. He finally felt free of the stench of the dumpster, and there was the odor of sex to be rid of; it wouldn't do to climb into bed with his wife, smelling like Melanie. He often showered after a long night at "the office" for that very reason.

By the time Douglas had finished, taken another handful of ibuprofen, and gotten ready for bed, Faye was sleeping soundly. He climbed stiffly into the bed beside her, afraid that his awkward movements would wake her again, but she barely stirred. The bedroom was very dark after the bright light of the bathroom. For a long while, he lay rigidly and listened to Faye breathing. When she was deeply asleep, she would start to snore gently—a soft, delicate sound that Douglas had always found endearing. Tonight it seemed an unconscious remnant of the Faye he'd fallen in love with—the Faye he was betraying.

Exhausted as he was, sleep did not come to Douglas. His back wasn't bothering him quite as much after the shower, but he still felt a severe twinge with almost every movement. And so he tried to lay still—also not wanting to wake Faye—a prisoner in his own bed. He could close his bleary eyes and pretend, *try*, but he could not entice sleep to claim him. He listened to his wife's husky breathing, tried to let the easy rhythm slow his heartbeat; that failing, he tried to block out her sleeping sounds, to place himself in a cocoon of sensory deprivation. Again, without success. Each time he glanced at the bedside clock, he wished he hadn't. What seemed like hours were but minutes, although soon enough the hours, too, began to slip past.

Eventually, agitated by his failure, he climbed out of bed and staggered through the dark. The murky silence of the house pressed down upon him, hemmed him in and made breathing difficult, much as the stifling heat within the car had earlier. In the living room, he poured himself a large glass of Scotch, took a sip, then swallowed more of a mouthful. He smothered a cough, but the tightness in his chest eased somewhat. Breath came more easily to him.

Outside, the wind had picked up again and was moaning as it whipped around the corner of the house. Douglas trudged into the family room. In the darkness, the impossible thoughts came back to him unbidden: the lion, the lurker. He took another swallow of Scotch. Holding his breath, he carefully pulled back the curtain on one of the French doors. Of course there was only the snow-covered swimming pool, he told himself. Those other things were impossible. He had not seen them before; he wouldn't see them now. He snorted at himself and sipped at his drink. The wind blew powdery snow from the roof and transformed the Sands' back yard into a scene in one of those tiny globes with a shaken blizzard. Douglas didn't want to see his world shaken just now, however. He lowered himself gingerly into the recliner. Perhaps the Scotch, and being away from Faye, would allow him to sleep.

His eyes closed, as if of their own accord, and he concentrated only upon the warm trail of liquid fire in his chest. He willed the alcohol to his back, his head, his hand, to all of his raw nerves. He took another large sip; the trail of fire burned anew. Douglas was too tired to think anymore. He held his attention to the spreading warmth in his chest—that and nothing else. For a few moments, there was no Faye, no Melanie, no work waiting for him tomorrow morning—*this* morning; dawn was not far away.

Douglas started awake suddenly. He glanced around quickly. Footsteps. He'd heard footsteps. Or was he dreaming? He'd finally drifted off, but his mind was not yet content to let him sleep. He sat perfectly still, listening. There was no sign of Faye. Breathing. For a moment, Douglas was certain that he'd heard someone breathing as well. Footsteps and breathing.

He picked up his glass. There was less Scotch remaining than he would have preferred, but he was too bone-weary to get up for more. He swigged down the last of it. *Damn dreams*, he thought. Even when he fell asleep, he couldn't rest. He'd been thinking about Faye's breathing—*her damn snoring*—and it had followed him into his dreams. Faye and her damn questions had dogged him awake and asleep.

But some nagging, just-out-of-reach-memory tugged at Douglas, told him that the breathing he'd heard was not the gentle snoring of his wife, nor were the imagined footsteps hers.

In the end, the shadow-filled family room was of no more comfort to Douglas than his question-plagued bedroom had been. In the darkness, the black television screen stared at him like some piece of alien technology; pictures of his smiling son, always smiling, watched Douglas not sleeping; and the wind, bored with the swirling snow, called to him: *"Daddy,"* it called. *"Dad-dy…"* trailing away like water down a drain when Douglas thought he heard it clearly. He pretended *not* to hear it, not to recognize the disturbingly familiar voice. Guilt and liquor—those were the culprits. A few hours of sleep would clear his mind, but rest was not to be had that night.

❖　　❖　　❖　　❖　　❖

Eventually, Sands did get up for a refill, and then another. But uneasy sleep did not come to him until after the sun had risen, and the wind had died. Even then, he dozed fitfully. He feigned sound sleep when he heard Faye stirring, preparing for her day of work and manic activity. After she had left, he called work to let them know he wouldn't be in, and then he crawled, stiff and despondent, into his empty bed.

CHAPTER 5

"Don't you agree, Douglas?"

Sands snapped back to the here and now, but his mind took a few seconds to shift gears. Recently, he often seemed a few steps behind, his thoughts distant. Almost two weeks had passed since the night he'd staggered home from Melanie's apartment and heard the voice on the wind. That was the first time, but not the last. He'd heard it every night since. Awake or asleep, drunk or sober, *wind or no wind*—the small, plaintive voice had called him every night. *Dad-dy*.

But this was work, Iron Rapids Manufacturing, and the only voice calling him now was that of Caroline Bishop. "Douglas? Are you with us?"

"I…" He glanced at the report before him on the conference table, then at the papers in front of Caroline and Albert, and was relieved to see that he was on the correct page, at least. "You lost me there with your graph, Caroline."

Caroline frowned. She was a small black woman with arms so thin that her bones were practically visible beneath her skin. But she was strong, hard as iron, after raising and educating four children, and her disapproval carried the weight of the Old Testament. "It's very simple, Douglas." And she patiently explained the graph again. She was a stern woman, but not unkind.

Sands looked at Albert Tinsley, who gave him a knowing raise of the eyebrows. Caroline was infamous for her computer-generated graphs and charts. Although junior to Sands in the corporate hierarchy, she was the glue that held the Personnel Department together. The daughter of share-croppers in Alabama, she had worked at IRM for thirty-plus years after moving north, and during that time had lived the American dream: moving up from the production line to management, and at the same time paying for the education of her four boys.

When computers had begun to come along, rather than foundering and becoming obsolete, she had embraced the developing technology like an asthmatic thrust suddenly into a room of pure oxygen. She had thrived and prospered and transformed herself into one of those indispensable persons without whom the day-to-day operations of the office simply would not happen. She had also developed a penchant for creating a chart when a brief sentence or notation would have served equally well—not because she wished to flaunt the fact that she could coax whatever she needed from software that defied Sands or anyone else, but because utilizing all the nifty bells and whistles of the computer age was now second nature to her.

"...So the numbers for the third fiscal quarter should be right on target."

"I see," Sands said. "You're right. That is fairly simple. Did we really *need* a graph for that?" Sands knew instantly that he shouldn't have said it, that his frustration and lack of sleep were talking.

"Pardon?"

Sands tried to strike a diplomatic note, to sound more professional and less petty: "I just hate to think of you spending a lot of time on—"

"It took thirty seconds," Caroline asserted, obviously irked that he would question her usage of time.

"Oh. That explains it," Sands said with a self-deprecating grin. "I was thinking about how long it would have taken *me*—probably two hours."

"Probably two days," Caroline said, collecting her papers.

"Excuse me?"

But Caroline merely smiled sweetly. "Is there anything else you need, Mr. Sands? I wouldn't want to be sitting here when I could be using my time productively."

"No, no thank you. But could you close the door on your way out, please?"

She did so, leaving Sands and Albert in the conference room. "A wise strategic retreat," Albert said, smiling. "You're right that we didn't need a graph for those figures."

"But she's right that it didn't take her any time. Should've held my tongue," Sands said. "I hate to think what would happen to this office if Caroline were mad at me."

"A fate worse than death," Albert agreed. "But how are *you* doing, Douglas?" His manner remained casual, friendly, but his words were more serious. "You seem tired. You *look* tired." Albert was the *person* side of Person-nel, handling interviews, placement, interdepartmental reviews, and conflict resolution. He'd been around almost as long as Caroline, and whereas she was the hard-edged matriarch of the department, he was the comforting, reasonable father figure. The noticeable wrinkles at the corners of his eyes and mouth softened his strong features, and a thick, grey beard only partially hid the onset of loose skin on his jaw and neck that was one of the undeniable gifts of age.

"I haven't been sleeping well," Sands said guardedly. He watched Albert closely. What would even an understanding person say if Sands told him that he was hearing voices? *He'd say what I would say*, Sands thought. *I'm cracking up.* "Nothing a good night's sleep won't fix," was all Douglas could bring himself to say.

Tinsley accepted that without comment. He nodded sympathetically. Douglas started flipping through his papers, trying at the same time to watch Albert surreptitiously. *Does he know? Can he tell somehow?* Did it show somehow that Sands heard things, saw things? Was that why Albert was asking—to catch Sands in a lie? Or did Sands just look tired? He flipped a few more pages and found the sheet he was looking for.

"I need to ask you about Gerry," Sands said, changing the subject. "I know certain matters are confidential, and I'm not asking for details, but can you tell me if he's being cooperative? Is he in counseling? You can tell me that much, can't you?"

"Has his performance improved?"

"Not a hell of a lot." Sands handed the pertinent report to Albert. In the past year, Gerry Stafford had misrouted electronic paychecks for ten IRM employees. *Ten.* It was a simple enough piece of information to double check for a new employee, to make sure the account number was entered correctly, and it was one of many duties that Gerry had performed without problem for years. But now it *was* a problem, understandably dating to a horrible car accident in which Gerry's wife of fifteen years had been killed and he, miraculously, had walked away. But, still, it was a problem.

Tinsley studied the report gravely. "He *is* in counseling, but it's going to take some time."

"I'm not unsympathetic to that, believe me," Sands said, and Tinsley nodded. "But I could approve a medical leave of absence for him. He could get more intensive treatment if he needs it."

When Albert looked up again, Sands could read the unspoken comments in the older man's eyes. *But you never took a leave of absence, Douglas. You never sought counseling.* But that had been ten years ago, and Sands was not Gerry Stafford. Still, it wasn't something Douglas wanted to talk about, or even to *avoid* talking about, with Albert Tinsley.

"Check with him, Albert. Let me know." Sands left the conference room a bit too brusquely. He couldn't escape the irony of him recommending treatment for someone else. *Is Gerry hearing voices?* he wondered wryly. But at least Sands was keeping up with his work; he wasn't the one screwing up his job. So let Tinsley stick his sympathetic nose in somebody else's business.

Sands practically stomped past the rows of office cubicles. He passed Melanie's desk without saying a word and closed the door to his office. Before he'd gotten settled into his chair, he heard her knock, quiet but firm, not the least tentative. "Yes?"

She came in and closed the door behind her. Melanie was extremely competent at the office; she had a professional bearing. Today she was wearing slacks and a blouse. A delicate locket hung from a gold chain at her open collar—it was the locket Sands had given her as a Christmas present last year.

"Two things," she said. "First, Mr. Grogan called to find out if you were going to be able to play tennis this week."

"Let him know yes, and could you reserve the court for us?"

Melanie nodded and made a quick note. "The second thing," she said, capping her pen and holding her notepad to her chest, "is...more personal."

Douglas shifted in his chair. He rubbed the back of his neck. This was the type of thing that was uncomfortable about sleeping with his executive assistant. They'd agreed from the start that business would remain business, and the rest would be separate. Neither one of them wanted to quit his or her job, and it would just be too weird otherwise. They didn't sneak around and kiss in the supply closet, or leave notes in each others' desks. For almost a year it had worked, with very few exceptions, this being one.

"Is there something wrong?" Melanie asked.

Douglas shifted again. "Wrong? No there's not...nothing is..."

"It's just that…you haven't been over for a couple weeks, and recently you barely talk to me here at work." She wasn't teary-eyed; that wasn't her style, but she was troubled. "I just wondered if…"

"No…there's nothing wrong. I've just…" *I've been too scared to come back, scared of what I might see. It's crazy.* "I've…not been sleeping well. I'm just tired. That's all."

Melanie watched him like a hawk, but managed to avoid being pushy. She had an ability to be both demure and vaguely predatory at the same time. "Doesn't Faye have another realty conference coming up? You could come over and stay. I could help you sleep."

She could wear him out until he collapsed from exhaustion, was what she meant. Sands couldn't pretend that he didn't notice the line of her bra beneath her slightly sheer blouse, or the curve of her slacks, but neither could he forget what he'd seen at her apartment the last time. "No, she's not going to the Phoenix conference this year."

"Denver."

"You're right, Denver. She's not going. She'll be here for the Christmas party."

That made a difference to Melanie. She still didn't tear up, but she was closer; she was forced visibly to maintain her composure. "I see."

"Tomorrow night," Sands said. "I'll come over tomorrow night."

She nodded and smiled weakly. "I'd better call Mr. Grogan."

Sands let her go and sighed loudly after the door was closed. He slid his fingers through his hair. The bruise on his forehead from Melanie's coffee table was gone, and the raw patch on his hand from the frozen handrail was mostly healed over. Trying hard to forget all of it, he turned back to his work.

CHAPTER 6

Douglas Sands could not remember ever having derived such pure, visceral satisfaction from smashing a furry, green ball. He might not be able to sleep, he might not be able to make a happy marriage, but he could beat the living hell out of a tennis ball. "Thirty-love." Sands fired a serve down the center T for an ace. Mike Grogan took a weak stab at it but was nowhere close to hitting the serve, much less getting it back over the net.

"Forty-love." With the next serve, from the ad court, Sands pulled Mike wide and charged the net. Grogan got a racket on the ball, barely, and slapped a desperate backhand, which floated perfectly for Sands to put away with a cross-court volley. Game.

"Man, whatever drugs you're taking for your back, give me some," Mike said in only partially joking frustration as they switched sides and took a breather. "I tell you, you hurt your back and take a week off, you're supposed to be rusty when you come back out—not smacking the ball better than you ever did."

"It feels pretty good today," Sands said. He'd taken a hot shower and spent extra time stretching to make sure his back was good and loose before they played. He'd opted against his kick serve, too. It was possible to hit a spin serve with relatively little effort and get it in consistently, but Sands knew his own competitive nature, and to get enough kick on his serve to give Mike trouble, he'd have to arch his back and swing hard enough, and twisting at the same time, that he was sure to throw his back out. He'd been there before. So he'd gone with his flat serve, and it was dropping in like nobody's business, with a lot of pace, and enough control to keep Mike guessing— guessing wrong for the most part, and getting back only weak returns even when he guessed right. Strangely enough, Sands owed it all to concentration; he was so tired of thinking about what was going on in the rest of his life that he'd shut it all out once he stepped onto the court. The Iron Rapids Racquet Club was out beyond the perimeter highway, not technically in Iron Rapids city limits. Maybe that helped—to be so separated from everything and everyone that was so *wrong*. Maybe a vacation was in order, maybe one of those winter Caribbean cruises.

"How's Faye doing, Doug? I haven't seen her in forever."

"She's…you know…fine." Sands watched Mike as they toweled off and drank water. *What's that supposed to mean?* Sands wondered. *"How's Faye doing?" She's doing how she's always doing, you son of a bitch.* Did Mike know something he wasn't saying? Had he talked to Faye? Had she confided her suspicions to him?

Sands shook his head sharply. He took another gulp of water. *Good God, what's wrong with me?* It was just an innocent question, small talk. His own lying and sneaking around was making him paranoid of everyone else's motives. Douglas and Mike, and Faye and Mike's ex-wife Barbara, went way back. Mike had started as floor manager at one of the IRM plants a few years after Douglas had started in Personnel. The two couples had played bridge and mixed doubles on occasion, but the bridge and most of the social interaction had dissolved with Mike and Barbara's marriage years ago. Only the tennis, intermittent over the years, had survived. Mike probably *hadn't* seen Faye in forever, and didn't deserve Sands' harsh thoughts.

"What's that make it?" Sands asked, heading back onto the court. "Four-one?"

Mike took the other side. "One-four, my serve."

"Right."

Douglas needed only a few points to know, without a doubt, that whatever intuitive zone of Zen tennis he had inhabited for the first set and a half, he was now an outcast from it. His forehands started flying long, and his backhands into the net. He flubbed what should have been an easy, put-away volley, and hit an overhead off his racket frame. No string at all. The ball landed three courts away and forced four crotchety, octogenarian, doubles players to call a let. Sands' serve, which had gone so well all morning, promptly deserted him. He couldn't hit a first serve in to save his life, and his second serve was erratic at best. The harder he tried, the worse it got. In what seemed like no time at all, but was actually two switchovers later, Mike had tied the score at four all.

"*How's Faye doing, Doug?*" Sands mimicked under his breath as he got ready to serve the next game. He'd managed to work himself into a foul mood, and he'd had more than enough of Mike's cheerful banter. Mike could not have more completely wrecked Sands' concentration if he had tried. *Easy for him to ask about Faye. His marriage fell apart fifteen years ago. Mine is falling apart now!*

Without thinking, Sands tossed the ball and put everything he had into a kick serve that was going to take Grogan's head off—and as Sands sprang forward and snapped his wrist, something else snapped in his lower back. At least he would have sworn that it snapped, or ripped, or tore, or maybe someone stabbed him, or stuffed a cattle prod up his ass and played the xylophone on his spine.

Mike was at his side before Sands was able to get to his feet. In fact, he might not have been able to stand unassisted. "Jesus, Doug. Are you okay?"

"What do you *think?*" he snapped, jerking his arm away from Grogan. Sands wasn't sure if his ears were ringing, or if what he heard was his yell of agony echoing throughout the cavernous tennis complex. He saw the octogenarians watching him, scowling as if perturbed that he'd interrupted their play a second time. "What the hell are you looking at?" he yelled at them. "Let me know how you like it when you break a hip!"

Mike was trying not to laugh. Sands whirled on him and hurt his back in the process. "Faye's just fine, you son of a bitch. But I'm leaving her." Mike was not laughing anymore as Sands, hunched and cursing, stalked off the court.

CHAPTER 7

Sands stood and stared at Melanie's door for a long while. Partially, he entertained the unrealistic hope that she would, for no special reason, look through the peephole, see him, and open the door. Not that he *expected* that to happen.

Mostly he was staring at the knocker, the faux-brass lion holding the ring between its teeth. He stared at the engraved number of the apartment, "3031," and tried to see the other numbers he had witnessed, "666". He didn't concern himself with *how* or *why* he'd seen them. He wanted to convince himself that he had *not* in fact seen them; he wanted to prove, once and for all…what? He wasn't sure what he wanted to prove about himself: that he was crazy, that he'd been hallucinating, that he'd been delirious because of his injured back? He couldn't decide; he didn't think it mattered in the long run. What mattered was that, tonight, the doorknocker was merely that, and that the apartment number was the apartment number. He was worried less about himself than about the world around him. Sands could accept that he'd seen things that weren't there—that fact was less ominous than if the things *were* there.

The wind tore through the breezeway numbing Sands' nose and ears, but he hardly noticed. It was enough that here the wind did not call to him; there was no lingering, mournful, *Dad-dy.* His hands were stuffed into the pockets of his overcoat despite his new pair of gloves. He'd not been back to Melanie's apartment since that night, and that was a problem. He had told her two days ago that he would come over *last* night, and he had not. It hadn't been a lie, not when he'd said it, but last night had come and he hadn't felt able to face that door again, to walk past the blue tarp where a dark figure had stood (there was no one on the balconies near the tarp when he arrived tonight). And so he had stayed home, and not slept, and listened to the wind.

But tonight, it was home he wasn't sure that he could face—home and Faye. Douglas was in pain as he stood before the threshold—as he'd been last time. His back was throbbing. He wasn't sure why he'd blurted out what he had to Mike that morning. Could Sands blame that, too, on his painful back? Maybe the fact that he'd said it aloud—that had been rather impulsive. But to leave Faye…? He was sure that he must have considered that route, at least in passing, at some point in past few years, but he couldn't recall a specific instance. Leave Faye? Was that what he wanted to do? Was that what he needed? It might be best for *her*, he considered. He certainly hadn't been much of a husband recently, not for quite a while. He'd left Faye to her personal torment and been satisfied that it didn't interfere with his daily life. But, of course, it did. Those were the jumbled thoughts that were struggling for attention in his mind as he stared at the door: lion, lurker, wind, wife, mistress…

The last of those, his mistress, was the most immediate problem (assuming that the lion, directly before him, behaved). Sands had stood her up completely last night, not called, and when he'd hobbled into work this afternoon after his morning of tennis, she'd not been there. She'd left a message with Caroline that she was taking a sick day.

And so here Sands was…why? He seemed to be distinctly unsure of his direction tonight. Had he come to sooth Melanie's temper? To tell her that he was ready to leave his wife? To have sex and see the girl naked (that much, at least, he knew he hoped for)? *Or just to stare at the damn door?* he asked himself eventually.

Finally, he raised his gloved fist and, not touching the lion, knocked. Melanie's expression was noncommittal when she opened the door, but her words less so: "You're a little late."

She didn't help him to the couch this time, nor did she take off his shoes and socks and place them by the space heater. She did, however, by the time he'd taken off his coat and sat, bring him a beer: "I bought a sixpack when I thought you were coming over last night," and then sat down in the chair across from him. She folded her hands in her lap—it was a forced gesture, almost dainty, not at all like Melanie— and looked at him expectantly. After a few seconds of strained silence, she craned her neck forward and peered wide-eyed at him. "Well?"

"Well?" Sands tried to shift in his seat, but his back was having none of that. If he tried to push with his feet, the barbs of lightning shot up his side and down his leg. Finally, he was forced to place his hands, palm down, on the cushions on either side of him, and lift his body to shift it slightly. Even this was awkward, as the cushions gave quite a bit under his weight. "Melanie…" he said as he loosened his tie, but then he faltered. He took a swig of beer.

"I've got all night," she said.

I'm going to leave my wife, Sands almost said. He took in a breath to say it, he opened his mouth, but the words caught in his throat. He'd said it to Mike, but this morning it had burst from his lips without forethought. Did having said it, Sands wondered, make it true? Was he leaving his wife? Would saying it to Melanie make it more real than saying it to Mike? It would certainly raise the stakes. But Sands couldn't say it to Melanie. The words, already caught, withered in his throat and threatened to choke him. He sighed. "I…I don't have a reason for not coming last night. Not a good one. I've been having a rough time. I just couldn't face…"

"Me?" Melanie ventured, neither timid nor confrontational, yet full of regret, resignation.

"No," Sands said softly, smiling sadly. "It wasn't you." *It's me.* It wasn't about Melanie at all. It was him. It was the guilt that was churning within him and twisting everything he saw and did. "I couldn't face…this place." That was as close as he could come, even if the place was only a symptom and not the disease.

Melanie was perplexed. "I don't want you to say something because you think it's what I want to hear, or *not* to say something because it's not what I want to hear."

"No. I'm not." *It's not you. It's not about you. It's me. I can't say any of it. I can't believe any of it.*

"I see." They sat silently for a while.

Sands did not meet her gaze. He stared at the floor, at the door; he wondered if the lion was calmly holding the ring, or crawling about on the other side, the demon of the threshold, pressing its metallic eye against the wrong side of the peephole.

"I want to thank you," Melanie said eventually, "for not coming last night."

"Thank me."

"Yes. Thank you. It was good that you didn't come. Oh, I was angry, and I cried, but after a while I started thinking, and I kept thinking." As she spoke, Melanie got up from the chair and began walking around the apartment. She grew more intense, more animated; this was more normal, more *her*—not sitting quietly with her hands folded in her lap. "You have stuff going on with you, I know. Some of it, maybe I figure into; some of it, maybe not. Well, I've got stuff going on too. I know it makes you uncomfortable when I talk about us having a future together, so I'm going to talk about us *not* having a future together—that's a lot of what I thought about last night. Because you've got a life, a wife, that doesn't involve me, and maybe what we have right now is all we'll ever have.

"No, be quiet and listen. Sooner or later, we'll know if we don't have a future. Maybe you know that already. If that's the way it happens…then fine. I'll meet somebody else—maybe somebody who's not older, not married. It'll be fine. You'll go back to your wife, and maybe that'll be fine, and maybe it won't. That's your life. But I've got my life too. I just want you to know that. If you come over, fine; if not, fine."

Douglas watched her pacing about the apartment, and he felt as if the couch were made of sand and crumbling away beneath him. He'd said that he was going to leave his wife; he'd begun, slowly, to accept that fact. He had told himself that maybe it would be best for Faye, maybe it would be best for Melanie—that's what he was suddenly convinced that he'd decided, although his thoughts had been completely jumbled, were still rather jumbled. Having made that tortured leap of logic, the next step was fairly modest: He was doing this, leaving his wife, all for Melanie. And she was telling him, as he understood, that she didn't care what he did. He couldn't quite grasp her full meaning, couldn't appreciate her perspective from within her own life. *Doesn't she realize the chances I've taken, everything I've sacrificed for her?* Apparently not. Sands was convinced in that instance—as surely as he was, at times, convinced that the lion had moved, that the wind called for him—that he'd done it all for her: risked bodily harm coming to this hellhole, neglected his marriage. All for Melanie. And now she said she didn't care.

Most nights, Sands would have flown into a rage; he would have yelled at her and stormed out of the apartment. But tonight, after weeks of sleeplessness, wracked by physical pain, and unable truly to believe his own eyes, he was too weak for anger. Not only the couch but the whole world felt like sand crumbling away beneath him, and despair washed in, a violent riptide tearing at the castle walls he'd built. Sands was not accustomed to dealing with tears; they had welled up in his eyes before he realized what they were. He couldn't remember the last time he'd cried— he sure as hell couldn't remember the last time he'd cried *in front of someone*—but the tears were streaming down his face. Once the realization struck, he couldn't stop the sobs that suddenly wracked his body.

His breakdown caught Melanie as off guard as it did him, maybe more so. After her initial shock, she joined him on the couch, put her arm around him, and began to stroke his hair. "Oh, baby," she said softly. Douglas tried to push her away, but his attempts merely aggravated his back, and she persisted in trying to comfort him.

He knew what she thought: that he couldn't stand to lose her. And maybe that was mixed up in his turmoil. Mostly, though, he felt that he had lost *everything*, all at once; she was one attachment of many. Maybe she was more of an emotional attachment than he'd realized. He didn't *think* he loved her—he'd never thought that—but wasn't she part of what was being taken from him? He didn't know;

he couldn't be sure of anything anymore. He couldn't say any of this aloud. He couldn't say *any-thing* at the moment; his nose was running, and he felt that he was choking on each breath. Finally, he gave in to the comfort of Melanie's arms. She held him to her chest and stroked his hair, and after a few minutes when he was able to speak again, his words—like his words that morning, and like this exhausting emotional outburst—were not what he expected. They were not what he planned to say to anyone: "My boy calls me."

"What?" Melanie asked. His voice was muffled against her chest.

"*My son, Adam,*" Sands whispered urgently, unable to pause now that he'd begun. "*He calls to me at night.*"

Melanie held him more tightly. "Oh, my God," she said breathlessly. "Douglas."

"*Sometimes it sounds like the wind, but it's him. He's calling me. He drowned. Dear God. Ten years ago. He drowned in our pool.*"

"Oh, my God," Melanie said, and Sands could feel her tears now, running down her face and dripping onto his. "Oh, Douglas." She held him as he sobbed and choked.

Sands wasn't sure how long he cried. His tears seemed to flow forever; his eyes and nose and throat grew raw. His stomach ached; his back was throbbing. At the end, like at the start, he wasn't sure what had brought on the attack: him leaving his wife, Melanie leaving him, his sanity crumbling, his dead son calling to him on the wind, all of it hopelessly tangled together and intertwined? Melanie was still holding him when he was finally able to breathe almost normally again; she was still stroking his greying hair.

Without a word, she eased him away from her and stood. She took him gently by the hand and led him to her darkened bedroom. There, she placed her hands on his cheeks and kissed him. The tenderness of her lips nearly overwhelmed him, but he had no tears left. Sands was exhausted; he couldn't remember ever having felt so weary, between the recent sleepless weeks and tonight's unforeseen outburst. Then Melanie took his still quivering fingers and slipped them beneath her shirt. He sighed, almost moaned, as he worked beneath the edge of her bra. She stepped back from him and pulled her shirt over her head. Sands eased his suit jacket from his shoulders; he realized now how hot he'd been, sweating through his shirt. He draped the jacket over a chair and, from habit, reached to close the blinds on the nearby window—

And he saw the shadowy figure. On the balcony beneath the blue tarp, not fifty yards away. Watching. He saw more than a vague outline this time; he saw a face: glaring eyes beneath a pale, hairless scalp; a smashed nose, strikingly narrow jaw, and a cruel, twisted mouth. It was an unimaginably grotesque face—and far less than human.

Sands was gone before Melanie could ask him where he was going. He staggered down the hall, his back protesting every step of the way. In the living room, he snatched up the forgotten beer bottle, still two-thirds full, and rushed out the door. The wind whipping through the breezeway tried to hold him back, but he pushed through it. He took the bottle by the throat, upside down and spilling beer, and at the top of the stairs smashed it against the metal railing. The glass shattered, leaving only the top of the bottle, a jagged weapon, in his hand.

He made his way painfully down the stairs, risking the ice, hurrying, but trying not to fall and slit his own throat. He lurched through the deep snow toward the other building, stopping only when he stood before it. With each gasp for air, his escaping breath billowed into the overcast night. The condemned building was dark and silent, the balconies empty.

"Come out here, damn you!" Sands yelled. There was no response; there was no one *to* respond. Perhaps someone peeked out a window of the building behind him, Melanie's building, but Sands' was fixated on the abandoned structure. He wasn't sure how many minutes he stood there, watching, waiting—but eventually the frantic pounding of his heart began to slacken, and he could feel the cold seeping through his sweat-soaked shirt. His cheeks and nose felt frozen, where the remnants of his tears had turned to frost.

"Douglas! What are you *doing?*" Melanie was behind him, but Sands couldn't pry his gaze from the condemned building. He waited for something—something inhuman—to move, to show itself.

"Go back inside. Lock the door."

"The hell I will." She was tugging on his arm now; she saw what was left of the bottle. "Oh, my God. What are you…? Douglas, come back inside. Now. Right now."

He was struck at first by her lack of faith in him. Couldn't she see that he was doing this for her? But then he realized: Of course she couldn't. No sane person would have any reason to believe what Sands had told her, much less what he'd left unsaid, and the lurker fell in that latter category. Melanie had already proven herself unappreciative; she was ready to cut Douglas loose despite all he'd risked for her.

Now here he was, armed only with a broken bottle against some God-knows-what kind of fiend, and she was insisting he come back inside.

"You have to get away from here, Melanie." Sands could be just as insistent as she was. "You have to move."

"*What?*"

"You have to move. You're not safe here."

"What are you…Douglas, come back—"

"*Promise me.*" He wasn't looking at her; he was watching the dark, empty building, as if condemned balconies themselves might charge at any instant.

The intensity of his demand brought Melanie up short. She sputtered, let go of his arm, but she wouldn't give in. Not completely. "I'll think about it. I promise I'll think about it."

From the tone of her voice, Sands could tell that she wasn't merely humoring him; she *would* think about it, and that was probably the best result he could hope for at the moment. He congratulated himself on this bit of negotiation, on his willingness to be reasonable; it was comforting to him, a signpost of his sanity, which he was doubting more and more each hour.

"All right," he said. There was no sign of the lurker. *But I saw it*, he told himself. The pain in his back was unbearable now that the adrenaline of shock was wearing off. Sands dropped the bottle. He let Melanie help him back inside.

CHAPTER 8

It was late, almost midnight, by the time Sands got home. He hadn't told Melanie anything else about what he'd seen. Not exactly. "A stalker," he'd answered to her persistent questions about who on earth he'd been chasing with a broken beer bottle. "There was a stalker outside. I've seen him here before."

"He probably *lives* here," Melanie had said.

"No. No."

"How do you know? How are you so sure?" But Sands had said nothing else. They'd spent a couple of tense, awkward hours dancing around various subjects. In retrospect, Sands couldn't believe that he'd told her about the wind, the voice. He suspected that he was crazy more for telling her than for hearing the voice. In the end, he'd left her. They hadn't had sex; she hadn't even kissed him again. He'd hobbled away, hoping that he might at least have startled her into being careful; maybe that small bit of good could come from the hell he was going through.

He didn't have any actual evidence that the…*thing*, the lurker, was stalking Melanie, but then again, he couldn't explain any of what was happening to him. Not really. Every time he thought he had discovered a reasonable excuse for the tricks his addled mind was playing, something else inexplicable happened. He saw something; he didn't see anything. He believed his eyes; he didn't believe his eyes. He doubted his own sanity; he was convinced that each succeeding paranoid delusion was incredibly real. Dancing back and forth over that line between conviction and skepticism, he went home. Faye was never up this late, but there she was, waiting for him.

"They don't pay you enough to work as much as you do," she said before he'd even had a chance to hang up his coat.

The habitual defenses tried to kick in—did she mean what she said, or was she hinting? did she know? but Sunds was too tired. His mind was too full of swirling possibilities, of insanity and of lurkers demonic. He was numb to his wife and her complaints. He was beyond caring. But the tired, flat words came all the same. "Internal audits are hell," he said. "They take a lot of time."

"Could you let me know when you're going to be late?"

"I lose track of time."

"And you don't check your voice mail."

"And I don't check my voice mail."

She was wearing a royal blue sweater and jeans that fit her well; she had a terrific figure, even into her forties. She should—she went to aerobics at least three or four times a week and ate like a bird. She was curled up in Douglas' recliner and made no move to cede her position to him. He took his time in the living room pouring a glass of Scotch, then eased himself onto the couch next to the recliner in the family room.

"Are you almost done?"

"What?"

"With your audit. Are you almost done? They can't expect you to work all these extra hours through the holidays."

"Almost done," Douglas nodded. "Although these things have a way of dragging on sometimes."

"It's already dragged on too long."

For the first time in perhaps months, Douglas looked into her green-grey eyes. Was she talking about his fictitious audit or about their marriage? "Yeah, well…"

"You said you'd get the decorations down this evening. Christmas is only ten days away, and we haven't so much as put a wreath on the door. I'd like to get the tree up and the candles in the windows before it's time to take them down."

"Can't you reach them? They're in the—"

"I know where they are. You said you'd get them down."

"I'll get them tomorrow."

"No, you won't." Her stark, raw contradiction struck Douglas like a slap across the face. Resentment seeped from her words like fluid from an infection.

I came back too soon, Douglas thought. *I should have driven on by when I saw the lights on.* But here he was, and he was too exhausted, too spent, physically, emotionally, and mentally, to avoid her. Instead, he laughed under his breath. "Do you mean no I won't because I'm going to get them right this damn minute, or no I won't because I never do anything I say?"

"Take your pick."

Douglas licked his finger and made an imaginary tick mark in the air. "Touché." He took a large swallow of Scotch.

"Don't you even *care?*" she asked, the cold fire of her eyes bleeding into her manner at last. "Don't you care about anything?"

"Right now," he said, enunciating each word precisely, "I care that my back hurts like hell. I threw it out playing tennis this morning, thank you very much for asking. I care that if this audit doesn't turn out well, it could mean my job."

"They wouldn't fire you."

"They damn well might. Who knows what those stuffed shirts might do? That's what I care about right now: keeping a roof over our heads—"

"And food on the table, and shoes on our feet." Faye rolled her eyes. "Please, you're going to make me cry. You know perfectly well that we could get by on my salary and commissions if we had to for a while—which we *won't*." She was slow to heat up, but Faye was rising to a full boil now. She pulled her feet from beneath her and sat forward on the chair. Aside from surprising Douglas, her fierceness rekindled her beauty, which had seemed blunted for quite some time. He remembered how beautiful she had always been, saw how beautiful she still was, and felt the color of shame rising to his cheeks.

She'll think I'm angry, he thought, and then realized that he *was* angry. She didn't know what agony he'd been going through; how dare she judge him and flay him with her sanctimonious tone? Douglas sucked Scotch through clenched teeth.

"If you *have* to work late," she went on, "that's fine. But you could damn well have the courtesy to let me know! We can even do the decorations tomorrow if you want, but if you're that concerned with keeping a roof over our heads, then trying doing something around *here* sometime." She tossed her hands in the air and let them clap to her thighs in exasperation. "You said you were going to take care of winterizing the pool how many months ago? And now the cover is torn from the weight of the snow—"

"I never wanted the damn pool in the first place," Douglas shot back. "If it were up to me, it wouldn't even be there. It *never* would have been there!" He didn't need to say the rest: *And our son would be alive!*

That ended it. Faye looked away from him. She couldn't face him and keep her lip from quivering. She wagged her index finger at him, as if she were truly about to unleash her fury upon Douglas, but her ferocity failed her. She rolled her lips in until they seemed to be gone and then covered her mouth with her hand. She left Douglas there on the couch. The slamming bedroom door shook the entire house. Numb, Douglas sipped his Scotch, and as the night grew later, listened to the wind.

✛   ✛   ✛   ✛   ✛

The next morning, Faye was gone before Douglas awoke on the couch. He was cold and stiff. Later, when he left for work, he noticed a strange mark on the roof of his car, just above the door. A gouge, maybe from a file or a chisel, someone attempting to pry the door open. Some social deviant must have tried to break into his car while he was at Melanie's last night. Looking more closely, he found a similar mark above the passenger's door. *Damn parasites*, he thought. Only briefly did he entertain—and then completely discard—the idea that the gouges could be from claws, from something holding on to the top of his car.

CHAPTER 9

John Hetger parked just off the road on a curve fifty yards before the railroad crossing. He had driven this stretch of road at least a hundred times, practically every time of the day and night. This time he walked. He noted every dip and curve, every crack in the asphalt and pothole that might be large enough to affect the trajectory of an automobile.

State route 217 was not busy. Ever, as far as Hetger had observed. Not during what would be the morning rush hour in the city, not now in the late afternoon, certainly not in the middle of the night. Probably because the winding, two-lane road didn't go particularly anywhere. It did go *somewhere*, of course, but not in a hurry, not very efficiently. It meandered northward, in the general direction of Flint. *But who the hell wants to go to Flint?* Hetger wondered idly. And for anyone who did want to, I-75, which more or less paralleled 217, provided a much quicker, if less scenic, route.

Visibility, for a driver, was not good approaching the railroad crossing on route 217. Hetger walked past the day-glow railroad crossing sign. The sign was new. The old sign had apparently been stolen and was missing the night of the accident.

He continued around the two sharp curves following the sign. Hetger wore a white windbreaker; he didn't mind the cold. He listened carefully for any car coming behind him. Light was fading quickly; his white jacket would help make him visible, but a driver speeding around these particular curves, even seeing the white jacket, wouldn't spot him in time. No driver, speeding or otherwise, did come around the curves. Route 217 was not busy.

The crossing arm had been replaced. It stood at attention beside the pair of darkened red lights. Hetger stood perfectly still and studied it. He imagined it down, and the red lights flashing rapidly, one and then the other. (It wasn't difficult to imagine; he'd watched trains cross here several times.) He imagined Father George Stinson, asleep at the wheel with two other priests in his car—that's what the police report stated: that he'd fallen asleep. Somehow, if the report were accurate, George had fallen asleep in the few yards since the last curve; a nodding driver, in Hetger's estimation, would have been very unlikely to make it through the sharp curves and all the way to the tracks. But George, according to the police, had fallen asleep. He'd run into the crossing arm near the base where it attached to the metal upright that supported the lights. The wooden crossing arm splintered. The front of the car smashed against the metal upright.

None of the priests were wearing seatbelts. Hetger had ridden with George Stinson on several occasions, as both driver and passenger different times, and had never noticed the priest *not* wearing a seatbelt. The police, however, asserted that Stinson and his two passengers that night were not wearing seatbelts when George fell asleep after the sharp curves and crashed into the crossing arm and pole. The car had spun onto the tracks. *All three* priests must have been stunned, because none of them had fled the car despite the freight train bearing down on them.

It was possible. All of it was *possible*. If numerous unlikely events had all occurred one after another after another. Although he was doubtful,

Hetger wasn't willing to take that possibility lightly. He'd seen his share of unlikely things—and that was putting it lightly. Father Stinson himself was a proponent of (in Hetger's mind) the unlikely: George believed, *had* believed, that bread and wine, through the sacrament of Eucharist, were transubstantiated, that they became the flesh and blood of Christ. That had been but one of Hetger's and Stinson's spirited yet friendly and respectful debates over the years.

Why not just go to a buffet or a flea market? Stinson had written on one occasion when Hetger had been contemplating the Unitarian faith. *I'll take this Christian tenet, and maybe a little Buddhism, and oh, what the heck, a little paganism too. It's such a good deal, I can't pass it up. What do you believe, John? A community without shared beliefs is not a community.*

And, Hetger had responded to his friend, *a community that for hundreds of years maintains unanimity of thought by burning "heretics" at the stake is not a community for me. Is the acknowledgement and reverence of universal human dignity not a shared belief?*

Hetger had spent hours reading over the letters after he'd learned of George's death. Only upon learning more of the details had John grown uncomfortable about the reported circumstances of his friend's accident. Wasn't it the case, though, that lives were snuffed out every day as a result of happenstance, of stupid chance? There was often no meaning in death, it seemed. Only in life.

But Hetger couldn't let it go at that. Why had Father Stinson been riding along that road with two associates? Had they all three suddenly craved a scenic drive to Flint in the middle of the night? Had they uncharacteristically decided, on this occasion, that God would be their shield, therefore seatbelts were not necessary?

Hetger was not satisfied with the answers he had so far. It was his nature to question. George had once accused him of "wielding a question mark like a sword." Perhaps that was true. But the things he had seen and touched and smelled in recent months had convinced him that there were forces at work in the world of which most people hadn't the faintest idea. Someone had to show them; someone had to ask the questions, *to find out*.

State route 217 was completely shrouded by night as John Hetger walked back to his car. Darkness was the great deceiver, but it gave shelter in its house to greater deceivers still.

CHAPTER 10

Peace on earth, goodwill toward all men. Christmas was supposed to smooth over all differences. For one brief holiday season, everyone was supposed to love and be kind to his fellow man and woman. If it was such a good idea, Douglas Sands had always wondered, why didn't people do it all year long? The truth was that a great many people weren't worth an ounce of love or kindness. He suspected, increasingly, that he was one of those great many people.

If all was not forgiven, he and Faye put on their civil faces for the office Christmas party. To all outside observers, the couple's twenty-three years of marriage had been a stroll down the lane of marital bliss. There was, of course, the horrible accident, the young son who had drowned, but no one spoke of that. Many of the newer employees at IRM, and even a few of the old-timers, had no idea it had happened. There was nothing in the manner or bearing of the handsome couple to suggest the scars of tragedy in their lives. The touch of stiffness with which they regarded one another and interacted was, no doubt, merely a hint of formality, a by-product of good breeding.

Douglas, despite his greying hair, was relatively youthful in appearance. He might not be as fit as he once had been, but the slight portliness suited a man of his age and stature; he still cut a fine figure in his Brooks Brothers suit. Faye was stunning in her emerald gown, with its plunging back and neckline tastefully cut yet sufficiently low to attract the attention of the uncouth.

Similarly to the way that the season resolved the difficulties of mankind, a bit of holiday decoration was supposed to transform the square footage of daily tedium into a festive oasis amidst the corporate and industrial desert. The cubicles were decked with chains of red and green construction paper, tinsel icicles, and ten-year-old cut-out Santas and reindeer, if not boughs of holly. The punch ran plentiful and, more importantly, *strong*. The spread was respectable and suitably rich for holiday fair. Someone was playing a Don Ho Christmas album over the intercom system.

Almost before the elevator had closed behind Douglas and Faye, Melanie, like a heat-seeking missile, was pressing glasses of punch into their hands. "Merry Christmas!" she beamed, her cheeks, Douglas suspected, rosy not from makeup but from punch. Melanie was not a drinker, aside from the occasional wine cooler or glass of Chardonnay, but she seemed full of holiday spirits tonight. She wore a black and grey cocktail dress, a bit more provocative than her usual business attire but tasteful; the dress, like her budding inebriation, was understated, not showy.

"Merry Christmas," Faye said, taking but at the same time ignoring the glass of punch.

"Thanks," Douglas said, watching his hopes for an uneventful evening fading away to nothing, like so many of his forgotten promises. He took a large gulp of punch. His eyes watered.

"Aren't the decorations great?" Melanie said a bit too cheerfully.

"They're very nice," Faye said.

"The music..." Melanie rolled her eyes. "I don't know."

At that point, Douglas reached up and patted Melanie on the shoulder. "Merry Christmas, Melanie." There was nothing of the sensual or flirtatious about the gesture; he patted her as one might a small boy, or a pet. He nodded toward several of the younger employees nearby, many of whom had hit the punch much harder than Melanie. "You and the kids have fun." Then he ushered Faye past the younger woman and between the rows of festive cubicles.

"She's very attractive," Faye said.

"Hm? Oh, Melanie?" Douglas shrugged, then nodded. "She's a nice girl." As Faye turned to greet another of his co-workers, Douglas downed the rest of his punch.

The Christmas party was a particular brand of torture to which the IRM employees were subjected each year. Individuals who had managed to establish stable working relationships were thrust into forced social interaction with only munchies and alcohol to smooth the way; it was like locking the entire department in the break room and filling the water cooler with Jim Beam. Few careers were made at the Christmas party, but a significant number were derailed. Douglas could rattle off the names of young bucks who, over the years, thanks to an unfortunate comment or flirtation, had not made it through the first few months of the new year. That was the crowd that he'd pointed Melanie toward. He and she had survived one Christmas party indiscretion; they could ill-afford another.

"Sands!" boomed a familiar, baritone voice. A meaty hand latched onto Douglas' arm and gave it a good squeeze. "Sands, good to see you. Merry Christmas!" Marcus Jubal, vice president in charge of Personnel, was a bear of a man. If they'd wanted someone to play office Santa, he would have been the choice. "And, Faye, you're as beautiful as ever."

"Why, thank you, Marcus," she said. "Are you and Annie enjoying the house?"

"Most certainly. It was a splendid buy."

Douglas was constantly surprised at how many of his co-workers, even his boss, knew Faye. Not through Douglas, but through her job—she'd sold Jubal and his wife a new house two years ago—or through blood drives, or her work at the homeless shelter, or with the Women's League. Douglas sometimes felt that he was the stranger at these office get-togethers.

Stranger or not, he felt distinctly ill at ease this year. As Jubal wandered off to greet other employees, Douglas kept scanning the milling crowd for Melanie. He hoped that the worst had past, but he couldn't be sure. He couldn't relax.

Last year, Faye had been away at a realty conference in Denver the week before Christmas. Melanie had been his executive assistant for almost two months at that point, and Douglas had thought he'd detected interest from her. It was tricky, sexual harassment having become the social force that it was. Fifteen years ago, when Douglas had launched his first affair, scouting out the field was much simpler; there were seldom repercussions for a rebuffed advance, a pat on the fanny or a suggestive comment. But now, a misplaced pat could lead to dismissal, demotion, or litigation.

Enter the office Christmas party: all of the personnel department stirred into a brew of fruit punch, vodka, and gin. Add a few of the plant managers to the mix, a smattering of suggestive outfits.... The wonderful, and horrible, thing about alcohol, Douglas had found, was that it gave people license to say and do things that they would have *liked* to have done anyway, if they had more courage or less common sense. Drink away a few inhibitions and suddenly hitting on that young, perky executive assistant seemed like a perfectly good idea, and if she'd had enough, she might not mind the advances; she might even enjoy it and reciprocate. That had pretty much been the way of it at last year's party: A few thinly veiled comments, and before he knew it, Douglas was in an out of the way supply closet with Melanie's skirt up over her waist and her panties around her ankles.

That was the absolute last time they had done or said anything remotely sexual at the office, not even a kiss or innuendo since. Their discipline had served them in good stead, and for Douglas, there was a certain eroticism in interacting on a perfectly normal, everyday level with a woman he knew he was going to see naked in a few hours. The anticipation was generally as exciting as the actual sex, and there was always the pleasant afterglow, when he simply watched Melanie.

Considering the history of their affair, Douglas wasn't totally surprised by Melanie's list tonight toward confrontational spirit, rather than holiday spirit. He did not, however, approve, and he planned to keep Faye as far away from the girl as possible. Toward that end, Albert Tinsley, bless his bleeding heart, was a godsend.

"Faye, it's been *ages*."

"Albert, how have you been?" Faye said, with the first genuine smile that Douglas had seen grace her features in quite a while.

"Merry Christmas, Albert." Then Douglas turned to his wife. "Honey, would you excuse me for a minute?" Tinsley was the most easy-going, *comforting* person Douglas had ever met, and Faye was fond of him as well. Albert was probably the one person in whose company Douglas could leave Faye and not catch too much grief about it later. And almost as much as Douglas wanted to keep Faye and Melanie apart, he wanted to get away from Faye himself.

They had put up Christmas decorations last night, the night after Douglas had "chased" the lurker with a broken beer bottle. Douglas had threatened the seen and then unseen apparition, but it was his wife he'd wounded the most deeply; he'd hurt her as badly as he knew how, and for what? For daring to point out a few of his lesser shortcomings?

So Thursday after work, after normal hours of work, he came home and helped her with the artificial tree, the wreath, the mantle decorations, the candles for the windows. If taking part in the decorating was Douglas' attempt to atone for his sins, it was Faye's vehicle for his punishment. The two had exchanged scarcely a dozen words over the three hours of activity. Eventually, struck by the distinct chill in his own house, Douglas had retreated outside where the cold, if just as cruel, was not stifling. He'd hung the garland on the lamp by the driveway and then stared again at the strange scratches on the roof of his car. He'd wandered back inside and warmed himself with a few glasses of Scotch, but Faye's icy silence had lingered. It persisted tonight relatively unchanged.

Let her talk to Albert, Douglas thought. *She'll enjoy that more than ignoring me.* He was glad, relieved, that Albert had come along when he had. Also, Douglas had caught sight of Mike Grogan, and felt he owed the plant manager an apology of a sort that could not be extended in Faye's presence. So Douglas slipped away from his wife, and she hardly seemed to notice.

"About yesterday, Mike," Douglas said, once Phil from Payroll had eased on to another cluster of co-workers, and the two tennis partners were alone amidst the throng.

"Merry Christmas, Doug."

"Um, right. But about yesterday—"

"Don't worry about it, friend." Mike was stoking his own Christmas glow, though he was far from drunk.

"I've been under a lot of pressure recently, and not sleeping," Douglas went on. "And I hurt my back on that last serve, but I shouldn't have blown up at you. It was wrong."

"Think nothing of it," Mike said with a pat on the back, the kind that is the extent of physical contact between athletic men. "It was worth it to see the look on the faces of those old codgers on court two." Amidst everything else, Douglas had forgotten the seniors on the other court. "But look," Mike said, more seriously. "I know how it is. I've been there. If you need anything, just let me know…but I hope you and Faye can make a go of it. It seems like you two have a good thing going."

Douglas shrugged. "It seemed like you and Barbara had a good thing going." This time Grogan shrugged, but he didn't argue. "But thanks," Douglas added. "I appreciate it. I really do." There wasn't much to say after that. They attempted some tennis talk, and Douglas asked about the plant—Mike managed the facility that made the emergency jacks, which were then shipped to Detroit and installed with the spare tires in trunks—but the conversation quickly dried up. Douglas wasn't the sharing type, and even if he had been, the Christmas party wasn't the environment for a satisfying heart-to-heart. They drifted apart with a departing "Merry

Christmas," and Douglas headed purposefully for the punchbowl to refill his glass.

He stepped past a group of the young turks, who had taken up a station near the refreshments, to find Gerry Stafford ladling the very red and very pungent juice into his glass. He was making a mess of it—punch was dribbling down the outside of his glass, over his fingers, and back into the bowl—but he didn't seem to notice particularly.

"Hitting the punch?" Douglas asked. It was one of those inane bits of small talk, stating the obvious, that made him cringe as soon as he said it.

Gerry nodded drolly. "Yes."

Of course he's hitting the booze, Douglas thought. *The poor guy's wife hasn't been dead a whole year*. This would be Stafford's first holiday season on his own after fifteen years of marriage. That couldn't be easy. Gerry was several years younger than Douglas but looked at least ten older. He seemed to have aged considerably over the past months. His beard, once kept trimmed and neat, was now a collection of wild hairs sticking out in random directions. He had more wrinkles; his skin seemed to have lost much of its elasticity. He had dark circles under his eyes that rivaled Douglas' own. The most striking change in Gerry, however, were his eyes; once reflecting a permanent smile, now they were dull, listless, and watery, as if he were constantly on the verge of tears.

Douglas wanted to say something else, something comforting, but he couldn't find the words. He felt hypocritical, trying to console this co-worker while Douglas himself was busy actively driving his own wife away. That was when it actually struck Douglas: that what he'd said the other morning to

Mike was true, real. More than two days after he'd spoken the words, Douglas knew that he was going to leave his wife; there was no point in continuing to put himself and Faye through such pain. Better to have it done with. He *would* leave Faye. Looking at Gerry, Douglas wondered if it would be easier for himself, since it was his fault, since he was driving Faye away, and she wasn't going to be stolen unjustly from him. Would it be worse?

On the intercom, Don Ho had given way to Elvis who, from the captured moments of his thin years, was crooning "Blue Christmas". Caught up in his own personal revelation, Douglas remained completely at a loss for anything to say to Gerry Stafford, and finally settled for a pat on the shoulder and a lame, "Merry Christmas." It was a sincere, if distinctly inadequate, gesture, but when Douglas' hand touched Stafford's shoulder, his fingers tingled and were suddenly as cold as they had been the night his skin had frozen to the metal handrail. A harsh chill ran up the length of Douglas' arm. He examined his hand, thinking it might fall off, as Stafford, evidently unconcerned or unaware of what had transpired, meandered away.

Douglas stretched his fingers, which were practically numb; he repeatedly squeezed and opened his fist. He watched Gerry walking away. *What the hell…?* Douglas had experienced brief numbness in his leg on occasion, because of his back, but this was different—this was *cold*.

The sensation shook Douglas badly. He couldn't imagine Gerry Stafford having anything to do with the numbness, and considering the string of bizarre maladies that had beset Douglas, it seemed likely that this was something else wrong with *him*. Had he suffered some type of nerve or mental damage? Was he becoming schizophrenic? Were these the first signs of Alzheimer's?

As Elvis surrendered to "Grandma Got Run Over by a Reindeer," Douglas decided that he'd had enough frivolity for one night, for one *year*, maybe two. He was ready to retrieve Faye and head home. He gulped down his punch and left the empty glass on the table. As he worked his way back to where he'd left Faye, however, Melanie stepped abruptly in front of him. Douglas stopped on his toes to avoid knocking her down.

"I think Elvis is so romantic. Don't you?" Melanie said. Her words were just a little thick, not yet slurred, but her cheeks and nose had taken on a rosy shine that would have challenged St. Nick himself.

"This isn't Elvis anymore," Douglas said curtly, but even as he said it, he remembered having heard Elvis playing in the background when they'd screwed in the supply closet last year.

Douglas looked around; he peered over a row of cubicles. Faye was still talking with Albert; Caroline Bishop had joined them, as well as Lavonda from Marketing. They all seemed intent on their friendly conversation, and no one else appeared concerned with the Personnel executive and his wobbly assistant. Douglas grabbed Melanie's elbow and led her forcefully away from the crowd. "Come here."

Turning a corner, they ran practically headlong into a young black man Douglas didn't recognize. He was dressed more shabbily than seemed appropriate for the party, in khakis that looked too tight, and a worn leather jacket. "Excuse us," Douglas stammered, but the man continued on briskly without acknowledging them. *Must be a plant worker*, Douglas thought.

Sometimes a manager reserved one of the larger meeting rooms downstairs for his factory Christmas party; the setting was a bit more relaxed than an equipment-laden assembly line.

Douglas led Melanie a little farther down the hallway, far enough to be sure they were out of earshot of the party. "The supply closet's that way," Melanie said with a grin, pointing another direction.

Douglas slapped her. Not incredibly hard, but sufficient to sting and get her attention. "You have got to *stop* this," he hissed. Melanie's shock quickly turned to anger; she tried to jerk her arm away, but Douglas held tight. "Do you hear me? You're acting *crazy*." He struggled to keep his voice down. "I know things are…weird right now, but we can't let any of that intrude here. Do you understand?"

Melanie's eyes were completely lucid now, the alcohol in her system taking a back seat to her wounded pride. Douglas was relieved that she didn't burst into tears or scream or make a scene. Instead, she took a deep breath and said, "I'm sorry." She took another deep breath. "Let go of my arm," she said calmly. When Douglas had, she added, "And don't you *ever* hit me again."

He self-consciously pulled his hands away from her. He felt justified in having slapped her, but he was not a violent person; he couldn't remember having hit someone before, ever, not even as a boy.

"Don't *ever* hit me again," she repeated.

Douglas had had enough of being made to feel guilty for what she had forced him to. "I'm going back," he said. "You take a minute to collect yourself."

"I *am* collected," Melanie snapped. "*You* take a minute." And then she stalked off without him.

Fine. Douglas didn't care if she waited or he did. The important thing was that they went back to the party separately. No point in taking more chances. He took a deep breath and sighed. As uncomfortable as that had been, it could have been worse, all things considered: no public scene, no screaming fight. *I've pushed my luck about enough*, Douglas thought. *Time to get out of here*. He'd made his appearance and met the expectations of his superiors and subordinates alike—that was enough.

"There you are," Albert Tinsley said when Douglas got back to Faye. Lavonda was still there as well. Faye had nothing to say about Douglas' return, but he could tell that she was bored and angry. Apparently there was only so much comfort that good old Albert could give.

"You about ready to go, honey?" Douglas asked.

"You shouldn't call me that in front of your wife," Albert joked.

After Douglas and Faye had said their goodbyes and were walking toward the elevator, Faye said casually: "I had an interesting conversation with Caroline earlier."

"Did you?" Douglas was scanning the clumps of people, hoping that Melanie wasn't going to try one last confrontation. The Sandses reached the elevator to the strains of Bing Crosby. Douglas stabbed at the button. He was almost out of this.

"I said that she must be relieved that the audit was almost over. Do you know what she said?"

Douglas' mouth suddenly went dry. His mind was racing, but all he could come up with to say was: "What did she say?"

"She said, 'What audit is that?'"

Douglas jabbed at the button again; he studied it intently, and the numbers above the doors. "There's only three floors. You'd think it would be here by now." He faced Faye. "What did you…oh, Caroline. Right. She's keeping up with the current quarter while we…the rest of us, straighten out the numbers from the last. Quarter. You know," he rushed on, "this elevator is taking way too long. I could use the exercise. Let's take the stairs." He escorted his wife around the corner to the stairwell and held the door for her.

"But surely Caroline *knows* about the audit, even if she's not working on it." Faye's questions were particularly pointed tonight, less innocent than they usually were. Douglas was struck by the image of a cat toying with an insect. "As much time as it's taking the *rest* of you…"

"What? Oh, yes. Of course she does. She was probably joking with you. You know, because she's not the one having to spend time on it."

"Still," Faye insisted, "it seems that—"

They turned the corner and saw Gerry Stafford. Sitting on the landing of the stairwell. His head split open down to the bridge of his nose. Douglas felt suddenly weak in his legs. Faye screamed.

CHAPTER 11

For once, Melanie lay beside Douglas in bed rather than tromping around the apartment talking. She was teasing the curly black and grey hairs on his chest and belly. He was occasionally brushing his fingers across her breast, watching as her nipple hardened, then relaxed slowly, then hardened again at his next light touch. Their sex tonight—it was always *sex* to Douglas, not *lovemaking*; their coupling had to it more of the primal and instinctive than the emotional—had been impassioned, almost desperate. Perhaps it was a reaction to—a reaction *against*—their harsh words last night at the party; perhaps they each realized at last that they could very well lose one another. Or perhaps it was in response to Gerry Stafford's broken body in the stairwell, an acknowledgement of their own mortality.

"So they think somebody did that to him," Melanie said, after two hours of avoiding the subject.

"He didn't fall down the steps." Douglas had only seen one dead body before last night: that of his drowned son. The memories were agonizing, unavoidable, and they didn't sit well; they didn't sit well with Faye either. She had taken mild sedatives tonight and was sleeping now. Douglas had known better than to trust sedatives or even his familiar Scotch, and he knew what would be in store for him if he managed by some miracle to fall asleep. He wasn't sure if the wind or the dreams would be worse, but he hadn't been about to stick around for either one. And so he had come here, into Melanie's arms. He'd taken hold of the ring in the lion's mouth and knocked.

"I'm so sorry you had to find him," she said.

"Somebody had to find him." Douglas caressed her arm, rubbed until her goosebumps went away. "There wasn't much blood," he said absently. "I would've thought there'd be more blood the way his head was split open." Melanie shuddered. "I'm sorry. I shouldn't talk about that."

"Why would anyone want to kill Gerry?" Melanie wondered. "He was so...harmless. He always seemed so sad."

"You didn't know him before the accident, did you?"

"Not very well, but I could still see the difference after."

Sands nodded, but it wasn't the change in Gerry Stafford he was thinking about. He was thinking of Faye's devastation after Adam drowned, of the vibrant spark that had been extinguished along with her son's life. She had filled her days with meetings and activities, civic groups and exercise, but her numerous commitments after Adam's death had struck Douglas as more manic than enthusiastic. *Goddamn pool*, he thought. *None of this would have happened....*

"Could it have been a robbery, a mugging, you think?" Melanie asked.

Douglas was lost for a moment, confused by the non sequitur of a swimming pool and a mugging, but then he remembered poor, hapless Gerry. "I don't know. The police were asking a lot more questions than they were answering." That had been almost as bad as finding the body: having to stay around and answer questions. It had aggravated Douglas, but it had been much harder on Faye. She had been so close to hysterics eventually that the police had let them go. "*You have our address,*" she had practically screamed at them. "*We're not going to skip town. You don't think we* killed him, do you? Why don't you go catch who did, instead of tormenting us?"

"I don't want to talk about it. I don't want to think about it anymore," Melanie said.

That was fine with Douglas; he didn't want to think about it anymore either. But he did: about Gerry, and Faye, and Adam. Even when Melanie crawled on top of him again, he was still thinking about it. She teased him to arousal, then mounted him and rode him relentlessly. Douglas was aware of the rising sensation; the pleasure wasn't completely lost upon him, but he was thinking of Gerry's head split open, his shattered skull; of Faye's hysteria, her red eyes; of Adam's floating, lifeless body. As Douglas' and Melanie's bodies rocked back and forth, he saw waves lapping against the side of a swimming pool. As Melanie pressed her weight down on him again and again and again, he imagined the incredible force required for a blunt object to have done what it did to Gerry's head. As Melanie arched her back and moaned, Douglas heard the animalistic cry of pain that had escaped Faye's lips when she'd learned of Adam.

The tragedies were hopelessly churning in Douglas' mind. He grabbed the sheet beneath him, balled it in his fists, and closed his eyes. The sudden pounding at his temples joined with the heavy vibrations of rap from next door. Melanie was so small, yet she weighed on him like a smothering ocean. She rammed herself down on him, and he rose to meet her like a collision of oncoming traffic. Then the timeless instant, balancing on the precipice between heaven and oblivion. And impact, release, surrender. Melanie collapsed on top of him, and they lay still, bodies along the highway. Except they were breathing, gasping, their hearts pounding one against the other.

Eventually, Douglas realized that he still held the balled sheet clenched in his fists. He uncurled his fingers and felt the last strength drain from his limbs. Melanie was still on top of him, breathing in his ear. The passage of time was marked only by her breath, and their slowing heartbeats, and the pounding bass from next door. Douglas let his head roll to the side and glanced at the clock on Melanie's bedside table, but instead of numbers, he saw digital letters: **TO KILL**.

Douglas blinked hard, trying to clear the red haze around the clock face, and the letters did change. But not to the numbers that should have been displayed. Instead, different words: **IT WAITS**.

What the…?

And as he watched the clock that did not show him the time, the words changed back and forth to the rhythm of his beating heart: **TO KILL-IT WAITS-TO KILL-IT WAITS-TO KILL**.

He started to reach for the solid metal lamp beside the clock, but his gaze slowly focused beyond the lamp, on the window, and the blinds that were lowered all but a few inches—and he saw eyes. Red, glaring, watching. Douglas jerked up, bumping heads with Melanie, but he paid no attention to that.

Everything was happening at once. The conscious part of his mind couldn't comprehend most of it. *There's no balcony…* His thoughts were sluggish, but strength flooded his suddenly tense body. Melanie was asking him what was wrong.

IT WAITS-TO KILL.

The lurker was clinging to the outside wall of the building, and the fiendish beast would kill Melanie if given a chance, if Douglas didn't interpose himself. In that instant he knew it for a certainty, as the clock blinked hellfire at him: **IT WAITS-TO KILL-IT WAITS-TO KILL**. He was already steeped in memories of the dead tonight, and he would not let Melanie join them, no matter the cost.

The eyes seemed to have noticed Douglas at the same time he noticed them. They jerked back from the glass. Douglas shoved Melanie to the side and this time did reach for the lamp. He didn't turn it on, but grabbed the solid, metal light above the base and yanked the cord from the wall. Melanie's scream echoed in his mind as he threw the lamp—not letting go but launching himself *with* it! Fire seared through the veins of Douglas' body. He was propelled by righteous indignation. Suddenly the world was shattering glass, a tangle of limbs and cheap blinds and a broken lampshade.

And for what seemed a very long moment, he was weightless, though the earth was rushing up to meet him. Douglas and the lurker fell, and he saw it for what it was: *dead*. As dead as Gerry Stafford had been. Dead and seeking life, seeking blood, Melanie's blood. The creature hissed. Its hate-filled eyes were no longer human, nor its jagged fangs and twisted countenance. Its claws, which seconds before had been hooked into a vertical wall, now tore at Douglas' face. Even as the two fell, Douglas swung the lamp at the bloodthirsty demon. He was awash with supernal might, invigorated for the first time in so many years by a sense of purpose—

And then they struck the ground. The snow was not nearly deep enough to cushion the bone-jarring impact. There was a flash of pain, and then nothing. Douglas' vision flickered. He saw the worthless lamp, half-buried in snow, several feet away. He saw the demon, limping, as it scuttled away into the darkness. He vaguely felt the cold wet snow melting against his feverish body. And then nothing.

CHAPTER 12

The Christmas lights shone through a haze of prescription painkillers. The doctors had said that he must sleep; they had forced sedatives upon him, and Faye had ruthlessly seen that he'd followed the doctors' instructions. Douglas was spared from the wind, but plunged helplessly into the torment of dreams. Lately, he'd been palming the sedatives and doubling up on the painkillers. His theory: If 600 mg was good, then 1,200 was great. Other than dozing restlessly, he hadn't slept for the past two days, and he was groggy enough most of the time to pretend that the plaintive voice was not calling him.

Much of the week since his fall was a muddled collage of hospital white—a flurry of doctors and nurses; the cast encasing his right arm; Faye, pale without makeup—but through the swirl of washed-out memories, a sentence that his wife had spoken during one of his brief rendezvous with lucidity stood out clearly: "When you're able…when you're well enough, I want you to move out."

The insurance company had seen to it that he'd moved out of the hospital soon enough, so he assumed that she meant from their home, the house where they had lived for twenty-three years, and where their son had died. Faye had not elaborated on her request, and Douglas had not asked for clarification, at the time or since, but it was galling for him: He had decided to leave her, yet she had kicked him out. She'd beaten him to the punch, when he was in the hospital, no less.

Not that he could argue with her decision. After all, the EMTs had found him unconscious, naked in the snow, amidst broken glass and a tattered Venetian blind, three floors beneath the shattered window of a lithesome and attractive, if somewhat hysterical, subordinate co-worker who claimed that he'd taken a swan dive out of her bed and through the window, with only a heavy lamp to break his fall. Didn't look good.

He couldn't even blame Melanie for not lying. She had been frantic, and she hadn't known the whole story—as if her telling the EMTs and the police (oh, yes, the police had been quite interested; an executive "finds" the body of a murdered co-worker one night and then throws himself out of a window the next) that a blood-drinking monster had been clinging to the side of the building and watching them have sex would have made the story more innocent, or believable.

Sands hadn't volunteered that information, after all. Not to Detective Havelin, who was investigating Gerry's murder, and not to Faye, and not even to Melanie. Melanie had come to visit him in the hospital once. Douglas had been surprised to see her initially, but then again, their secret was no longer a secret, so her presence was more gauche than stupid. She was as confused as anyone about what had happened; she hadn't seen the thing outside the window, and Douglas hadn't bothered to try to convince her that the stalker had been back. There was no way, short of a ladder or a rappel, that *anyone* could have been at that window. There was no explanation that Douglas could give. No reasonable explanation. And so he was left with his own private, unreasonable explanation. The worst part was that, this time, he knew that it was true. He knew that the lurker had been there—he had 128 stitches around his eye from its claw as proof—and that it would have drunk

Melanie's blood. But who would have believed him? The gash in his face was "obviously" caused by broken glass from the window through which *he* had thrown himself.

As certain as Sands was that the lurker had been present, he was just as mystified by something else: He hadn't set out to dive through the window. At least, he didn't think so. What *had* he been trying to do? Chase away the lurker? Kill it? Surely almost killing himself wasn't the best way to accomplish either of those goals, or to protect Melanie in the long term. And there was the matter of *how* he'd done it. He should never have been able to shoot through the window that way—not from the bed, not without a running start and brandishing a large, heavy lamp. Sands couldn't explain it to his own satisfaction, but he was left to make up explanations for everyone else.

He'd decided early on that his best bet was to convince them that he'd been asleep and having a nightmare. That was why he'd flung himself out the window. The psychiatrist who had evaluated him in the hospital had been skeptical.

"Night terrors are not uncommon," the doctor had said, "but Ms. Vinn says she didn't think you could have been asleep." He was flipping back through the pages on his clipboard, checking his notes.

"She thought wrong."

"She says that the two of you had just finished making love."

Douglas had tried to raise himself onto his elbows and met with limited success. "Look, Doctor…what did you say your name was?" He tried to see the name pin but couldn't focus properly.

"Laney. Dr. Laney."

"Okay. Well, look, Dr. Laney…are you married?" Dr. Laney nodded. "Good. So what is one of the first things you do after you screw your wife—or somebody else's wife, for that matter? Hm? You go to sleep. Whatever Ms. Vinn thought, she was wrong."

Dr. Laney had evidently found Douglas to be sane, if not cooperative. He hadn't been kept for extended psychiatric evaluation. The powers-that-be at Founders' Memorial Hospital had sent him home with his wife. Perhaps they decided that was a sufficiently disagreeable treatment for a decidedly disagreeable patient.

Douglas had spent the first night home in their bed. Alone. The next day, he'd made his way out to his recliner and decided that was the most comfortable place he could stay. And he had—aside from occasional trips to the bathroom. Comfort was not a simple matter, not with a broken wrist that required a full arm cast, a sprained neck, a severe concussion, 128 stitches, and broken ribs. Everyone agreed that he'd been remarkably lucky that he hadn't broken his neck, or his back, or punctured any internal organs—almost everyone agreed, rather. Douglas thought everyone else had a distorted sense of what was lucky. Ironically, in throwing himself through the window and careening three stories to the ground, he had not hurt his back.

So Douglas' recliner had served as his throne and his bed. He wouldn't let Faye feel superior by giving up her own bed and sleeping in the guest room. Instead, he, injured as he was, staked out the high ground. He didn't want to sleep, anyway. He wanted to sit and stare at the damn Christmas lights; he wanted to look at the ornaments and try to remember which year they'd been new; he wanted to relive some of the early years of his marriage and remember exactly what it was he'd thrown away. He sat, and brooded, and pulled a blanket tight about his shoulders as a shield against the wind. Faye took care of his physical needs but didn't speak to him otherwise—not until tonight, Christmas Eve.

She had gone to bed a few hours ago, but now she reappeared wrapped in a thick bathrobe. She didn't seem surprised that Douglas was still awake; she didn't acknowledge him but, instead, walked past him and into the living room, where she poured herself a shallow glass of Scotch.

"You don't like Scotch," Douglas said. She turned up the glass and drained it, grimacing, then poured herself another. "Well, at least pour me a glass."

"You can't drink with your medication."

"Good God."

Faye came back into the family room and sat down on the couch, curling her feet beneath her. She took a deep breath and sighed. She traced the rim of the glass with her finger. The silence was tiring and heavy, like a wet, smothering blanket. When finally Faye did speak, her words were hesitant: "Do you love her?" she asked. "Are you going to marry her?"

The questions caught Douglas off guard, but he supposed that they shouldn't have. He hadn't really thought about the future, about what he would do now that he'd made such a wreck of things. The phantasms that haunted his thoughts were of the past: a little boy, a prowling monster. The past, however, was the one thing that Faye could not face; she kept her face pointed bravely to the future, though it was the past, try as she might to ignore it, from which she could not disentangle herself. She was trying to find, desperately grasping for, something noble in the sordid mess their lives had become; she wanted Douglas to give her that much. But he found that he resented her, and the blinders she had worn for years, almost as much as he resented himself.

"Marry Melanie? No." He shook his head slowly, so as not to aggravate his neck. Faye, eyes downcast, accepted that without comment, but Douglas wasn't done. "And, no, I don't love her. Nothing that honorable."

Faye flinched. Then she looked up at him, glared.

"It was just the sex," he continued. "She was insatiable. I'm surprised I didn't have a heart attack. And, oh, if you're taping this for your lawyer, she was the fourth. The fourth affair." *You had to have known,* he thought. *I couldn't have fooled you that much unless you wanted to be fooled.*

Faye's glare evaporated almost as quickly as it had appeared. Her eyes were tired, sad. She finished the last of her Scotch, left the glass on the coffee table, and, saying nothing else, headed back toward the bedroom. Douglas recognized her retreat for what it was: If he wasn't going to help her salvage even a small portion of her dignity, then she wasn't going to give him the satisfaction of an argument. She didn't care that much anymore, and Douglas knew that he didn't either, not about their marriage. But the prospect of night, of his need to sleep, frightened him.

"Do you hear the wind?" he asked her quickly as she turned the corner.

Faye stopped, turned back to him; she didn't understand what he was asking. "It whips around that back corner of the house sometimes," she said, puzzled. "Sometimes it makes a moaning sound. Why?"

Because it's not always the wind, Douglas wanted to say. *Sometimes it's Adam. Calling me. Does he call you?* Douglas wanted to say all that, but he couldn't. Not to Faye, not after everything. *Because if that other monster is real, a blood drinking...a vampire, for God's sake...if that's real, does it mean the voice is real too?* "So...you hear it?" he asked her.

Faye sighed again. "Goodnight, Douglas." She turned away from him, and he let her go.

✢   ✢   ✢   ✢   ✢

Douglas awoke to a light touch on his arm. He should have been terrified; he should have run screaming. But instead of the revulsion and fear and indignation that had consumed him at the sight of the lurker, he was now overwhelmed by despair, by pity.

Adam stood by the recliner, his hand on Douglas' arm. The boy looked worried, his bottom lip pouched out in an exaggerated frown. "Daddy?" he said, quizzically. "Dad-dy?" Still looking worried, he turned and walked away with that awkward gait of a toddler. Douglas watched him as the child waddled to the French doors—and then through them.

Even that did not shock Douglas. As tears streamed down his cheeks, he was mortified to know that he could no longer pretend. The voice was not merely the wind whipping around the back corner of the house, like he wanted very desperately for it to be. The lurker was real; the gash on Douglas' face was from claws, not glass, like everyone assumed. And Adam was real.

Douglas pulled himself up from the chair. He held the blanket tightly around his shoulders. Each movement was an agony, but he would not stay there. He could not. He found his wallet, and his car keys, and he staggered out the front door into the dark and the cold and the wind.

PART TWO:

Mr. and Mrs. Kilby

CHAPTER 13

Sands awoke with a sudden jolt. The crystalline white sky was pressing down upon him, smothering him. With a cry, he threw out his hands to ward it off and struck slick, frosted glass. Only the pain was familiar: The precise blade of a stiletto stabbed again and again into his neck, the sprain offended by his sudden, jerky movement. Less familiar was the throbbing in his knee; he'd banged it against the steering wheel.

The plumes of his breath filled the interior of the car as he panted, not because of nightmares this time, but because of the realization that he'd fallen asleep. *I should've stayed awake! I should've stayed awake!* Despite weeks without proper rest, he had promised himself that he would stay awake. But, again, he had proven unable to keep a promise.

Anxiously, he scratched at the inside of the windshield, which was covered with a thin film of ice, his breath, captured and frozen while he slept. His right arm, with the cast, was incredibly awkward; he knocked the rearview mirror cockeyed. He was able to make only narrow gouges in the ice with the fingers of his left hand. The world beyond was an indistinct grey.

Trying to ignore the jagged complaints from his ribs, he reached down and felt under the seat, casting about frantically until he found his scraper. It peeled the ice from the windshield much more easily, but still Sands could see nothing. A light snow had fallen during the night—light, but enough to thinly blanket the outside of the glass. He turned the ignition part way, flicked on the wipers. He was still breathing rapidly. Despite the mundane nature of his tasks, he feared what he couldn't see; he feared what, momentarily, he *might* see.

As the wipers followed their metronomic arc, scraping over the bottom-most layer of frozen moisture, the powdery snow on top cascaded down the windshield to be shoved aside by the metal and rubber arms. At last, Sands could see, not completely through the frozen splotches clinging tenaciously to the glass, but enough.

He could see the darkened apartment complex: Melanie's building, the stairs that led up to the breezeway, the shrubbery oppressed by weighty snow and ice, the dumpster and it's spilling refuse with a delicate frosting of white, the condemned building, the blue tarp. According to the clock on his dashboard, it was later in the morning than he would have guessed. The veil of clouds was so solid, uninterrupted, that the sun might not yet have risen, for all the good it did. But the sun *was* up there, and that the meant that the lurker was held at bay...didn't it?

Wasn't that the way vampires worked: They came out at night, and sunlight—even cloud-obscured sunlight, he hoped—turned them to a pile of steaming goo if they were caught out? He'd never seen the lurker during the day, but then again, Sands had never been at Melanie's except at night. He tried to remember all the relevant details from movies and books: a cross, garlic, stake through the heart, sunlight.... Wasn't there something about they couldn't come into your home unless you invited them? He wasn't sure. It had been so long—probably thirty years since he'd read *Dracula*, and it might have been ten or fifteen since he'd read a few chapters of one of those Anne Rice books everyone had been talking about at the time.

They're just books, stories! he told himself, seized suddenly by a sense of profound absurdity, as he seemed subject to every few hours. But he'd *seen* the lurker and known it for what it was: dead and lusting after Melanie's blood! That made it a vampire, right?

As he watched the apartment buildings that Christmas morning, Sands didn't probe too deeply into *how* it was that he'd known what the lurker was. He'd been sure—in a way he'd never been sure about anything else in his life. He might have struggled with other questions—would he leave his wife? did he love her? did he love Melanie?—but he'd been *sure*, without question, that the thing he'd hurled himself at was a vampire. Sure, at least, of what the monster was, what it did. "Vampire" was the only name he knew to give it.

Sands wiped the inside of the windshield; it was fogging up. Feeling keenly now the cold that permeated his every bone and joint, he turned the car on, cranked the heater, and pulled the blanket that had fallen around his waist back up to his shoulders. He turned the radio on and listened to Christmas music. Barely hearing the *rum-pa-pum-pums* of the "Little Drummer Boy," Sands thoughts drifted to another little boy, a little boy who should not have touched Douglas' arm last night, should not have spoken to him. Douglas and Faye had shared two Christmases with Adam. Only two. He had grown old enough to enjoy receiving presents, tearing open the shiny paper and ripping off the bows, but still had had little idea of the holiday concept.

Douglas had already started shaking his head violently to clear his thoughts before he remembered his neck. A spike of pain shot from his jaw, behind his ear, to his temple, promptly reminding him. So many of his habits, his natural responses, seemed to cause pain—for him or for someone else.

But this pain, physical pain, helped distract him. He wasn't going to think about Adam; there was nothing he could do. But the lurker, the vampire, that was different. Last night, when Sands had walked out of his house with the blanket around his shoulders, he'd

ad no clear destination in mind. He'd simply walked.
Away from there. An hour had passed before he'd come
back, and though his battered body ached and
throbbed, he still hadn't managed to face his wife, his
home, his son. And so he'd gotten into his car, taking
with him only the blanket and an old baseball bat that
leaned dusty in the corner of the garage.

Sands' left hand drifted to his face, his fingers
tracing the stitches beside his eye. He well remembered the lurker's glaring red eyes, the bestial hiss,
the mouth full of jagged fangs, the claws raking his
face. Sands turned off the car and climbed out, Louisville Slugger in hand. He set off across the treacherous parking lot, not sure what he hoped to accomplish. He had come here last night to safeguard
Melanie, to watch over her, and he had fallen asleep.
He needed to know that she was all right.

He moved carefully over the icy pavement, trying
not to jar his neck. His ribs hurt no matter what; a deep
breath was enough to set them off. If he did meet the
lurker, what, he wondered, could a one armed man do
with a baseball bat? He tested steadying it with the fingers of his right hand that peeked out from beneath the
cast, and took a few tiny, awkward swings. The results
were not inspiring. He'd best hope he was right about
vampires not coming out during the day, he decided.

He didn't go toward the stairs and the breezeway but, instead, around behind the building. He
could have faced the lion today—if worst came to
worst, he could beat the hell out of it with the bat—
but he couldn't face Melanie. There were too many
unsettled emotions vying for supremacy within
Sands' abused body. He felt a certain steadfastness
of purpose in his need to protect her, and he didn't
want lust or love or whatever he felt for her to get
in the way and confuse the issue.

The snow behind the building was marred by hundreds of footprints; last night's dusting had not been enough to cover them. The largest flattened area was where Sands had landed. Perhaps, in retrospect, flinging himself through the window had not been the wisest of moves, but there'd been no time to think to calculate, and he'd been overcome by his surety of the evil thing lurking outside. He still didn't *think* that he'd meant to throw himself through the window, but it was so difficult to reconstruct precisely what had happened, and *why*, after the fact.

He thought he could still pick out where the lamp had landed and poked a deep hole in a drift. Otherwise, the ground was tangle of footprints from the EMTs and, later, Detective Havelin, no doubt.

Sands stared beyond the "accident scene" at the condemned building, devoid as it was of trees or lights or decorations; only the blue tarp lent a glimpse of color to the dour grey and brown landscape of snow, ice, and winter-stripped trees. He turned and looked up at Melanie's replaced window. Her blinds were open— *hasn't she learned anything?*—and warm and inviting light streamed out, defying the gloom. As he watched, Sands saw movement inside, someone passing in front of and momentarily obscuring the light. He didn't catch sight of Melanie herself, but he felt sure it must be her—not unquestioningly *positive*, like he'd been sure about the lurker, but enough. He hurried, as much as he could, back around the building to his car.

Before he left, Sands scribbled a brief note, left-handed—*Keep the damn blinds closed. And down ALL the way*—and stuffed it part way under her door.

❖   ❖   ❖   ❖   ❖

Downtown Iron Rapids was moribund and nearly deserted on normal business days. On Christmas, it

as a veritable ghost town. Most of the shops had
ed years ago to the suburbs and to malls beyond the
erimeter highway. Pockets of grand old houses that
ad once been home to genteel society had been sub-
ivided into apartments and left to rental squalor.

The years had not been kind to the city, nor to
he industries that supported it, that were its reason
or being. The iron mines had petered out decades ago,
nd shortly thereafter the steel mills they had spawned
ollowed suit. Only the foresight of the city fathers and
he rugged determination of the inhabitants had kept
he place alive. Many of the mills were converted to
nanufacturing, and Iron Rapids had become another
f those satellite communities supporting the almighty
uto industry in Detroit. And as in those other cities,
lint, Pontiac, the near collapse and subsequent reor-
anization of the industry in the early eighties had
truck Iron Rapids like a runaway luxury sedan. As far
s Sands could see, those earlier, ruggedly determined
ron Rapidians had given way to generations of the
vorking poor and welfare-dependent.

Sands was surprised to find anything open down-
own; he'd was driving through the empty streets for
no real reason, just driving, when he'd spotted the
ights at Zahn's Bakery at the corner of Main and
Burlington. Parking was an imprecise exercise on the
vinter streets. He pulled his car as close as he could
o the mound of grimy, frozen snow that concealed
parking spaces and meters alike.

As soon as he opened the door to the bakery and
vas awash in the wholesome smell of fresh bread,
Sands realized how incredibly hungry he was. He'd
elt compelled to leave his blanket in the car, and so
he was in only his shirt sleeves, sweat pants, and
sneakers, but the girl behind the counter didn't seem

to think anything of it, despite the bitter cold and occasional flurries outside. Sands ordered a baguette and coffee and settled onto a hard wooden chair at a table in the corner. Christmas music played over the speakers in here too, a different radio station than he'd had on in his car.

The bread was still steaming as he broke it apart. He closed his eyes and sighed as he chewed. Despite the coffee, he felt an intense lethargy sweeping over him. He wasn't sure if it was the warmth and food, exhaustion, or the pain pills, of which he downed another handful. He tried to concentrate on immediate questions like that, on things trivial and inconsequential: What radio station was that? How many loaves did these people make in a day? Good coffee, what kind? Did he remember this building being a Chinese restaurant a few years ago? How much sugar sludge would be in the bottom of his coffee cup? He tried to think about anything in the here and now; at the moment, he couldn't face the past, things he'd seen and done, or the future, where he'd go from here.

The familiar figure that walked through the door shortly after Sands' started on his second cup of coffee seemed out of place; several seconds passed before the synapses fired and Douglas realized who he was seeing. Albert Tinsley seemed to have much the same reaction. His gaze passed over Sands, went on to the menu board mounted behind the counter, then jerked back to Douglas. "Douglas? You're out of the hospital. Merry Christmas! Is Faye with you?"

"Go ahead and order," Sands nodded toward the girl behind the counter and tried to hide his fatigue.

"Good idea," Tinsley nodded. "Hi, Michelle," he said to the girl. He was wearing jeans, boots, and a heavy woolen sweater, apparel much more appropriate for the weather than was Sands'. Dressed like he was, Albert's grey beard made him look like a mountain man, and the deep wrinkles at his eyes and mouth seemed more a testament to hours spent exposed to the harsh elements rather than signs of age. His mood was, typically, pleasant as he joined Sands. "How are you, Douglas?" He paused for a moment as he took a closer look at his co-worker. "You look like hell."

"Thanks," Sands said, raising his coffee cup in salute.

"No, I'm serious. You *do* look like hell," Tinsley said, concerned. "Have you been out of the hospital long? Are you sleeping any?"

"Not long, and not much. I did sleep last night. Some. Look, can we talk about something else?"

"Sure," Tinsley said, but he couldn't hide his worry. Still, he tried his best to sound casual. "So, what brings you downtown to Zahn's? I haven't run into you here before."

"You come here a lot? You live near here?"

"Not far at all. A few blocks."

"Oh." Sands was surprised to learn that. Nothing around here was the greatest part of the city, and he knew that Albert pulled in a decent salary. "Well, me...? Faye kicked me out."

Tinsley laughed—then, mortified, realized Sands wasn't joking. "Oh, God. Douglas, you're serious. I'm...so sorry. But at Christmas...?"

"She didn't specify when, exactly," Sands said dryly. "But I figured, hey, no time like the present."

They sat in morose silence for a few minutes. The coffee suddenly seemed bitter, and the odor of baking bread not so comforting. Tinsley, his earlier attempts at conversation having met with disaster, was obviously at a loss, and Sands wasn't feeling chatty. But Albert was nothing if not resilient, and was soon ready to try again: "Do you need somewhere to stay? I mean...you look like you slept in your car."

"It was a long night. I was hunting vampires."

"Excuse me?"

Douglas sighed. "Never mind. And no thanks. I couldn't put you to that trouble. I'll get a hotel room."

"I'm not asking to be polite, Douglas. You don't have anywhere to stay—come to my house. Even if it's only for tonight."

"Aren't you afraid I'll throw myself out the window?" Sands asked.

Tinsley paused, then: "I did hear an odd story to that effect. But I don't have an upstairs, so it might be the safest place you could go."

❖   ❖   ❖   ❖   ❖

Albert lived in one of the shotgun shacks near the Iron River. The cramped and tightly packed structures had originally housed mining families, hard-working, short-lived men and women who had generally owed lock, stock, and barrel to the company store. The steel workers had never deigned to live in this neighborhood, which they dubbed "the Islands," because of the tendency of the river, a tame tributary of the Grand River most of the year, to flood in the spring, transforming the inundated river basin into a tiny archipelago of shingled roofs. A series of culverts designed by the Army Corps of Engineers in the seventies had alleviated that problem, though the dirt cellars in the Islands still flooded regularly. By then, however, the mines were dead, the mills closed, and the workers from those two industries inhabited the poverty-stricken area in equal numbers. Some managed to purchase their homes, but most of the shacks were now rental houses, snatched up by some of the established money families in the city: the Pecks, the Schneiders, the Ellsworths, the Gordons, among others.

Albert's shack was what Faye would have called a "bungalow," meaning that the roof didn't leak much, and the structure had both some insulation and indoor plumbing. (The Islands had been the last neighborhood to receive city water and sewage services, when social activists had finally brought to public attention the severe health hazard caused by outhouses during the spring flooding each year.)

"How long have you been here?" Sands asked when they entered. Despite his initial misgivings, he could tell at once how much work Tinsley must have put into the place. It was warm and comfortable, lived in.

"A few years," Albert said. "I did have a newer place out at Spring Cove, but I didn't need something that big, and after fixing this up, I've been able to do other things with my money." As he spoke, Tinsley showed Sands to the closet-like guest bedroom.

"You must have done a hell of a lot of work," Sands said, suppressing a yawn. He climbed onto the bed, just to test the springs; he eased back and propped up his feet.

"Yep. Ripped out the walls. New plumbing and wiring. Tore up the linoleum, put in the hardwood floors. Pretty much re-did it from the ground up."

Sands yawned again. He couldn't hold it in this time. "Excuse me. It's not the company. He stretched, carefully, so as not distress his various injuries, and groaned. "So, tell me this, Albert…." But before he could completely formulate the question, much less ask it, Sands was asleep.

CHAPTER 14

Detective Eric Havelin rapped a knuckle against the frosted glass on the door to the medical examiner's office. Her "Come in" was noticeably curt. She didn't offer him a seat, but he sat anyway. He kept his coat on; the place was so cold he wondered if maybe she was keeping the stiffs in her filing cabinet. He'd met the good doctor before, briefly. She was the all-business type. He guessed that she was a little younger than he was, maybe mid-forties, but still quite the looker, in a severe sort of way.

"Dr. Vanderchurch, I'm really sorry to bother you on the holiday," he began, trying to strike a conciliatory note.

"There is a reason I have an unlisted phone number, Detective," she said sharply.

"That's okay. Don't worry about it. It wasn't any trouble for me to find it. Just a little detective work, heh, heh. That's what I get paid for." Havelin, glancing around, didn't think he'd ever seen an office kept so meticulously: no stacks of papers or files, except for a few in the out box on her desk, and one file on the desk top beside Nissa Vanderchurch's computer terminal. "That for me?" he asked, indicating the singled out file with a nod of his head.

Vanderchurch handed it to him. "I don't see why this couldn't have waited. I generally spend Christmas day with my husband and children."

"Yeah, like I said, I'm really sorry about that," Havelin said, beginning to flip through the pages of the autopsy report. "I *generally* bother Lois for this kind of thing," he said, appropriating the doctor's syntax, but with an almost flippant, not-quite-mocking tone. "But she said you did this autopsy yourself, and you had the file, and you were going to take the whole week off. You see, I'm looking for clues about a murder weapon, and I can't wait until after New Year's." He looked up from the report, at Vanderchurch, and spoke more solemnly: "So you see, that's why it couldn't wait. And I appreciate your trouble. Oh, and you should give Lois a raise. I told her that the easiest thing would be for her just to get this for me, but she wasn't having any of that. She wasn't going through your files for anything."

"I should think not," Vanderchurch said.

"She's a good kid." *And a lot easier than you to badger into doing what I want—most of the time*, he thought. He smiled at the grim doctor, her hair pulled back into a tight bun. She seemed fit and well-endowed, but Havelin saw her as cold and rigid. He wondered if she'd found the perfect job, or if it was the job that had turned her into an ice queen.

"I don't think you're going to find much to help you there," she said, nodding to indicate the report now in his hands, mimicking precisely Havelin's earlier gesture.

Cold, rigid, and sharp, Havelin thought. "And why's that?"

"Because I have no earthly idea what caused that injury."

Havelin frowned at her, then turned back to the report. "Massive trauma to the skull from a blunt object…" he read.

"The cranium," Vanderchurch recited, "was fractured from the crest of the frontal bone vertically to the glabella by a single blow."

"*A single blow*. Geeze Louise." Havelin whistled and shook his head. "What could have made that kind of break, busted through damn near half his skull, without crushing the whole thing?"

"Like I said," Vanderchurch again mimicked him, "I have no earthly idea."

"How about unearthly?"

"Whatever it was," she continued, "it was very hot. There was very little bleeding. The wound seems to have been cauterized very quickly, maybe as it was made."

Havelin studied the report and tried to ignore Vanderchurch. Her smug satisfaction irritated him; she seemed pleased by the prospect that his disrupting her holiday might not do him any good. The least he could do, he decided, was to occupy as much of her time as possible. "Can you show me the body?"

"It's already gone to the crematorium," she said.

"Oh. I see," Havelin said, thwarted. He looked over the report for a few more minutes and asked what questions he could think of. Eventually, he closed the file. "Well," he said with a forced smile, "somebody sure had it in for Mr. Gerald Stafford. And since I know it wasn't me, and it wasn't you, I guess I better go look elsewhere."

"That would seem expeditious," Vanderchurch said dryly.

"Vanderchurch. Is that Scandinavian? You don't look Scandinavian."

"It's a Dutch name."

"You don't look Dutch either, heh, heh."

"My husband's name," she said with an impatient sigh.

"Oh. Right. Well…" Havelin stood and moved to the door. "You have kids? You said that, didn't you?"

"I would like to go home to them, Detective."

"Right. Well…sure you do. Thanks again." He half-saluted her with the file folder, and then closed the office door behind him.

❖   ❖   ❖   ❖   ❖

A few minutes after the tiresome detective left, Dr. Vanderchurch removed the notes regarding the autopsy of Gerald Stafford from her desk and placed them into her briefcase. They would go home and join her private files. The official report did not state, and the police did not need to know, that many of Stafford's internal organs had apparently not functioned for, as far as she could tell, close to a year *before* the mysterious blow that had supposedly killed him last week. She didn't know who had struck that blow, but she hoped any trail that might lead to that person was sufficiently cold.

CHAPTER 15

"Going out again?" Tinsley asked.

"Yep." Sands was still wearing his long-sleeved T-shirt, sweats, and sneakers. He'd traded his blanket for a winter coat that Albert had lent him. The house was warm, but Sands held his arms and the coat firmly against his body; he hadn't asked permission to borrow the flask that was tucked in his left armpit, and he was in a hurry, though he couldn't imagine Tinsley objecting. As Sands headed for the door, he noticed that Albert was lacing up his boots. "You too? Going out?"

"I am, in fact," Tinsley said.

Sands had the door open, but he felt that a moment of small talk was the least he could do after Albert had been kind enough to put him up—and to put up with him. "With your friend who called earlier? Your *lady* friend?"

Albert chuckled. "I *am* meeting my friend, and she does happen to be a lady."

"Well…enjoy."

"Douglas," Tinsley called as Sands stepped out and started to pull the door closed behind him. Sands poked his head back inside. "Where are you going?" Albert paused uncomfortably. "What I mean is…I hate to think of you sitting alone at a bar or something. You're welcome to come along with us. It's not a date or anything like that."

"I appreciate that, Albert. I really do. But I'll be fine. You have a good time with your lady friend." Sands pulled the door closed before Albert could protest further—and as he did so, the flask slipped from beneath his arm and the coat, and clattered onto the porch. He snatched up the container as quickly as he could, keeping his neck and ribs in mind, and hurried down the shoveled walk.

The hazy gloom of dusk had given way fully to the more complete darkness of night. With such a thick cloud cover, what little light there was during the day went very quickly once early evening arrived. The sun may have set spectacularly somewhere, but here there was but a brief deepening of murkiness, and then night. As Sands pulled away in his car, he felt that the overcast sky was pressing down upon him; it seemed so close with its heavy clouds stretching in every direction. Maybe that was why the blue collar folks never seemed to escape Iron Rapids, even when the jobs were gone, and it would have seemed in their best interest to go elsewhere: The horizon seemed so close and impenetrable all around, he could see how they might think this city was the whole world.

Sands set the silver-plated flask in the passenger's seat beside his Louisville Slugger. He'd found the flask in a box in the guest room closet — actually, the closet was more of a cubbyhole; the guest bedroom itself probably qualified as a closet with a single bed stuffed in it. But the lodgings had seemed a palace—if a small palace—to Sands. He'd fallen asleep Christmas morning just after arriving, and slept all day, all that night, and all the next day as well. Upon waking, he'd felt somewhat stunned but greatly improved. Rightly or wrongly, he'd slept the sleep of the just, of the dead—better than some of the dead that he'd seen recently. Perhaps his body had finally taken as much as it could, or maybe being away from Faye and the house and the pool had made the difference. Whatever the reason, Sands felt like a human being again. The circles under his eyes were not quite so dark. He was still nursing his aches and pains, but just knowing that he *could* sleep made the discomfort much more bearable.

"God bless Albert Tinsley," Sands said with a wry smile. Albert had provided a roof, a bed, food, and last night, like tonight, he'd offered his company as well. Douglas didn't want to seem ungrateful, but the truth was that he wasn't sitting around pitying himself—or, at least, not *just* that. He appreciated Albert's offer, but Sands had yet to come up with a satisfactory way to explain where he was going and what he was doing: *Well, you see, there's this vampire stalking my girlfriend…* just didn't seem the right approach somehow.

The day before, Sands had woken up around late afternoon and, despite how good it had felt, been horrified at how long he'd slept. He'd left Melanie on her own for a night! Never mind that she'd been on her own for more than a week while Douglas had convalesced in the hospital and at home, and she'd lived by herself for several *years* before that. Sands' need to be there, to stake out her apartment, had grown to a fairly compulsive level of intensity. He recognized that. But it didn't change the facts: He was the only one who knew about the lurker; he was the only one who might be able to stop the monster, though it might cost his own life. *That's probably what I deserve*, he thought, *after everything I've done*. It wasn't like anyone would miss him.

And so he'd fended off Tinsley's attempts at care-taking again tonight, and now was on his way to Melanie's. He stopped only once, at a package store to buy a bottle of Scotch, part of which he poured into Albert's flask. The flask had been full of water, but Sands poured that out onto the frozen parking lot of the store. He'd grown distinctly cold and stiff during last night's uneventful watch and decided that a few nips would raise his spirits and relax his sore muscles.

Quite a few people were out for a Monday night. Many of them, especially at the package store, were in pickups with fishing gear in the back. They were probably getting back from a long weekend of ice fishing. *That would be enough to drive anybody to drink,* Sands thought, taking a sip of his Scotch.

There was a lot of activity at Melanie's apartment complex too: more pickups trolling parking lot, country music blaring in competition with the rap emanating so forcefully from other neon-bedecked cars that Sands' rearview mirror vibrated. Unlike during his former visits to see Melanie, he steered clear of the few functional streetlights and found a shadowed parking spot. He backed in and sat unobtrusively watching the parade of stereophonic malcontents. *How in the world can she stay in this place?* he asked himself for perhaps the two thousandth time.

As an hour passed, and then another, and the parking lot traffic grew more sparse, Sands' thoughts shifted to another track. Gradually, his resentment of the other drivers grew duller, and he wondered of them: *Do any of them know? Am I the only one?* As another low-riding, purple, vibrating-to-the-music car cruised past, Sands tried to peer through its tinted windows and glean something, *anything*, about the driver—but he could see nothing beyond the darkened glass. This was the first that Sands had thought about the lurker in a broader context. *Have any of these people seen what I've seen?* The idea, the hope that someone else could confirm and validate what he'd been going through, was heartening at first. Sands' spirits rose; for a moment he didn't feel quite so isolated, so alone—but then his mind, not willing to leave well enough alone, continued the progression to its next logical step: *If I'm not the only one who's seen an actual monster, then isn't it just as possible that the lurker, my lurker, isn't the only one of those out there either?*

Sands' burgeoning philosophy of hope and comfort almost instantly twisted itself into a cruel mockery. He was suddenly cold, through and through. The other drivers, who for a few brief moments he'd started to view as potential allies, were now suddenly alien and hostile again. They were probably *all* lurkers, predators of one sort or another. Sands had encountered his share of human predators; maybe they weren't all as human as he'd thought. He wished that his own windows were tinted, that he could be completely invisible sitting in the darkness.

I must be the only one who's seen it, he decided. *It must be the only one, the only lurker, the only vampire.* That had to be the truth. He couldn't begin to comprehend a world full of those creatures. He pushed the entire, unsettling question from his mind.

Earlier, Sands had turned the car on once or twice to run the heater. With so much traffic and noise, he'd felt fairly inconspicuous. Now, he was sure that if he did so again, someone or some*thing* would take notice. So instead, he reached for the flask, uncomfortable with even that slight movement. He tried to remain as still as humanly possible, and, despite the Scotch, he felt the cold seeping through his clothes and into his bones. Wool socks and sneakers were little protection; over the next hour or so, feeling began to retreat from his toes. His neck grew stiff as well, and his face became so cold and lifeless that he feared the skin might contract and tear the stitches apart.

But there was very little traffic now. An idling car would be too noticeable. The clock on the dash read: 12:18. Sands wondered suddenly if he should cover the clock; would the wan green light it gave off reveal him to the lurker? After all, the creature had stared at Melanie and him with its red eyes from a balcony of the condemned building.

Then another terrible thought came to him: The monster could climb up the side of the building and break in through the window while Sands was sitting here watching the steps! *Good God!* He reached for his bat, not sure exactly what he should do, but knowing he needed to check the apartment more closely, at least make sure that neither the door nor the window nor the sliding glass door on the balcony was smashed in. *How stupid could I be?*

As if in answer to his question, at that moment, Melanie drove up and pulled into the parking spot next to his. As she got out of her car, she did a double take. "Douglas?" She'd pulled in forward, so their driver's sides were right next to one another.

Sands sat in shock. He pressed himself back into his seat, but it didn't do any good; crawling onto the floorboard wouldn't have helped at this point. Not only had he been discovered, which was bad enough, but he'd been watching Melanie's apartment, supposedly protecting her, *and she hadn't even been home*.

"Douglas?" Melanie tapped softly on his window.

Sands sighed, and he felt as if the mist of his breath was all the air being released from a balloon. He pressed the button for the window, but nothing happened; he turned the key part way, and then pressed the button again. He lowered the window just a few inches. "Uh…hi."

"What are you doing? Have you been waiting long?"

It's not you that I'm waiting for, he thought. But he couldn't tell her. There was just too much to explain. "Uh…no. Not…long. Not too long." She just stood there looking at him. She wouldn't go away. Sands wanted more than anything for her to go away.

Instead, she wrinkled her nose and sniffed. "What's that smell? Have you been drinking?" Sands didn't respond. "Well…" she said after a few seconds, "would you like to come in?"

"No. I mean…I *can't*. I…I'll walk you up."

"Uh…okay."

Sands wanted, at the least, to make sure that her apartment was safe, but he wasn't going to stay; he couldn't let himself be distracted.

"I'm sorry I wasn't here," Melanie said as they started walking. "You should have called. I was out with a friend." She didn't notice the baseball bat until they were about half way across the parking lot. "Douglas, what's that?"

"What?"

"What you're trying to hide behind your back—that's what."

"Oh, this." He sheepishly showed her the bat. "Nothing. Just a…uh…a…"

"Baseball bat."

"Right."

"And you have it…why? Isn't spring training still a couple months away?"

"Let's go up, Melanie." He scanned their surroundings as he took her by the arm and ushered her toward the steps.

"What's *wrong* with you?" she asked, but Sands didn't pause. She jerked her arm away—he had the bat in his left hand, and the cast didn't allow him to get a firm grip with his right—and stopped. "Quit that. What is going on?" Sands looked at her only briefly. He was more concerned with trying to penetrate the darkness of the condemned building, but he couldn't make out any shadowy, lurking figure. Only the blue tarp. "*Douglas?*"

"Look. Can we talk about this upstairs. Please."

Melanie relented, but she wouldn't let him take her arm as they climbed the steps. As she unlocked the door, Sands clutched the bat in his hand and glared at the faux-brass lion, silently daring it so much as to twitch. "Let me go first," he said when the door was open.

"What are you…?"

But he'd already stepped past her and was examining the living room and kitchen. Then he saw that she was standing in the breezeway, *alone*, watching him. "Good God. Come in. Shut the door and lock it. No…*wait.*" Should he have her lock the door? What if the monster was already inside, and they needed to make a quick getaway—as opposed to it sweeping in behind her from outside?

Melanie, however, seemed to have little patience with his indecision, and she wasn't waiting for instruction, regardless. She closed the door and locked it. "How long have you been out of the hospital?" she asked. "Are you still taking medication?"

"Wait right there. By the door," Sands said. He quickly but thoroughly checked the rest of the apartment: bathroom, closets, under the bed. Realizing that he'd neglected the balcony, he hurried back to the living room and found that Melanie had not, in fact, waited by the door. Sands muttered curses under his breath as he lifted the curtain and peered out onto the balcony.

"I still have beer in the fridge," Melanie said, brushing her hair out of her eyes, "but you smell like you've already been hitting the booze. Are you taking some medicine your not supposed to drink with?"

"I can't stay," Sands said, heading for the door. "Everything looks okay here."

"Oh no you don't." Melanie blocked his way to the door. "You sit out in the parking lot waiting for me, and now you're going to turn around and leave? I don't think so. Not until you tell me why you're being such a freak."

Sands only partially heard her; he was trying to decide what was the best location from which to watch the building. He couldn't see much beside the steps from the parking lot. Maybe the woods behind the building; then he could see her window, balcony, and door, as well as the condemned building.

"Douglas? Hello? What's going on?"

"I've got to go. It's the stalker," he said. *The lurker, the vampire*.

"What? You saw him? While you were waiting?"

"Yes," he lied. If that was what it was going to take… He'd lied for much less noble reasons.

"Okay. Then we'll call the police."

"He hasn't *done* anything," Sands objected. "Like you said before, he probably lives around here."

"There are anti-stalking laws on the books," Melanie said, "if it's not just your imagination."

"It is *not* my imagination."

"Fine. Then at the very least the police could identify him. That would probably scare him off."

"They won't find him," Sands said. "They'll never find him."

Something in the way he said that worried Melanie. She stepped away from him, glanced down at the bat in his hand. "I don't think you should be driving, Douglas. Why don't you stay here?"

"I can't." He stepped past her to the door. "I can't be distracted. I can't."

"What? What are you talking about? You can sleep on the couch if you want. I just don't think you should be driving. Not tonight."

"I can't," he said again, opening the door. "And make sure to lock this behind me. And keep the curtains closed and the blinds *all the way down*."

Melanie cocked her head and gave him a hard stare. "I *thought* you wrote that note, but it must have been left-handed," she said, looking at his cast, "and I wasn't sure. What were you doing here Christmas morning? How long have you—"

But Sands pulled the door closed. He suddenly knew exactly what he had to do, and set off for the condemned building next door.

CHAPTER 16

All of the first floor windows on the condemned building were boarded up. The precaution seemed to have thwarted most of the potential vandals, but a few had made a point of lobbing rocks or shooting out the glass above the first floor. Sands, like an ardent vandal, was not dissuaded by plywood. His feet were cold to the point of numb as he crunched around the building in the snow, but he hardly noticed. He was too intent on getting inside.

Melanie had not followed him, for which he was thankful. She couldn't seem to grasp that he was doing all of this for her, taking all these insane chances for her. He didn't blame her for not understanding—she hadn't seen what he had seen—but a little faith would have gone a long way. Her skepticism was a personal affront against him, but, again, he supposed that he hadn't given anyone much reason to respect his integrity.

He climbed the stairs to the third floor breezeway of the condemned building. From the railing there, he decided that he should be able to climb to the balcony beneath the blue tarp; there were only two or three feet separating the breezeway railing from the balcony railing. Without snow or ice, and for a moderately athletic person, it would have been a fairly simple climb—more a step across. But there were both snow *and* ice. And Sands, even though he considered himself *at least* moderately athletic, had one arm in a cast, and was recovering from a sprained neck and broken ribs.

He used the bat to scrape the two railings as clear as possible. That was the greatest challenge, to avoid slipping, he thought. He found, however, that climbing up onto the first railing wasn't as simple a matter as he'd believed, not with only one fully functional arm. He decided quickly that he could not climb and hold onto the bat, so he tossed it over onto the balcony. Now, with only the corner of the building to steady him, he struggled up onto the railing. He could have straddled it easily enough, but he needed to stand on it. Sands was distinctly aware of the fierce pounding of his heart as, face pressed against the icy building, he worked himself up onto his feet and, finally, standing.

The two or three feet separating the railings he now estimated as four or five feet, as he looked down at the void and the hard-packed snow on the ground beneath. He'd already fallen three stories once this holiday season; he didn't relish the idea of a repeat performance.

Aside from the corner of the building, which he would need to hold onto with his largely useless right hand, there was a light fixture mounted on the wall above the balcony; he didn't know how much weight the fixture could take, but he hoped it could help steady him if he didn't lean fully on it. He'd still have to step over to the balcony railing before he could reach the light fixture, though.

Standing on the railing, shivering, and surveying his immediate future, Sands was filled with a sense of foreboding. Despite the cold, he was sweating profusely. If his right foot or right hand slipped as he stepped across with his left foot, he would fall. If his left foot slipped and he missed grabbing the light fixture, or if he grabbed it and it didn't hold his weight, he would fall. If he fell, he might not be so "lucky" this time; he might break his neck, or his back, or his other arm, or both legs, or…

Good God! Sands thought, disgusted with himself and his doom mongering, and he stepped.

His right foot slipped; the fingers of his right hand, peeking from beneath the end of the cast, scrabbled ineffectually at the siding; his left foot stubbed the balcony railing; and, flailing for and grabbing the light fixture, he discovered how much weight it could hold: not enough.

The only thing that did go Sands' way during those few, elongated seconds as he tumbled across the void, was momentum. He managed somehow to get enough of a push-off with his right foot, as it slipped, to propel himself toward the balcony, and though he missed his step and stubbed his left foot, he fell into rather than away from the balcony. The light fixture, trailing wires like the veins of a decapitated beast, pulled free from the wall. The brief resistance it offered, however, was sufficient to spin Sands around. As he spun, the outside of his right knee cracked against the balcony railing, and he toppled over it, onto the floor. He landed hard on his back. On top of the baseball bat.

For quite a while, he lay stunned.

The dark, overcast sky seemed very close to the corner of the building's roof, maybe a few feet above it. Sands stared vacantly at that corner of roof, and the thick clouds, and the bare tips of trees that poked into his field of vision. The first sensation he slowly became aware of was cold. The back of his head was cold; his face was cold too, as a matter of fact, as the wind whisked away the last feeling from his nose and lanced his cheeks with hundreds of tiny pins, but the back of his head was resting in several inches of snow. Pain followed cold in rapid succession when he tried to move his head. His neck was having none of that, or at least wasn't taking it quietly. Sands let his head fall back to the snow, surrendering to the white-hot barbs. Perhaps in sympathy with his neck, his knee began to throb. Sands also became painfully aware of the bat lodged, quite uncomfortably, beneath his back.

He forced himself to start slowly, experimenting, carefully moving this part of his body then that, making sure that nothing was broken. His right knee gave him the most trouble, but it seemed still to work for the most part. Even being cautious, sitting up was a torment; the sharp pains in his neck made his eyes water. He sat there in the snow for several minutes, his butt becoming as numb as his face. His head slowly cleared.

This is crazy, he told himself. But *crazy* had ceased to hold meaning for Sands, or at least the term was not nearly specific enough for his needs. Or maybe the subject/object distinction was what lacked proper specificity. Was *this* (the fact that he had risked life and limb to jump/fall onto the balcony of a vacant apartment) crazy, or merely stupid, and *he* was crazy (read: insane)? Was the very fact that he had repeatedly seen the lurker crazy (impossible but true), or was Sands, again, crazy (insane)? What (or who) exactly was crazy: the situation, or the unfortunate bastard caught up within it? Or both?

It would be so much easier, Sands thought, if it were him, if he'd just nearly killed himself for no *real* reason. A brief stay in the appropriate institution, and then everything would be better, back to normal, not crazy, sane. He *wanted* to believe that was what was happening—wanted to, but didn't. He couldn't discount his own sanity, even though to do so would place the burden of insanity squarely with him and not, more disturbingly, with the rest of the world.

Either way, he decided, *I'm here, damn it*. He climbed to his feet and began to examine the blue tarp above him: It was fastened across the opening in the wall that had been covered by sliding glass doors before that fourth floor balcony had fallen and taken the doors with it. The tarp was not fastened so tightly, however, that a person couldn't slip under the bottom edge and into or out of the semi-exposed, vacant apartment behind it. Sands stood where he had seen the lurker stand. He turned and looked at Melanie's building, at her window, and saw that her blinds were closed and lowered all the way. He allowed himself a brief, self-congratulatory smile.

Turning back to the tarp, he noticed that the siding beneath it, just above him, was marred by several curious scratches—gouges, really. Their shape was vaguely familiar to him, but if Douglas Sands was growing gradually more sure of his own sanity—or at least more sure of the internal logic within his own psychoses—he was still not willing to make certain connections, and so he attributed the scratches to the disaster of the balcony collapsing—which was possible.

He pressed his face against the cold glass doors on his level. The apartment within was dark and deserted, though whoever had vacated it had not bothered to take all of his or her furniture before leaving, and management had not bothered to clean out the condemned apartments. Not pausing to give himself time to reconsider, Sands smashed his baseball bat against the large pane of glass of one of the sliding doors. His swing was one-handed, left-handed at that, and awkward; it bounced harmlessly off the glass. The covering of snow on the buildings, the trees, and the ground muffled the crack of the bat somewhat. Now that he had a better idea of how hard he needed to swing, and steadying the bat with the fingers of his right hand, he hit the glass again. A crack several inches long appeared. Sands hit the door again; the crack lengthened and split into a series of branching veins, or tributary rivers. Three more blows and that portion of the glass shattered, leaving the rest of the pane intact, except for an expanded series of cracks.

Sands peeked out from the balcony at the other, occupied building. Silence had reasserted itself after the thunderclaps of the bat and the tinkling of broken glass. As far as he could tell, Melanie wasn't peeking through her blinds, and he didn't see anyone else investigating the noise.

There was no need to break out the rest of the glass. Sands reached through and unlocked the door. He decided that an abandoned sofa inside suited his purposes, but maneuvering it proved fairly difficult. The sofa wasn't heavy, but it was bulky, and Sands, with his one good arm, had trouble getting a grip. If he shoved too hard with his body, his sore ribs acted up. All the while, he was trying not to jar his neck, and then a nail on the bottom of the sofa gouged the palm of his good hand. In the end, Sands had to prop the sofa upright on its side and drag it through the open door onto the balcony. The way the evening was going, he wouldn't have been at all surprised if *this* balcony gave way beneath him, and he and the sofa went crashing down onto the balcony below, and then that one gave way, and then the next, and the next, ad infinitum, until he ended up on the crushed balcony of the ninth level of hell.

Finally, he got the sofa situated how he wanted it: on end, propped against the wall beneath the blue tarp. He retrieved the bat and then climbed up the sofa, using the springs and underside like a ladder. He would have preferred for the sofa to have been longer; as it was, he could reach the opening beneath the tarp, but just barely. Climbing through was not easy. By grabbing hold of the tarp itself, he could do it. Again, barely. But like getting onto the balcony, he had to toss the bat ahead of him. And when he finally managed to scrabble up and over the edge and into the balcony-less apartment, he found himself face to face with the inhuman lurker.

CHAPTER 17

One particular listing on the commercial real estate web page caught Nathan's eye. He'd gone to the site out of little more than idle curiosity. Yes, he did have a vague notion about renting office space somewhere, but no firm plans nor even a tentative timetable. The idea seemed like an unjustifiable extravagance, not to mention an unnecessary risk. On the other hand, multiple locations would allow flexibility, as well as making his and his allies' operations more difficult to trace. Also, at some point, he was going to want to go to multiple servers, and there was only so much room in his current "office."

He'd poked around looking at the small-fry office space for a while, then clicked over to the more industrial-oriented listings. His interest in this particular page was, pure and simple, morbid fascination. Industry did not start up in Iron Rapids; factories downsized or closed, industrial space became available, and prices dropped. Nathan checked back every few weeks to see how much owners had lowered their asking prices. It was a guilty pleasure, watching white moneybags take it on the chin; Nathan felt like a rubbernecking motorist driving past the auto wreckage of somebody he *really didn't like*.

None of those prices, of course, had come anywhere near low enough for him to think about, nor would they ever. Nathan wasn't a venture capitalist. He made out well enough day trading and with a few other investments on the side, and that served his purposes. Get any bigger, and he'd attract unwanted attention. Nope, he wasn't in the market for industrial real estate.

What caught his attention was that somebody else apparently was. In Iron Rapids. *Hm. Go figure*, he thought. The old Hadley factory, which had sat vacant for years right down in the heart of the city, had been sold. The web site he was perusing was just realty listings; there were no details on sales, except that the location had indeed sold. Merely a temporary inconvenience, that.

Two searches and one insultingly infantile security code later, Nathan had the name of the company that had purchased the Hadley plant: Synthetic Solutions.

Hm. Nathan had heard of them, of course. He was active on NASDAQ as well as the New York Stock Exchange, among other exchanges. Like a great many technology stocks, SynSol had had a volatile year, but overall was gaining in value; it wasn't one of the overnight dot-coms, here today, gone tomorrow. He couldn't remember much more about the company, but he made a mental note to keep an eye on it. He also made a bet with himself on how many months would pass until the CEO came to his senses and backed out of the Iron Rapids market. Available labor was plentiful, considering the unemployment rate in the city, but workers with the education and training for a tech company...?

They'll never make a go of it here, Nathan thought. *They won't stay long. Nobody with any brains stays here.*

CHAPTER 18

"*Who are you?*" the beast whispered. "*Who are you to judge me?*"

Sands had just crawled and pulled himself under the tarp, into the abandoned apartment. The baseball bat, which he had tossed up ahead, was a couple of feet beyond his reach. He'd not yet sat upright when he saw the lurker—and it saw him.

Sands' lungs seized up and his breath caught in his throat. A putrid stench filled his mouth and nostrils—it was like the foul stink of the dumpster the first night that he'd seen…seen this *thing*.

The lurker was huddled in a corner. It's eyes seemed to glow red in the murkiness of the apartment's shadowy interior. The creature was as Sands remembered it: It's bald head was white as bone, the skin coarse and pasty; the flattened, crooked nose looked broken; it's jaw was hardly wider than its gaping mouth, which was overcrowded with jagged fangs. The stalagmite- and stalactite-like teeth rubbed together making a sound like scraping metal when the lurker spoke.

"*Who are you to judge me?*"

Sands didn't absorb the meaning of the words. He was too shocked that the thing was *speaking*. It was *dead*, but it was moving and talking. There was no life in the creature except what it had stolen. Sands couldn't spare more than a second or two to wonder how he knew all this: How did he know it was dead, that it drank blood, that it was unnatural, *wrong*? He wasn't sure; he simply *knew*. And he knew, also, that he had more immediate problems.

Idiot! he berated himself, glancing at the bat. He lunged for it, but the lurker was faster. Despite having been on the other side of the room, the monster reached the bat the same instant that Sands did. Clawed fingers dug into the thick wooden barrel just as Sands' hand grasped the handle. The lurker pinned the bat to the floor. Sands couldn't budge it.

"*What are you?*" the lurker asked. Speech was difficult for it; it struggled and over-enunciated each word, its teeth scraping like a mouthful of razor blades. The thing's clothes were little more than tattered rags; pale skin showed through in several spots.

"What am I?" Sands repeated, dumbfounded. "What am *I*?" His fingers gripped the handle of the bat as if his life depended upon it—and it might. The lurker had not tried to jerk the bat away from him, but neither did it allow him to pick it up. Sands forced himself to breathe. He was mere feet from the monster, but the stench didn't seem any stronger than before. He could feel his own eyes bulging in terror, growing dry from the cold air. *It didn't attack me*, Sands told himself, trying to keep calm, trying to keep from running and screaming. *It could have attacked me before I even looked up. Maybe it doesn't want to kill me.* He wanted to believe that; he wanted to believe it very much.

With a supreme effort of will, Sands climbed to his knees, all the while keeping his eyes on the lurker and his hand on the bat. His own forced calm seemed to upset the lurker; its ribbon-thin tongue flicked in and out among its crowded fangs. Sands wanted to stand up—he wouldn't feel quite so vulnerable standing—but he wanted more to keep his hand on the bat.

"What am I?" Sands said again. "What the hell are *you*?"

It hissed. Sands flinched. He might have turned and run had he not been clutching the bat like a lifeline. He noticed, almost distractedly, that the lurker's fourth and fifth finger were fused into one misshapen claw digging into the wood of the bat. Sands pictured that claw slitting his throat; he could almost feel the point digging into the flesh at his neck, tearing his throat open. *It doesn't want to kill me*, he told himself hopefully. *It doesn't want to kill me*.

Then he saw the bat again: Instead of "Louisville Slugger", it suddenly read "Louisville Killer" in the same flowing script. Sands' hopeful thoughts disintegrated. He knew he was being stupid. This thing would drink his blood if he gave it a chance. *It didn't attack me because it was surprised!* he suddenly realized. Not surprised that he'd shown up— he'd made enough noise to awaken the dead, if the lurker had been sleeping—but surprised that he'd *seen* it. *It hides*, Sands thought. *It hides, it waits, it kills*. The writing on the bat was back to normal now, "Louisville Slugger", but he could see again the flashing words on the face of the clock: **IT WAITS-TO KILL**.

Maybe, Sands thought. *But it's not going to kill Melanie*. "You want to know who I am?" he said to the lurker. "I'm the one who can see you." The monster stiffened and snarled. "You got that?" he rushed on, the unbidden revelations flooding into his mind as he faced the lurker. "You hide, and you wait, and you kill. You drink blood, you sick bastard. But they never see you, do they? Not until it's too late. Not until—"

Sands' eyes rolled upward. He watched the monster, but the beast was no longer in the condemned building. It was in a cramped, dark place, looking out at ankles and feet. A car. It was under a car. Watching someone walk past. In the parking lot. The parking lot just outside. The lurker slipped from beneath the car with amazing speed. The pedestrian was a young man, half drunk. But still he should have seen the creature coming at him from the side. But he *didn't* see, *couldn't* see. The lurker was on him, fanged maw at the man's throat—

Sands was back in the apartment, his knuckles white against the smooth wood of the baseball bat. The beast still held the other end. Sands blinked. He licked his lips but couldn't feel them; they were numbed by the cold. He wasn't sure what he'd just seen—except that it had happened. He was haunted by the image of feet receding beneath a car, a body dragged away. His gaze focused on the lurker again, on the here and now.

"Not so easy when we can *see* you, is it?" Rage gripped Sands. It wouldn't always be a nameless man the lurker killed; in time it would be Melanie. "I'm the one who can see you," Sands said again, thumping his chest with his cast. "I'm the one who's not going to let you have her. I'm the one—"

The back of the beast's hand struck Sands squarely across the face. His head whipped around. The world was suddenly spinning. He landed on his back. He thought at first that his head was ripped completely off. No. He was coughing, the wind knocked out of him, his ribs throbbing with each spasm. And the stabbing pain in his sprained neck—it couldn't hurt that much if his head were ripped off.

He opened his eyes just in time to see *and* feel the monstrously strong foot slam into his gut. White-hot pain from his ribs. Dancing lights. Nausea sweeping over him. Another kick.

The lurker was standing over him, staring down with those bestial eyes and talking through the razor blades: "*You should worry less about your girlfriend and more about your wife.*"

Sands forced his eyes open, looked up at the evil crocodile smile. *Faye?* He stared at the claws, the fingers fused together. The car. The gouges above the doors. The same gouges on the side of the building below the tarp. Nausea overwhelmed him. Bile and partially digested dinner burbled up his throat and erupted from his mouth as the realization sunk in: *I led it right to Faye. Good God. What have I done?*

Another kick to the stomach. Sands choked on his vomit. He rolled in it as he curled trying to protect himself. *Not Faye.* The dancing lights obscured his vision. Consciousness began to flee. Life would not be far behind.

"*I feed where I want to feed,*" said the lurker, stretching his mouth to speak each word distinctly. "*I will have your girl's blood and then your wife's,*" it said with a sneer.

Not Faye! Sands reached out, feebly trying to ward off the next blow, and his hand brushed against something…the bat. The lurker must have let go to hit him, and the bat had rolled. Something like that. It didn't matter. He rapped his fingers around the handle—*Not Faye!*—and swung.

He was lying on the floor. No leverage. Swinging with his left hand. Yet somehow the bat sliced through the air as if it were propelled by the wrath of God. Sands never could have done that, never could have found that sort of strength…but he did. The barrel of the bat smashed into the beast's face. Its already flat nose caved in. Bone and cartilage crunched under the impact. The lurker's hands shot, too late, to its broken face. It staggered away from Sands.

Sands stumbled as he tried to climb to his feet. He wanted to be standing before the next blow fell— but there was no next blow. The lurker was a blur as it disappeared around the corner. Sands raised the bat, but there was nothing to swing at.

Not ready to believe the lurker had fled, Sands hobbled around the corner, farther into the apartment. To his right, across the entry hall, the front door was still locked; to his left, a thin metal grate, three-feet square, had been pulled from the wall. Sands edged closer to the naked hole. There was a water heater in the space, and behind that another, smaller hole that led only into deeper darkness. Speckles of blood led from the living room to the crawl space. Sands, not getting too close, gazed into the darkness behind the water heater. *No way in hell…* then staggered back to the living room.

As he turned the corner, the spasms began in his back. From just above his hip, all the way up his side, and across his shoulder to his injured neck. He clutched the bat, using it now for a cane instead of a weapon. He managed two more steps before he collapsed and lay in agony beside drops of the lurker's blood and the pool of his own vomit.

✛   ✛   ✛   ✛   ✛

Eventually, Sands was able to stand. He thought that he must have lost consciousness for at least a little while. *Stupid. It could have come back,* he thought, but with little conviction. He glanced at his watch. Almost 3:30 AM.

He could stand now, but he couldn't straighten completely; his back spasms had ceased, but the muscles were still incredibly tender. Sands had to walk in a semi-crouch. He continued to use the baseball bat as a cane and took his exit through the front door, which he could unlock from within, rather than by the balcony.

Good God! he realized as he staggered down the stairs. *It could have killed her while I was lying up there!*

He didn't think so; he'd bashed the lurker's face in pretty well—and that was another mystery: How had he managed to swing the bat like that? His first concern had to be Melanie, however. *And Faye,* he thought, condemning himself with each pained step. *I led that damn thing right to her!* But the lurker had been here most recently; Melanie was in the most immediate danger. *Hell, it could have killed Melanie and gone after Faye already!* But all he could do at that moment was check on Melanie and hope that nothing had happened.

Her apartment appeared secure: The window, the balcony, didn't show signs of forced entry. Sands hobbled around to the front of the building and laboriously up the three flights of stairs. The front door seemed intact.

The more he moved around, the more his ribs throbbed. Also, his knee that he'd banged on the balcony railing began to fail him. By the time he finally made it back down the stairs and to his car, all he could do was laugh. He imagined the sight he was: partially crouched as he walked with a limp and a baseball bat for a crutch, his neck at an odd angle to relieve that pain, 128 stitches along the side of his face, his right arm in a cast and held tight against his body and his aggravated ribs, his left hand bloody from where the couch had gouged him, pants and coat torn. And now add to that his slightly hysterical laughter. Anyone who saw him would assume he was insane—and they might not be far wrong.

Before getting in his car, he squatted down and checked under it, and under the surrounding vehicles. He looked carefully in the back seat. No lurker to be seen. *Would I see it all the time?* he wondered. Sometimes, like in the condemned building, he felt like he knew so much about the creature; other times, like now, he wasn't so sure. The Devil was in the details—and this devil had a mouth full of razor-blade teeth, and claws that matched the scratches on the roof of Sands' car. *Damn it all! I not only led it to Faye, I gave it a damn ride!*

He turned the engine on and ran the heater, but didn't let the car interior get too warm; he drank some Scotch, but not too much. He didn't want to fall asleep. He wouldn't let himself. He needed a few minutes to gain mastery over his sporadic outbursts of uncontrollable laughter. He was glad to finally stop; laughing was hell on his ribs. When his gallows humor had dissolved away, he was left with little more than despair. *I can't save both of them,* he thought dismally. *Hell, I probably can't save just one!* He rattled his bottle of pain pills but didn't take any; he wanted to stay alert, for whatever good it might do. He owed Melanie that much. And Faye. The pills would make him groggy. The pain kept him awake.

He wasn't sure when exactly the sun came up. The sky was so thickly clouded it was difficult to tell. Shortly after 8:00 AM, he realized that the murky night had been replaced by the murky dawn. As he pulled away, he prayed that the coming of daylight meant that Melanie and Faye were now safe, at least for a few more hours.

CHAPTER 19

Sands left the silver flask under the seat in his car and carried the half-empty bottle of Scotch into Tinsley's "bungalow." Albert was in the kitchen reading the paper. The sharp odor of bacon made Sands hungry, taunting his uneasy stomach. He tried to slip past the kitchen door and to the bathroom without alerting Albert, but Sands was moving so stiffly that Albert made it out of the kitchen before the bathroom door closed.

"*Douglas?*" Albert's concern about Sands' disheveled and battered appearance was obvious. "What *in hell* happened to you?"

Sands didn't think he'd ever heard Albert curse before. Douglas also didn't have the strength to think about what had happened to him, much less to talk about it. He didn't pause, but continued limping unsteadily into the bathroom. "I'm sorry I ripped your coat," he said, not able to make himself completely ignore Albert. Sands closed the bathroom door and locked it.

"Douglas?" Albert was knocking—not pounding and demanding to be let in; just knocking, hesitantly. "*Douglas?* Are you all right?"

Sands turned on the water in the tub as hot as he could stand it. He began the laborious task of peeling off his clothes. Every movement was agony; each turn or twist or seemingly innocuous motion hurt *some* part of his body. Albert didn't keep knocking; he seemed at least partially satisfied by the sound of the bath water. *Or maybe he thinks I'm going to drown myself, and he's calling the police*, Sands thought. *Was* he trying to kill himself? he wondered briefly. Not in the bathtub, but with the other insane, *stupid* things he was doing? He didn't think so. If he died, what would become of Faye and Melanie?

When his clothes were finally in a heap on the floor, Sands slipped into the steaming bath, propping his cast up out of the water. The tub wasn't quite as clean as he would have preferred—Albert wasn't the housekeeper that Faye was—but, at the moment, Sands was thinking more about the soothing, almost scalding, water than he was about the red mildew in the fiberglass corners and around the drain. Once he was settled, he took a swig of Scotch and, with much effort, set the bottle back on the floor by the tub. He sank down, trying to let the water massage his neck, but holding his cast out of the water was awkward and uncomfortable. His skin rapidly turned rosy pink. Much less rapidly, his back began to loosen. He thought that he probably should have iced rather than heated his knee, which was considerably swollen after banging against the balcony railing during his fall, but as with the mildew, he was too exhausted to be picky. Practically every inch of his body hurt.

All in a good night's work, he thought with a caustic smirk—which led to another thought, one that drained the half-hearted smile from his face: *I have to go back tonight. Every night. Good God, this is going to kill me.*

He could barely stand. How was he going to protect Melanie? How was he going to protect Melanie *and* Faye? The lurker had threatened them both: *I will have your girl's blood and then your wife's.* Sands submerged beneath a wave of helplessness and futility that was more palpable than the steaming water of the bath. *And I led it right to Faye.* He had seen the scratches on the car and ignored them; he'd let himself believe that some mere hooligan had tried to break in. He should have known, should have recognized the signs.

Faye wouldn't be in danger at all if I hadn't been sleeping with Melanie, he thought, but that was more blame than he was willing to accept. *Everything couldn't be his fault…he hoped.* Melanie would still have been in danger. The monster would have been stalking her whether Douglas was there or not. *Hell,* he thought, *it might have killed her already if it weren't for me!* That, to his fatigued mind, seemed a more equitable distribution of guilt. It was his fault that Faye was in danger, but the lurker had found Melanie independent of him.

Not that that changed facts on the ground—the thing still had plainly threatened to kill both women—but for Sands, there was a tradeoff there somewhere. If he saved them both, that would make up for the danger he'd put Faye in.

But despite his tortured logic and his vainglorious rationalizing, the question remained: How in hell was he going to save them?

As the bath cooled, Sands pulled the plug and then filled the tub again with nearly scalding water. He wished he could boil the pain out of his body— the pain and the doubt and the fear. He wasn't about to drown himself, no matter what Albert thought or didn't think, but he would have liked to have boiled the flesh from his bones. He was shriveled like a prune—*or like a desiccated corpse,* he thought. For the first time since early last night, no part of his body was numb from cold, although numbness seemed a more attractive concept as he took stock of his numerous contusions, scrapes, and strains.

Then he tried to put all those pains out of mind, to let his thoughts as well as his body float unencumbered. He was a fowl in a pot, boiling away to nothing; he was a suit hanging over the back of a chair, the steam easing away wrinkles. But the steam dissipated, the water grew tepid, and the lurker remained real.

❖   ❖   ❖   ❖   ❖

"Douglas, I want you to meet someone," Tinsley said.

Sands had just crawled under the covers; his head had barely touched the pillow. The bath hadn't been able to boil the pain from his body, but it had relaxed him beyond the point of fighting his fatigue. If he closed his eyes for as much as a minute, he'd be asleep. He kept his eyes shut, but Tinsley didn't give him that minute. Albert had heard Sands come out of the bathroom and followed him into the tiny guest bedroom.

"Douglas?"

"Let me check my social calendar," Sands mumbled. "Mmm. Sorry. All booked."

"Douglas," Albert said, placing his hand on Sands' knee, hinting that he wasn't going to go away or be ignored. "She can help you."

Sands sighed, opened his eyes. Exhausted beyond words, beyond anger, he looked up at Tinsley.

Albert was resolute. "I know you're tired…but you're killing yourself." He waited. He did not go; he would not go. "She can help."

Sands climbed from the bed. He was wearing only his underwear. His sweatpants and long-sleeved T-shirt lay where he'd dropped them on the floor. As he pulled them on, they were still cold and slightly damp against his freshly steamed and soaked skin. Goosebumps spread over his arms and legs. From habit, he ran his fingers through his wet hair, then he followed Albert into the kitchen, where the woman was waiting, standing.

She was shorter than Sands and Albert, maybe five-two or three. Her listless hair was cut boyishly short, but that was all that seemed slightly youthful about her. Her shoulders were thin, narrow; they looked too small, or too straight, for the rest of her. She was rounded: her face, her heavy breasts, her hips. Her shoulders should have been rounded also, slightly stooped, but they were fixed ramrods that held the rest of her body erect. She was remarkably plain—no makeup, nondescript sweater and pants—except for her eyes: They were bright blue, clear like a mountain spring, *too* bright and clear, too light and ephemeral for her rounded, earthy body. Sands didn't like the way she looked at him, like he was a hurt child.

"I don't need your pity," were the first words Sands spoke to her.

"It's not you I feel sorry for," she said.

"Douglas," Albert said, "this is Julia." The kitchen was not large. The three stood close together; any one of them could have touched the other two at the same time without moving.

"Sit down," she said.

"Are you a shrink or something?" Sands asked her.

"Something."

"Try to relax, Douglas," Albert said. "Please, sit down."

I was trying to relax before you bothered me, Sands thought, but he sat. The chair was wooden and straight-backed, rigid like Julia's too-narrow shoulders, not made for relaxation.

"Close your eyes if you want to," Julia said.

Sands didn't want to. Julia stood behind him. He looked at Albert skeptically as he felt her fingertips on the back of his head, sifting through his wet hair. Her fingers were strong; strong and…warm? Sands started to warn her not to press too hard—he had banged the back of his head more than once last night and had the beginnings of several respectable knots—but there was no pain as she pressed against those places. Only warmth. Like the comfort of the steaming bath, except deeper. Sands' eyes slowly closed.

Her fingers moved up and forward. He felt her tracing the line of stitches on his face. He hadn't covered them with a bandage after his bath. The lacerated skin, so tight in the cold outside and then puffy with warmth in the bath, felt cool and comfortable, almost numb; for practically the first time in days, it didn't itch the slightest bit.

She touched the other side of his face, where the lurker had hit him. Sands could smell the wool of her sweater; she was leaning over him, her breasts near his face. He could no longer detect the hard wooden surface of the chair. She was rubbing warmth into his neck. Sands had trouble holding his head up; it lolled this way and that, moving freely.

She was behind him now. She must have eased him forward, because she was massaging his back. The deep warmth spread along his spine and into his hips. She was in front of him again, pressing firmly with her fingers against his ribs. Those fractured bones should have sent searing pain and sucked his breath away, but there was only warmth. His knee—she was rubbing it above and below, working the lower portion of his leg up and down, slowly, painlessly, up and down, up and down....

❖　　❖　　❖　　❖　　❖

At some point, Albert whispered in his ear. "You should sleep now."

I'm not sleeping already? Sands wondered lazily.

Strong hands were helping him walk, easing him into bed, pulling blankets over him....

CHAPTER 20

"It's time to get up, Douglas."

Sands head was a leaden ingot he couldn't lift from the pillow. Albert's voice was calm, reassuring, but it was still an intrusion. It dragged Sands gently, incontestably, from dreamless sleep: "You can sleep more later, but I need to talk to you now." His hazel eyes were keen and sharp, watching from their cradle of wrinkles.

Sands' mind parted reluctantly with sleep. "What time... Is it tomorrow?"

"It's never tomorrow," Albert said softly. Sands must have looked confused. "It's still Tuesday," Albert clarified. "You've only been asleep for a few hours. But there are things we have to talk about."

"Right now?"

"Yes." Tinsley opened the blinds on the window, letting in meager light from outside.

"It's not dark yet," Sands said. From deep within the pits of his lethargy, he could feel his frantic thoughts trying to scrabble out—He had to protect Melanie, and Faye; he had to go soon; the lurker had said it would drink the blood of his girl and then his wife; did it *have* to be sequentially? did that mean Sands could afford to guard only Melanie at first?— but he was so tired.

"No, it's not dark yet," said Albert. In the space of a few desperate seconds, Sands had almost forgotten his host. "It won't be for a couple more hours. That's why we need to talk now." Sands tried to gather his faculties; he stared at Tinsley, but Albert didn't elaborate. "Here are some boots, and warmer clothes," was all he said, gesturing toward a chair beside the bed. He turned and left Sands to dress alone in the cramped room.

When Sands emerged, wearing sturdy jeans, boots, and a lined flannel shirt, Albert cautioned him with a finger over his lips. A woman was lying on the couch in the living room. Julia. Her back was to the room. The quilt that covered her made her shoulder and hip into patchwork hillocks. Tinsley handed Sands the borrowed coat, the one Douglas had torn last night, and they quietly left the house.

"I don't have my car keys," Sands said, outside. "You'll have to drive."

"Let's walk."

Sands had lived in Iron Rapids for most of his adult life, but he had never before walked through the Islands. The first snow this fall, six inches, had come in October, and the two months since had piled several more feet on top of that. The few clear days over that period had been crisp and cold, and the minute trickle that had melted had re-frozen the following night, only to have more snow fall on top of it, forming a treacherous foundation for driver and pedestrian alike. Tonight, Sands and Tinsley walked in the street. Many, but by no means all, of the shacks in the neighborhood had narrow paths shoveled from front door to the car out front, but none of the lateral sidewalks, connecting house to house, were cleared. Drifts and mounds of snow, aided by the efforts of the snow plows, seemed determined to blot out practically every trace of human civilization: Automobiles that were not used regularly were blocked in or buried; fire hydrants, mail boxes, and medium-sized shrubs were indistinguishable from one another; porch railings peeked out mere inches above white drifts.

Despite the cold, Sands could not shake the lethargy that lingered in his mind and weighed down his limbs. Each step along the slick street required an effort of will—but his movement now, he noticed, was largely painless. The sky, again tonight, was choked with clouds, and loomed close. As dusk and night approached and the grey clouds faded black, the smothering effect would only be heightened. The ambient light of the city seemed to draw the clouds closer still. Recognizing these harbingers of the night, Sands thoughts turned again to Melanie and Faye, but he couldn't make himself concentrate for more than a few seconds at a time. He was too tired; there was simply too much strangeness.

"You've been going through a rough time," Tinsley said.

Sands didn't know what to say; he didn't know what to make of that statement. Albert couldn't know exactly *how* rough the last few weeks had been; he must be talking about Sands' crumbling marriage— or was he? Had Tinsley, formerly the voice of calm and reason, become another part of the strangeness? He had brought Julia to Sands. *And what the hell was going on with her?* Douglas wondered. Not that he minded feeling better: His knee was no longer swollen and sore; he could breath comfortably, even the frigid outdoor air; his neck was not bothering him. He didn't mind, it just *didn't make sense!*

"What the hell is going on?" Sands asked. "I don't know what happened with Julia. I don't think I want to know. She's not dead is she?" His mind switched gears suddenly, revisiting ground he'd already covered, questions he'd already asked but could not quite recall. "What time is it? It's going to be dark soon."

"Julia's not dead," Albert said, as calm as ever. "She's just tired. Worn out from helping you."

"Helping me…giving me a massage?"

"Did it feel like just a massage?"

Sands didn't answer. He knew he shouldn't be as recovered physically as he was. *Maybe that hot bath did me more good than I realized*, he tried to tell himself. Or maybe she'd hypnotized him, and he simply didn't *feel* the pain. He struggled to find a rational explanation—but how much of what he'd seen over the past nights was rational?

"Why are you afraid of the night, Douglas?" Sands stopped. Albert stopped too, and faced him. "Let's keep walking. We have somewhere to be. And like you said, it's going to be dark soon." They resumed walking.

"Where are we going?" Sands asked.

"My question first. What are you afraid of?"

If Albert had still been wholly of the old, normal world, Sands would have walked away. What could he have said that anyone could believe? To explain was to confess his own insanity. But Tinsley had brought Julia, with her clear eyes and harsh words and healing fingers—*No*. It couldn't have been that. Sands didn't understand what had happened, but *something* had, and Tinsley was mixed up in it. He was part of the insanity that had taken over Sands' life. And so, under the roiling clouds in the gathering darkness, he told him,

"There's…something that threatened to kill Melanie. And Faye. It's… I don't know what it is."

"You do know what it is," Albert said. Sands stopped again. "Tell me."

Sands looked hard at him. Tinsley's eyes were still sympathetic, his underlying gentleness remained, but there was firmness in his expression as well; the strength of steel lay in wait beneath those grey whiskers. "It's not human," Sands said. "It…" but he couldn't say the rest, not even to Albert.

"The other morning," Tinsley prompted him, "Christmas morning, at the bakery. You said you'd been hunting vampires. You weren't kidding, were you." It sounded almost reasonable when he said it, not a question at all, not insane—not *completely* insane.

Sands shook his head. "No. I wasn't kidding. I wanted to be kidding. I wish I had been."

Tinsley took him by the elbow, ushered him along the street. "Tell me while we walk. We don't have too much time. Tell me what you saw."

Slowly at first, but then gathering momentum, Sands told him. He told him about the lurker: about seeing the shadowy, vaguely sinister form on the balcony; about seeing it more clearly and brandishing a broken beer bottle at the empty night; he told him about the face, the razor sound of teeth scraping one against another, the narrow jaw, the red, glaring eyes; about the bone-white skin; the claws; the fused fingers. Once Sands forced himself to begin talking, he couldn't have stopped had he wanted to. The pressure had been building for weeks; the dam had been ready to burst, and after the first cracks formed, it gave way rapidly.

Sands heard and felt the words streaming from his mouth. Tears of relief welled up in his eyes, but he fought them back. He would *not* cry in front of Albert. Sands was not so emotionally raw as he had been the night he'd cried on Melanie and confessed that his dead son called to him on the wind. (He did not mention Adam to Tinsley, not a word; Sands could not reveal himself so completely.) Much had happened since then; Sands was tired, in many ways numb. After the initial up welling of tears, the fatigue took hold and he spoke in almost a detached manner, describing the horrors that had befallen him as if they were the misfortune of some other person. The cadence of his words fell into the rhythm of his footsteps.

He told Tinsley of that other person's post-coital realization that the lurker was watching just beyond the window; of that other person's overwhelming need to interpose himself between the beast and the girl; of the subsequent, yet not completely intentional, fall from the window.

(He skipped any mention of the wind, of the voice, of Faye.)

He told Tinsley of the other person's clumsy attempts to safeguard Melanie (omitting the detail of the silver flask), and of the clumsier attempt to climb into the abandoned apartment. Sands recounted the confrontation with the lurker, every word that the creature had spoken, and every detail that the other person had *known*, independent of any discernible proof, about the beast. By the time Sands finished, his head pounded as fiercely as when the lurker had struck him; he was as spent as if Melanie had just climbed from atop him. He realized that their pace, like the flow of his words, had quickened. The boots Tinsley had given him had good traction, and he hadn't slipped. Now that he was done, he stopped, exhausted.

Albert placed a hand on Sands shoulder, almost as if holding him up. With his other hand, Tinsley took a cell phone from his coat pocket. He dialed a number. "...Right. Listen. I have two addresses that need watching. Definitely tonight. Probably beyond tonight. Maybe it'll keep Clarence busy.... Bloodsucker.... Right. First address..." He reeled off Sands' own address, and described Faye. "Second address..." He looked at Sands. "What's Melanie's address?" Sands told him, and Albert repeated the information to whomever was on the other end of the call. "...Right. Her name is Melanie Vinn. Early twenties, medium length hair, brown, petite…. Uh, hold on. Third floor apartment?" he asked Sands, who nodded. "Third floor apartment…. All right. Thanks." He slipped the phone back into his pocket.

"They should be fine," he said. "For a while, at least. Long enough for you to get…back on your feet."

They should be fine. This, to Sands, seemed the culmination of insanity. More odd than the lurker or the unreasonable lengths Sands had gone to thwart it. Tinsley had listened to him, had seemed not just to believe him but to *understand*, and he'd passed the information on to someone else who evidently understood, and who would protect Melanie and Faye. The insanity had come full circle, had turned in on itself and become *real*. Sands could continue to question his own sanity, but that meant he would have to question Tinsley's sanity as well, and Julia's, and whoever Albert had been talking to. The old world, Sands' old life, didn't exist anymore. The lurker and its threats were real.

"Come on," Tinsley said, continuing down the street.

Sands, falling in beside him, couldn't identify his own feelings about this new world around him: relief (because he was no longer alone), fear (because his fellow inhabitants were not all benign), dread of what the future would bring (because if the lurker was real, then the voice, and Adam's hand on his arm, were real)? Perhaps all of those things in various measures. Sands was at a loss; he was drained after telling his story and followed Tinsley helplessly for another block.

Then Albert stopped. They stood before one of the Islands' less decorous shacks, an edifice in ill-repair with cracked and peeling paint. It would have been interchangeable with at least a hundred other of the buildings in the area, but Albert stopped, purposefully. "This is where we're going," he said.

✢　　✢　　✢　　✢　　✢

They traversed the front walk, a foot-trodden canyon among the white hills. Tinsley had waited for Sands to go first. *Why's he brought me here?* Sands wondered, but he felt he owed Tinsley a certain amount of trust. Albert had taken him in, listened to him, understood. Darkness was full upon the city now. A biting wind was kicking up fine powder into Douglas' eyes.

The porch creaked beneath the weight of the two men. Sands glanced back at Albert, who indicated that they should continue. Sands grasped the doorknob and turned it easily enough—but the door would not budge. The latch wasn't hindering it. A bolt on the inside?

"It sticks," Albert said.

Sands shoved harder, put a little shoulder into it; the door gave with a crack and swung inward. He stood on the threshold of deeper darkness for a moment, trying to let his eyes adjust. Then they stepped out of the winter night—and into a cold far more intense.

Almost instantly, the inside of Sands' nostrils froze. Blinking his eyes was almost painful. He took another step inside. Through the plumes of his breath, Sands saw light from a street lamp reflecting against an interior wall—against a sheet of solid ice. He scratched away enough to flick a light switch, but nothing happened.

"The power's been cut off. Seems like that's always the case," Albert said. Sands wasn't sure if he meant always the case for this house, or if he was speaking more generally. "He's usually in the kitchen," Albert said, pointing down a side hall. "It's the coldest room." As if that explained anything.

Moving down the hall, Sands could see into other rooms. Every wall was covered by ice. Pictures were encrusted in it; icicles hung from lampshades and light fixtures. The painted hardwood floors crunched underfoot like frost-covered tundra. This was more than a house devoid of heat and abandoned to the elements—the elements would not be so cruel, so consuming here; maybe several hundred miles to the north, but not in Iron Rapids.

The cold was permeating, seeping through the warm clothes that Sands wore. He rubbed the fingers of his right hand; the cast made it too awkward to stick them in a pocket. Distracted by the preternatural cold, Douglas was not at all prepared to see the old man in a sleeveless undershirt and threadbare boxers sitting cross-legged on the kitchen table.

The kitchen was not as dark as the other rooms; the refrigerator door was open, but the light inside served merely to produce glare and lengthen the shadows, rather than to illuminate. The old man's panting shot a constant stream of clouds into the air. He was frail, with skin hanging on his bones, and more hair, grey and curly, on his shoulders than on his head. A flap of wrinkled scrotum hung from one leg of his underwear and rested, likely frozen, on the table. Nearby was a bowl of ice-encrusted pasta, the protruding spoon sparkling in the refrigerator light. The man watched them as they entered the room.

"She weren't no drunkard," he said.

"Hello, Mr. Kilby," Albert said, as if finding a half-naked old man in this ice-cave of a house were perfectly normal.

"Why isn't he frozen to death?" Sands whispered. He felt that he *should* whisper, despite the fact that the old man could undoubtedly hear every word.

"Look at him, Douglas. *Really* look at him," Albert said, his quiet voice amplified in the glittering kitchen.

But Sands wouldn't do it; something about the bitter hopelessness of Mr. Kilby unnerved Douglas. He wouldn't look at the old man, couldn't make himself. Instead, he busied himself with the details of the kitchen: the wooden chairs that would have been rickety had their joints not been frozen solid; the table, in similar condition; cabinets with thick paint, layer upon layer covered but never scraped, beneath the ice; stained and cracked linoleum covering the floor, except where it had peeled away from the wall in the corners; the dingy white interior of the open refrigerator. "How is the refrigerator light on if the power's off?" he asked, still whispering. He didn't hear a generator, or the hum of the refrigerator's motor, for that matter.

"*Look* at him, Douglas." Albert was speaking normally, but his voice seemed to echo and defy this arctic hell, as if human speech could break through the ice, as if the words themselves could puncture the sleek armor of despair, could create a fissure that would grow and spread until the entire ice cave, the house, imploded inward and was utterly gone.

"She weren't no drunkard," Mr. Kilby said again, oblivious to the tension between Sands and Tinsley. The old man's voice was at home in this place, his words fit. His breath suddenly cast no vapor, no moisture, no warmth. Sands could *hear* the ice growing thicker, could *feel* it happening.

He began to shiver violently. At the same time, he noticed a faint scent—growing stronger, rivaling and quickly overpowering the crisp, dry odor of ice. Sands recognized the smell, the stench of the dumpster, of decay, of death, of everything that was wrong. It fought its way down his throat and churned his insides. He fell to his knees, and though his stomach was empty, his body tried to retch. The bitter tang of bile filled his mouth. *She weren't no drunkard.* The words slithered through his mind; they attempted to force themselves from his mouth.

"*Stop it*," Tinsley said, not to Sands, but to the old man. Then: "Douglas, look at him. *See* him."

Finally, Sands lifted his face, met the gaze of the old man—and saw more than Mr. Kilby's pitted, bitter face. Another face glared back at Douglas. Another face that was where Mr. Kilby's should be, where Mr. Kilby's *was* still, yet Sands could see them both clearly somehow. The second face was meatier than the old man's, with fleshy jowls and a double chin, but equally as angry and contentious, perhaps more so. And the second face was that of a woman

"She weren't no drunkard," Mr. Kilby said—at least it was his actual mouth that moved, although the woman's mouth moved as well, and, to Douglas' ears, her voice overlapped that of the old man. Her words were distorted, they dragged out, one over the next. She gave off no breath-cloud either. The foul stench receded slightly now, and Sands no longer felt her words—yes, they were the woman's words, he realized—in his mind, in his throat. His stomach steadied somewhat.

"Douglas," Albert said, "meet *Mrs*. Kilby. Good evening, Amelia." In response, the old man pulled back the leg of his boxers, displaying more of his scrotum and his shriveled manhood in all its glory. "Amelia is not always the most...articulate of our clients," Albert said.

Sands slowly climbed to his feet. "Clients...? What are you talking about? It's...she's...she's a..."

"Davis, what is she?" Albert asked the old man.

"She's a bloated whore," Mr. Kilby said with only his own voice. "She…" But then his head jerked back and the next words died in his throat. His jaw twisted to the side, his scummy tongue lolled from his mouth, and gurgling noises interrupted his sentence. He continued with difficulty, and with another deep voice overlapping his own. "She's…my…sweetums." Sands could make out Amelia's sneer.

"Amelia," Albert said, "I need to talk with Davis."

"Sweet-ums…" Mr. Kilby said, a crooked smile and a confused expression on his face. He was, thankfully, no longer holding the leg of his shorts open.

"Amelia," Albert said, "I know Davis loves you, and you love him. Do you remember the time you spent with him? Do you remember? Back when you were alive?"

Back when you were alive? Sands looked on, dumbfounded.

Mrs. Kilby reacted less placidly. She stretched her mouth wide, as if to scream. Mr. Kilby's body trembled violently; his mouth jerked open also—but no sound emerged. Around the frozen kitchen, icicles began to burst, exploding in sprays of crystalline shards. Sands and Albert ducked and covered their faces—and then it was over. Silence.

Hesitantly, they looked up. Mr. Kilby sat calmly on the table as before. Sands saw no trace of Mrs. Kilby. The old man's face was again his own, his wife's visage not in evidence. His breath formed clouds that hung in the air.

"Are you being able to eat at all, Davis?" Albert asked.

Sands was completely lost. A superimposed, dead wife. Exploding icicles. An elderly man, who should have frozen to death long ago, instead flashing his genitals from atop the kitchen table. And now polite dinner conversation? Mr. Kilby seemed equally confused, or perhaps stunned. He stared at Albert through rheumy, grief-stricken eyes.

"Davis, are you eating anything?" Albert asked again. The old man looked at the frozen bowl of pasta on the table and shrugged apologetically. "I'll bring more tomorrow," Albert said.

Having now seen the grotesque overlap of Mrs. Kilby's face, Sands couldn't shake the feeling that something was missing now that she was no longer visible. He looked warily around the room. "Is she…?"

"Gone?" Tinsley said. "Sort of. But not for long."

"I was going to say dead," Sands said, forcing himself not to whisper.

"Is she dead? Oh, yes," Albert said. "Pretty sensitive about it too. I wouldn't mention it if you don't have to." While he talked, he approached Mr. Kilby and began examining the old man as a doctor might, looking in his eyes, squeezing his neck, arms, abdomen. Tinsley sighed. "He's losing a lot of body mass. He won't last much longer. I'd better try one of those nutrition drinks tomorrow. I don't know if he can handle solid food anymore."

Sands watched Albert and was struck by how matter-of-factly his friend conducted himself amidst all this insanity. Tinsley's normalcy was, itself, *abnormal*. But Sands had seen Amelia too; he'd felt her trying to speak through him—do more than speak through him, he realized. What would have happened if Tinsley hadn't been here? Sands turned away from the table; he stared at the ice formation that used to be an overhead light, at the gaping refrigerator and the light bulb within that should not have been burning but was.

"I'm going to wait outside," he said.

"We're all done here," Albert said, turning away from Mr. Kilby. "We can go."

Outside, Albert took Sands by the elbow, as if escorting him back home. Sands was glad for the support. The alien landscape within the Kilby's house had chased his fatigue for a short while, but now his body and mind were dragging, threatening to shut down altogether.

"I wanted you to see that they're not all bloodsuckers, Douglas," Albert said. "They're not all evil. You have to remember that. We all have to remember that."

Albert said nothing else the rest of the way back. Perhaps he sensed how far Sands had slipped into exhaustion. Or perhaps he heard what Douglas did: the howling of the wind, scared, angry, almost calling him.

At Tinsley's house, Sands trudged past Julia's sleeping form, struggled to remove his cold boots and coat, and then crawled fully clothed into bed.

CHAPTER 21

For the first time in what seemed like ages, Sands awoke fairly refreshed. He felt only the least bit stunned, and the disorientation faded very quickly once he realized that he was in Tinsley's house and not his own. Glancing at the date on his watch, he discovered why he felt so rested—he'd slept for two entire nights and the intervening day. This was the second morning after his and Albert's disconcerting meeting with the Kilbys.

With that thought, the full weight of memory slammed down upon him. He wished, for a brief moment, to be asleep again, to be completely devoid of past and future. He wanted to wake up in his old life, his *normal* life, not this new existence that resembled the old in many superficial ways but left him struggling to understand and survive. His thoughts jumped ahead: Melanie, Faye. He'd abandoned them; he had to check on them.

And then he realized that his cast was gone.

It had been there—on his right arm—when he went to sleep. He stared uncomprehending at his bare arm. Six to eight weeks it should have been in a cast. He looked at the date on his watch again. No. He hadn't slept *that* long. "What the hell…?" He pulled on a shirt; he was already wearing his sweatpants. *I had on a shirt…and jeans when I went to bed*, he recalled.

The house smelled like bacon and coffee. Sands' stomach ached, partially from the strain of retching at the Kilbys' house, but mostly from hunger.

"Ah, there you are!" Albert said, sitting at the kitchen table. Julia seemed to be gone. He piled several slices of bacon on a plate and handed it to Sands, then started pouring coffee. "Cream and sugar, right?" Sands nodded. "I have some biscuits I can make. Just out of a can, I'm afraid. I'm not that much of a cook to do them from scratch." He set the coffee on the table in front of Sands. "And I've got strawberry preserves and peach." Albert opened the refrigerator and peered inside. "On second thought, the peach preserves have seen better days. I'd stick with strawberry. You must be hungry."

Sands nodded again. He *was* hungry, starving, in fact, but he couldn't let that distract him. "Are Melanie and Faye all right?"

"They're fine," Albert said, as he squinted to read the instructions on the can of biscuits. He peeled the label until the can went *poof* and was open. "We've been keeping an eye on them."

"We," Douglas said, his patience suddenly deserting him. "Who the hell is 'we'?" He tossed up his hands, became aware of the gesture and then held up his right hand, wriggling the fingers. "What happened to my wrist?"

"It works okay, right?"

"Well…yes." Sands kept wiggling his fingers and rotating his hand.

"Good. You can thank Julia."

"What the hell…?"

"You have a lot of questions."

"*Yes*, I have a lot of questions. None of this makes any sense!"

"It does make sense," Albert said. "That's the problem. It just takes a while to sink in. But I have to tell you: It doesn't get much easier once it does sink in."

"What are you saying?"

"You'll see. Just ask. And eat. Don't let everything get cold."

Sands took a seat at the table. He sipped his coffee and took a few bites of bacon; he had to restrain himself from wolfing down the entire plate full. "Melanie and Faye are all right," he said after a moment.

"Yes."

"Who's watching them? The person you called the other night?"

"Among others," Albert said. "Friends."

"Friends." *Then there are others.* "You seem to know what I'm going through. Do you...?"

"...See things that shouldn't be there? Talk to dead people? Yes. I'm afraid so. We call it being imbued. Although it doesn't seem to be the same for everyone."

"And Julia...she sees these things? She's...imbued?"

"Yes. And my other friends as well. That's how they can watch over Faye and Melanie."

Sands took a long, slow sip of coffee. "I'm not crazy, Albert?"

"If you are, then many of us are, and it's some incredibly widespread, shared dementia."

"Widespread...?"

"Well..." Albert set the raw biscuits aside for the moment and joined Sands at the table. "I don't mean to exaggerate. I don't know that there are *that* many of us. We don't know precisely...a few hundred world-wide, maybe more. But the number and the geographical spread would seem to make some form of group psychosis unlikely at best."

"But there are more people like us...who see these things. Ghosts. Monsters."

"Yes."

Sands considered that for several minutes. Bacon crunching between his teeth was the only sound as he and Albert sat in near silence. As Sands' thoughts rumbled reluctantly forward, his mouth went dry; the bacon that had been so delicious a moment ago was now hard to swallow. "And the monsters…there are a lot of them. All over the place."

"Yes," Albert said solemnly. "There are a lot of them. All over the place."

Sands took a sip of coffee. It seemed colder than it should; not even the sugar and cream cut the bitterness. Monsters. A lot of them. All over the place. It was his worst musings come true. He remembered the night not so long ago: sitting in his car in Melanie's parking lot, watching the other cars go by with their tinted windows, imagining that every other driver was one of *them*, like the lurker, that every one of them wanted to kill him. "Good God," he muttered.

"Maybe," said Albert. "The jury's still out on that one."

"But how?" Sands wanted to know. "How can there be so many? Why doesn't everyone see?"

"That I can't answer. Most people just go on living their lives. Oblivious. Certain people seem to be chosen: you, me, Julia, my friends. There are signs."

"Signs? What the hell are you talking about?"

"When I became aware…enlightened, imbued, whatever you want to call it…it was at work, in the cafeteria, of all places. I never thought the biggest change in my life would happen while I was trying to decide between green and orange Jell-O. Anyway, it was the first day back at work for Gerry

Stafford after the car accident. You remember how he was before the wreck: lively, funny."

Sands nodded, agreeing. "He never got over Melinda's death."

"*He died with her*, Douglas. Gerry and Melinda Stafford both died in that wreck." Tinsley paused, let his words sink in. "Gerry just didn't *stay* dead, not all the way."

Sands blinked. And again. The lurker was one thing; Gerry Stafford was quite another. Douglas forced himself to suspend disbelief, to think about what Albert said in terms of this new, warped perspective of reality. "Don't tell me you killed Gerry," Sands said. "At the Christmas party."

"No," Albert said, his jaw tightening—it was the closest Sands had ever seen his friend come to getting angry. "That wasn't me. It should never have happened."

"But it was…one of us."

"Yes. A hunter," Albert said. "That's what we call ourselves, generally. Hunters. Some of us take it too literally, though."

"Like whoever killed Gerry."

"Yes. Some people don't know how to respond to something that's different, other than to fear it, to kill it. It's the same thing as racism, or sexism, or homophobia—"

"But the thing that's after Melanie," Sands interrupted. "You can't tell me that's—"

"I'm not saying they're all *good* either—but I hate to put it in those terms: good and evil. It's never that simple…or seldom, anyway," Albert said.

"What are you saying? You think a vampire can be…reformed?"

"Probably not. But is every vampire necessarily the same? You saw this one. You talked to it. I don't know."

"You know," Sands said, "it's weird enough that we're sitting here, two grown men, talking about vampires, but now we're debating good vampires and bad vampires. While we're at it, I say Superman would kick Batman's ass."

"Sarcasm doesn't help anyone, Douglas. If you know so much about how all this works, then I'll just leave you alone." Albert got up from the table. He found a can of Crisco and started greasing a cookie tray for the biscuits.

"Albert, I...I'm sorry. Look. This is all new to me, and not very...you know, comfortable. But I don't think anybody could convince me that that *thing* has an altruistic bone in its body. It wants to drink Melanie's *blood*, for God's sake!"

"Maybe it's just the blood that's the key element," Albert said, whipping around and gesticulating with a Crisco-laden butter knife. "Maybe the thing is fixated on Melanie, but if we supplied it with blood, it wouldn't be interested in her anymore."

"Oh, give me a break."

"I'm just saying maybe, Douglas. And if not this one, maybe another one. How will we know if we always try to kill them right from the start?"

"But they're already dead! Sort of. Or supposed to be."

"We don't know *what* is *supposed to be*. We just know what's *not* supposed to be. We see those things, and we just know that it's wrong, unnatural, that it's *not supposed to be that way*. Wasn't it that way for you?"

Douglas swallowed. He remembered seeing the lurker, and the pure revulsion that gripped him.

Merely thinking about it brought the knot back to his stomach. He nodded.

"That seems to be a constant with everyone, with all the Imbued. But the *reaction*…that varies wildly from person to person," Albert said. "You reacted out of fear and anger. You attacked that creature. And maybe that was necessary. I'm not second-guessing you. But even if what you saw was evil incarnate, does that mean that every single one of those things, unnatural and wrong as it is, is malevolent? Evil?"

Douglas sat silently. He wasn't ready to answer that. He had no problem thinking of the lurker as a beast that needed to be wiped from the face of the earth—but Sands had felt the touch of his dead son's hand, had heard his voice.

"I was telling you about Gerry," Albert said, calmer after a few moments. "I saw him in the cafeteria that first day he was back, and I knew he was unnatural. I knew he was dead. I didn't know *how* I knew, or how it could be true, but I knew. Before I saw him, though, I was looking at the stupid Jell-O." Having spread chunks of biscuit dough across the cookie tray, he slid it into the oven. "You know the sign on top of the counter, with the plastic letters, that tells you what everything is?"

"Yeah," Sands knew. "The one Ketricks had to start putting up because at least one entree is always unidentifiable."

"Right. Well, I looked at that sign, and instead of having the names of the entrees, the letters spelled: 'He is in pain.'" Albert held up his fingers as if framing the words. "'He is in pain.' Same plastic letters. The 'e' was even upside down, like it is half the time because Ketricks reaches over and puts the letters on from the top. I thought it was a joke. Maybe somebody who ate the meatloaf was trying to get back at Ketricks. So I look around. And I see Gerry. Nobody else seemed to notice, but the way I saw him, his head was half crushed, like he'd just five minutes ago hit the windshield. And his chest was caved in from the steering column. He was bleeding. Covered in blood. Unless I made a point not to, that's how I saw him every day for months."

Sands stared at his tepid coffee, said nothing.

"He was in the cafeteria, standing in line, and he was *dead*," Albert said. He paused and drank deeply from his own mug, not appearing to mind how warm the coffee was or was not. Lost in his story, he seemed to have forgotten that Sands was there.

"Dead—like Mr. Kilby?" Sands asked.

"Hm? Oh. No, not really. Mr. Kilby is still alive. His wife is dead, and she's possessed his body somehow. She was one of our employees, by the way. IRM. Gerry was different. He was…dead. Walking around and dead, and for whatever reason, whatever it is that keeps most people blind to the supernatural, he was able to pass for living."

"So you didn't confront him," Sands said.

"Not in the cafeteria, right in the middle of everybody," Albert said.

"What the hell was he doing in the cafeteria if he was dead?"

"I don't know. I think it was just what he was used to. He was still going through the motions of being alive. I watched him, and he just poked at his food. I went by his cubicle later and talked with him. It was strange. He didn't realize that I could tell what he was. He was just...himself. Quieter, sadder, but himself."

"What was it like? I mean..."

"What was it like when you talked with him the last few months?" Albert asked. "He was the same guy basically."

"Just dead."

"Yes," Albert said, nodding distractedly. Then he looked up, renewed intensity in his eyes. "But do you see why I don't think they can all be evil or malevolent or bad or whatever? Gerry was none of those things—not before, not after. Maybe this vampire of yours was a psychotic before he be-came a vampire. I don't know." His verve slowly faded away again, and he was his typical, calm self. "But I talked to him other times, quite a bit, in fact. About a week later, I told him that I knew. He seemed surprised, but not very. He didn't know what was going on any more than I did. He never acknowledged outright that he was dead, but af-ter I confronted him about it, he started talking about Melinda. He hadn't mentioned her or her death before, but after I told him that I knew he was dead, not a day went by that he didn't men-tion her to me. He cried sometimes, Douglas. His tears were blood."

"My God." Sands' words were barely audible.

"I don't know what I could have done to help him. Maybe nothing. I couldn't bring Melinda back for him. Maybe he would have been doomed to spend lackluster days going through the motions at work, and nights in a house with nothing but memories, but he wasn't hurting anyone."

"And then someone cracked his head open again," Sands said.

"Yes." Albert turned away and placed his palms flat on the counter. He stood that way for several seconds, with his back to Sands. Eventually, Albert stirred. He checked the biscuits, set his kitchen timer, and then left Douglas alone. Albert didn't come back when the timer went off.

❖   ❖   ❖   ❖   ❖

After breakfast, Sands went for a walk. He hadn't thought that he would be able to eat anything at first after hearing Albert's story, but when the timer sounded and he pulled the biscuits from the oven, his stomach, empty and neglected while he'd slept for a day and two nights, asserted itself. Albert had been right about one thing: The peach preserves were well past their prime. But a little butter and strawberry preserves were ambrosia to Sands. He ate ravenously, and had to force himself to leave three biscuits in case Albert decided he wanted some.

Albert had retreated to his room, and Sands, after eating, felt the walls of the small house closing in about him. He put on the warm clothes that Tinsley had given him—boots, jeans, flannel shirt—and found an extra pair of gloves. While he was dressing, he realized to his bemusement that he was holding his right arm at the same rigid, ninety-degree angle that it had occupied in the cast. He stretched his fingers and spent a few minutes reacquainting his elbow and wrist with freedom of movement.

Sands stepped out of the house just after noon. There was a hint of sun above the cloud cover, a lighter shade of grey that threatened brightness and warmth should the clouds relent even briefly. More drivers were out than had been last night.

The blue-collar workers were already at their jobs; they didn't get the whole week off between Christmas and New Year's. The Islands had a large enough unemployed population, however, that there were plenty of people around: digging their dilapidated cars out until the next time the snow plow went by, or making the mile and a half trek to the grocery store. (There were no grocery or clothing stores situated in the Islands; the owners were too worried about crime. There were, however, three liquor stores and a convenience store that sold gasoline and lottery tickets; all four establishments had, in fact, been robbed in the past six months, resulting in three fatalities.)

Sands watched the road and the tires of approaching cars as he walked. He didn't look at the drivers; he tried not to look at anyone at all. He was afraid of what he might see. How many weeks and months had he worked with Gerry Stafford, walked past his cubicle or said hello in the corridor, ridden on the elevator with him—and never known? It was creepy. But worse for Sands was thinking that he might never again have the luxury of not knowing. He doubted he could ever go back to his old, normal, *ignorant* life. This wasn't a matter of dealing with one impossible creature, one vampire, and then getting back to the way things were supposed to be. Things were *not* like they were supposed to be. Monsters were real, and they were out there. Lots of them. *Lots of them, and lots of us, to hear Albert tell it*, Sands thought. *Monsters. Hunters.*

And according to Albert, the monsters weren't all bad, *might* not be all bad, anyway. Sands had no illusions about the lurker, and he wasn't about to award a congeniality award to Amelia Kilby, but plenty of *living* people were obscene, infuriating asses, too. *But she tried to get into my mind, into me*, he remembered. Albert had called her off, or maybe it was Sands who had repulsed her when he'd seen her for what she was. He wasn't sure. Either way, he suspected that she didn't quite fit into Albert's category of unfortunate spirits who merely need an attitude adjustment.

But what about Adam calling for his father? *What about Gerry? For God's sake*, Sands thought, pushing his thoughts along, refusing to dwell on what struck too close to home. *Albert's right about that. Gerry never would have hurt anybody*. But someone had taken upon himself—*or herself; would Julia do something like that?*—to kill Gerry Stafford. Again. *Does that mean it's permanent this time?* Sands wondered. If it was, and Gerry's prolonged existence was nothing but suffering, then was his second death a bad thing after all?

Who are you to judge me? That's what the lurker had said to Sands. Douglas didn't think the question carried much weight for the vampire—it was planning to kill people, after all—but did it apply more reasonably to Gerry? *There are plenty of unhappy people around, but I don't just decide to kill them all for their own good!* If that were the case, he might have killed Faye, or *himself*, years ago. *Maybe Gerry would've snapped out of it sooner or later.* Now they'd never know.

Sands returned to the house having resolved nothing. If anything, he was more despondent than before. In addition to the vampire that was stalking his wife and mistress, there was a whole world of capering fiends out there. Tinsley was still in his room, which wasn't that much larger than the diminutive guest room. He was sitting on his bed reading.

"So where do we go from here?" Sands asked, standing in the doorway.

Albert closed his book. "I don't know. Where *do* you go? You're welcome to stay here as long as you need."

"I left you some biscuits," Sands said. He didn't know what else to say.

"Do you miss Faye, Douglas?" Albert asked.

"What?"

"Do you miss Faye? I'm not talking about worrying about her well-being. Do you miss being with her? Do you miss her?"

"I've missed her for years, Albert." Silence descended between them. Sands wanted to walk away—he didn't want to talk about Faye—but he couldn't quite make himself.

"You know you haven't talked to her since you walked out," Albert said.

"She *kicked* me out!"

"She asked you to leave when you were up to it. You were the one who walked away without saying anything. That was almost a week ago."

"How the hell do you know—"

"I called her a few days ago," Albert said, unapologetic. "Just to let her know that you were okay."

"You had no right—!" but Sands couldn't finish. He knew that *he* should have at least let Faye know that he was all right, but *should* and *shouldn't* were such slippery concepts; he shouldn't have been sleeping around on her for fifteen years, after all.

"You have to go on living," Albert said. "With or without Faye, that's up to you. I just called out of consideration for her. I'm not trying to play marriage counselor. But you have to go on living. You have a family, if you want to keep it. You have a job. You have holidays and vacation time, but I wouldn't try to stretch the medical leave too far—after all you don't have a cast or stitches anymore."

"Stitches?" Sands' hand shot to his face and felt smooth, undamaged skin. He'd noticed the absence of the cast, of course, but he hadn't looked in a mirror. He rushed to the bathroom to confirm that the gash on his face was completely healed, without the slightest trace of a scar. He went back to Albert. "Julia?"

Tinsley nodded. "She came back. You were so exhausted after your earlier session, you barely stirred. She cut open the cast, took care of your wrist, your face again...."

"What the hell is she?"

"She's one of us, Douglas. We have different gifts. Whoever or whatever decided to imbue us—"

"Hold it right there. I can do without the philosophical mumbo jumbo. I had enough ethical dilemmas before breakfast to last me a few years. You're right about Faye. All right? I should've at least called."

"It's a hard adjustment for all of us," Albert said. "If you—"

"No, let me finish. I'll talk to Faye. Tomorrow. I'll figure something out. And I'll help do something about the lurker, the vampire. God, I feel crazy just saying this. I appreciate your help, and your friends' help—I think I would've killed myself or cracked up if I didn't have a break—and I'm willing to see this thing through. I mean,

Faye's my wife, and Melanie…she's my responsibility. But that's where it ends, as far as I'm concerned. I don't care what happens to the Kilbys. That old guy can go wave his dick around till it freezes off, for all I care. I don't care about all the rest of it—ghosts, vampires, hunters—none of it. That's it."

"Only as far as it affects you personally," Albert said evenly.

"That's right."

Silence intervened again for what seemed like a very long time. The two men's gazes were locked. Sands was as tense as if he were watching for the lurker. Finally, Albert picked up his book. "If that's the way you want it, Douglas." He returned to his reading.

CHAPTER 22

Sands stood before the faux-brass lion for perhaps the last time. He wistfully wondered if there was some way he could sleep with Melanie first, and then break things off. He had wondered no such thing about Faye. That was where he'd just come from: his own home.

Faye had been taking down and packing away the Christmas decorations. Never mind that he and she had put them up just two weeks before. This was the afternoon of New Year's Eve, therefore the Christmas decorations had to come down. Faye had never felt that she could welcome the new year properly amidst the Yuletide flotsam of the old one.

"There are some boxes by the steps that are ready to go into the attic," she'd said, assuming he was crawling back for forgiveness.

"I'm not here to undecorate," Douglas said, walking past her to the bedroom. He stuffed several suits and dress shirts into a hanging bag, then tossed a suitcase onto the bed.

Faye stood in the doorway and watched him pack. "So that's it?" she asked.

"That's it." Sands concentrated on what he was doing. Socks, underwear, T-shirts, shoes, toiletries from the bathroom. He'd thought about coming later in the evening; chances were that Faye would be out with one of her realtor friends. But he'd decided that he'd rather face her than the wind he felt certain would whip around the back corner of the house after dark.

"You could have called," she said.

She was right; Sands had admitted as much to himself and to Albert, but he hated to give her the satisfaction. The old defenses kicked in; the same tired offenses, his and hers, were fresh, open wounds. "You're right. I could have," he said grudgingly.

"You could have been dead for all I knew. You could have thrown yourself out another window!" She was hurt as much as angry, though the two seemed to go together.

"Right again. I could have." He closed the suitcase forcefully, then took it and the hanging bag and stepped past his wife again, this time on his way out of their bedroom. He thought to stop in the living room. "Where's my Scotch?"

"I poured it out."

"*All* of it? You poured it *all* out?"

"I didn't want it in this house. You drink too much."

Douglas took a deep breath. "You're right again, Faye. I guess you're right about everything. Except the pool. I never wanted the damn pool."

She slapped him, then stomped back to the bedroom. He waited until the door slammed, then he kicked a half-packed box of Christmas ornaments and left. The silver flask was still under his driver's seat. He drank most of it, and stopped and bought another bottle of Scotch on the way to Melanie's.

Now, staring at the lion, he wished he hadn't said what he had to Faye. He'd been so angry—was *still* angry. She was the one who let Adam's death suck the life out of her. It *was* a tragedy, but they'd had their whole lives before them. But Faye's ability to love had died with Adam. "The vampire can *have* her, for all I care," Sands said, but even as he spoke the words, he knew they weren't true. He loved Faye, loved the person she *had been*; he would do everything he could to protect her, but he couldn't be with her. Not now. Maybe never again. Sands grasped the ring in the lion's mouth and knocked.

"Douglas. Come in." Melanie regarded him warily. He knew she could smell the Scotch on him. He didn't care.

"No. I can't." He paused, unsure where to go from there, but there was only one way *to* go. "We've got to stop. Stop seeing each other. Everything. It's over."

She considered that for a moment, not seeming altogether surprised. "Is that what you want?" she asked. Sands could read the undercurrent of anger in her: how she held her jaw, the way she crossed her arms.

"That's how it has to be. You'll have to transfer your position at work—"

"Already did," Melanie cut him off. Her words were clipped, abrupt. "You didn't give me a chance to tell you last time. It seemed like the only sensible thing now that…well, you know, now that everything's out in the open. They tried to get me to file a sexual harassment complaint against you, but I told them to go screw themselves. I'm a big girl. I had at least as much to do with all this as you did."

"Oh. Well…thank you."

"Don't thank me, you son of a bitch. I didn't do it for you. I'm not a victim in this. You know, I think I always knew it would come to this someday, and now that it has, I think it should have been sooner," Melanie said. That seemed to sum it up for her. She would cry after she closed the door, Sands could tell, but for the moment she was all indignation and spitfire. He couldn't blame her; she had no way of knowing what he'd gone through for her. They both stood there for a while waiting for the other to say something. "We're letting all my heat out," Melanie said finally.

"Well…I guess…goodbye, then," Sands said.

Melanie didn't say goodbye. She didn't say anything. She just closed the door and left Sands standing alone in the breezeway.

CHAPTER 23

IRM should have been a familiar, comforting place—that's what Sands had thought before he'd come to work. He'd figured it had to be better than New Year's Eve. He and Albert had spent it quietly at Tinsley's house: Albert with his book, Douglas with his bottle of Scotch. Sands had been in a foul mood after visiting Faye and Melanie. He didn't know what either of the women were doing. Maybe they were out with friends; maybe not. Faye might have been spending the evening quietly in their decoration-free home. After deciding that he did not want to talk about women, or anything abnormal or supernatural, Sands quickly discovered that he had nothing else to talk about; his life had been completely subsumed by the abnormal. So he'd been left to the television, and suffering through "New Year's Rockin' Eve."

"Have you ever seen Dick Clark in the daytime?" Sands had asked at one point. "I think he's a vampire. He hasn't aged in thirty years. In fact, I think he's getting younger."

Albert had chuckled, but he was more intent on his reading than conversation. His book was about the Russian czars—not exactly what Sands would have picked for holiday reading. "Right. And Rasputin was a vampire," Albert had said, joking. "Or maybe a werewolf."

"Would I be able to tell over television?" Sands had asked, staring suspiciously at Dick Clark. "I mean, if he *were*…something. Would I be able to tell?"

"I don't know. I've never seen one that way."

That had been about the extent of their conversation that night. Sands had drank and brooded, and drank some more. New Year's Day had held more of the same. By Monday morning, despite a slight hangover, Sands had been ready to go back to the office.

Work, however, proved little more relaxing than the rest of his tumultuous life. The drive, and the parking lot, and the lobby had all been fairly innocuous; the semblance of routine, of normalcy, was a pleasant distraction. But when he stepped onto the elevator, and the other people crammed in, and then the doors closed...

Sitting in his office, with the door closed and a wet cloth over his face, Sands was trying not to think about the sudden claustrophobia that had seized him—that and the certainty that every person surrounding him was actually a ghoul, zombie, or vampire. He had made his way between the rows of cubicles, greeting as few people as possible, trying not to make eye contact with anyone.

The entire morning had been like that. He'd waited as long as humanly possible to visit the bathroom. The thought of walking through the corridors had frozen him behind his desk. After all, with any turn of a corner, he might come face to face with a co-worker whose head had been crushed in a car accident months ago, or he might discover someone possessed, an unfamiliar face incongruously sharing the same space as that of the person he was used to seeing.

Sands wasn't sure how he was going to make it through the day. His new executive assistant, Sharon—an older woman, professional in appearance but not *too* attractive; Sands suspected she'd been assigned to him for that very reason, after the blow-up with Melanie—had been kind enough to bring him coffee, but that had exacerbated the bathroom problem. Sharon had suggested the damp cloth after Sands had explained that he was suffering from a *very bad* headache.

Caroline Bishop paid Douglas a visit to bring him up to speed after lunch—after lunchtime, rather. Sands didn't have lunch; he sat in his office with the damp cloth over his face. He wouldn't normally have taken the entire Christmas-to-New Year's week off. Fortunately, there tended to be little in the way of employee turnover during that period, so there was not too tremendous an amount of paperwork to catch up on. Caroline mentioned that he'd picked a good time to miss work. What she pointedly did *not* say was that he'd picked a good time to throw himself out of a window, but then again, Caroline was subtle that way. Sands was aware that some people knew the reason that Melanie had been reassigned. He assumed that Caroline was one of those people; there was little that affected Personnel that Caroline didn't know. Sands wasn't sure how many of the details Caroline, or anyone else, might have learned—like the fact that he'd been found naked in the snow beneath Melanie's shattered window. Perhaps, he mused, word of his incredible daring had made the rounds, and any vampires in the company would wisely keep their distance.

That afternoon, Sands called it an early day and slipped out of the office.

❖   ❖   ❖   ❖   ❖

Tuesday, overall, was a little better. The morning was not so good, however. Sands was still staying with Albert. Tinsley was not pressing for Sands to leave, and Sands didn't feel up to arranging new living arrangements just yet. Not after Monday. Actually, Tuesday's drive was slightly worse, because Sands was anticipating the anxiety that had overwhelmed him the day before. Every other driver was glaring with red eyes; every trunk was full of dead, decaying bodies. As Sands walked across the company parking lot, he took from his briefcase a memo and pretended to study it intently—a perfectly good excuse not to make eye contact with anyone. The memo proved useful in the lobby as well, without looking up, Sands grunted a response to someone, an unidentified male voice, who had the audacity to greet him.

Sands was pleased with how well he maintained his composure—until the elevator door opened. He was standing fairly anonymously, incommunicatively, in the midst of his fellow workers, but when the throng began shuffling forward into the confined space of the elevator, Sands panicked. He was seized by the sensation that a devious undertow had taken hold of him and was dragging him out to sea, or perhaps down the drain of some demonic plumbing system that emptied directly into the brimstone court-yards of hell itself. He was certain that any super-natural in the crowd would recognize his telltale rapid breathing, that he would accidentally look at the crea-ture, and *it* would know that *he* knew....

He bolted for the stairs, navigating around the heels of his co-workers, which was as much of them as he allowed himself to see. He collided with some-one who had started to step around him when he slowed, but who had not anticipated his sudden change of direction away from the elevator. A sheath of papers fell to the floor. The woman he'd bumped exclaimed in surprise.

"Excuse me," Sands said, not pausing or looking back.

The stairwell was not far. He stepped inside, let the door swing closed behind him, pressed his back against it, and loosened his tie. He took a deep breath. The memo in his hand was crumpled from running into the woman. Sands busied himself by assiduously smoothing the sheet of paper. Relief at having avoided the elevator gradually took hold, and he managed to breathe more regularly.

The stairwell, of course, carried its own challenges and potential terrors. Although, thanks to Julia's ministrations, he felt as well as he had in quite a while, and the steps themselves did not present a physical obstacle, this was where Sands and Faye had found Gerry Stafford. More precisely, the second floor landing, sixteen steps and one turn away, was the exact spot where they had found Gerry Stafford's body, his head split open. According to Albert, some hunter had killed Gerry—if it was possible to kill somebody that was already dead; Sands wasn't completely clear on that point. One point that he *was* completely clear on was that he'd traded a brief ride in a crowded elevator for an interminable climb up a twisting tunnel of death.

Good God, Douglas! he chided himself, disgusted. *How damn melodramatic can you be?* He started up the stairs. And stopped on the third step. *The elevator probably isn't as crowded now*, he thought, then, *No, no, no. You can walk up a damn set of stairs.*

And so he did. He traversed the next five stairs, took in a deep breath as he made the turn to the next eight…exhaled at the sight of *no body* on the second floor landing—*Of course there's no body!*—then continued on to the third floor. He even managed a few subdued greetings as he walked between the rows of cubicles to his office.

Sands asked Sharon to get him a cup of coffee; he felt satisfied from yesterday that she was not a vampire or possessed human being, and he felt equally satisfied, after his victory over the stairwell, that he would be able to endure the gauntlet to the bathroom later in the morning.

His in box was practically bulging. Caroline must have been irritated with his having left early yesterday, and she'd let him have it—passing along all the paperwork that she'd shielded him from yesterday. Sands knew her well enough to reconstruct that much; he also knew her well enough to be fairly certain that if he lagged behind for long, she would begin to remove items from his box, surreptitiously, one or two files at a time, and take care of them herself. The stuffed in box was her way of urging him to get his act together. But if it came to it, she would keep the department running. Sands suspected that she could keep the boat afloat almost indefinitely should he vanish from the face of the earth, and months might pass before upper management realized that he was gone.

For several minutes, Sands sat with his palms flat on his desk. He took deep, calming breaths and admired his own collected manner—at least the thin veneer he maintained on the surface. Maybe life could go on. Here he was. At work. Like nothing unusual had ever happened—more or less.

When Sharon brought him his coffee, Sands even turned on a bit of the old charm that had gotten him into the panties of several co-workers over the years—not that he wanted to get into *her* panties. Sharon was at least fifty. Sands had not slept with an older woman since his college days, and he suspected that, though Sharon was attractive for her age, her nakedness—should it ever come to that— would be disappointing compared to his recent memories of Melanie, or even his less recent memories of Faye, for that matter. For all practical purposes, however, the question was moot. Sharon seemed more wary of than receptive to his charm; she undoubtedly had heard at least *something* about Sands' inappropriate relationship—and the disastrous climax of that relationship—with his previous executive assistant. Sharon, who was more maternal, and who had been more comfortable yesterday when Sands had been significantly rattled and she could take care of him, was clearly determined not to repeat the mistakes of her predecessor.

That's fine with me, Sands thought. *Strictly business*.

He poked through the top files from his in box for a half hour or so, shuffling a few papers here and there, forming an idea of which tasks would likely require the most attention over the next week or two. Before long, though, he was on his computer, clicking his way through the network and searching through "inactive" employee files. Until he found one file in particular: Amelia Kilby. He stared at her name for several minutes before he opened the file itself. *Why am I looking at this?* he wondered. Pure curiosity, he assured himself. Just a way to procrastinate for a little while before diving into the daunting pile of work that Caroline had constructed. The electronic file had little enough information, regardless: name, address, dates of employment, Social Security number, wage, HMO subscriber identification number. Just the technical nuts and bolts of an employee's identity. Sands still had no firm purpose in mind when he buzzed Sharon.

"Yes, Mr. Sands?"

"Sharon, I need the personnel file for a former employee: Amelia Kilby. Could you get that for me, please?"

While he was waiting for Sharon to return with the actual file, which would have more useful information, such as performance reviews, Sands noticed an interesting fact on the electronic file: The plant that Mrs. Kilby had worked at was Mike Grogan's plant. "Hm." Sands reached for the phone.

CHAPTER 24

Sands was beginning to wish that he'd agreed to meet Mike some place, *any* place, other than the employee cafeteria. Too many people. And Sands couldn't stop thinking about Albert's story, about seeing Gerry Stafford walk in and knowing that the poor bastard was dead. What had Tinsley called it? His *imbuing*. Somehow that term seemed too clinical, too *theoretical* for what Sands had experienced. *Imbuing* sounded too much like some sort of graduation ceremony: Somebody hands you a sheepskin, flips your tassel, and—*bam*—there you are; you can see supernatural critters now. For Sands, the association he maintained for the first time he'd seen the lurker, and *known* what it was, was more along the lines of somebody sticking a fist down his throat and jerking out his stomach through his mouth. *That* was what imbuing meant to him. And it did not engender a considerable appetite, cafeteria or no cafeteria.

He'd at least thought to bring a few files with him. He figured he ought to toss *something* in his out box by the end of the day, to keep Caroline pacified, if for no other reason. Mostly, though, the presence of the files meant that he could stare at the pages and pretend to concentrate on them rather than greet people. A few irritatingly friendly individuals did say hello to him; Sands looked up, smiled and nodded, never quite focusing on the person's face—just in case—and then returned to his paperwork.

He didn't know what was for lunch today; he hadn't wanted to look at the sign on the counter, at the plastic letters that Ketricks, the cafeteria manager, arranged every day. What if, like when Albert had seen them, and when Sands had looked at Melanie's clock, the letters didn't spell what they were supposed to spell? What if they read: THE MEATLOAF LIVES, or YOU DON'T HAVE HEMORRHOIDS. THOSE ARE SPACE ALIENS. What then? What would he be left trying to explain afterward? He thought the cafeteria windows were probably too thick to throw himself through, but wouldn't it be more embarrassing to *fail* to throw himself through a window, to bounce back and land in someone's lunch, than to succeed? What if he looked at Ketricks and the elderly black man was possessed, or dead like Gerry had been? Would Sands try to drown him in the minestrone soup? Would he be able to control what he did, or would he just snap—like before?

Sands wished for a drink of Scotch. He wished he hadn't left the damn flask in the car.

"Doug, you look *great*," said Mike Grogan, weaving his way among the nearby tables to join Sands. When Sands had called that morning, Mike had said that he would be in the building for a meeting, so they might as well grab some lunch in the cafeteria after he was done. Sands, much to his chagrin now, had agreed. Mike was wearing a tie but not a suit; he could get away with that as a plant manager, since he wasn't above rolling up his sleeves and doing some hands-on mechanical work once in a while. "I heard you had a broken arm," Grogan said, hanging his IRM jacket over the back of a chair.

"Oh, that," Sands said. "My wrist. It wasn't as bad as they thought originally. They took the cast off."

"Really? Great. Well, why don't we grab some food?"

"Uh…you go ahead. I'm not really hungry."

"Suit yourself then. I'll be right back."

While Mike was in line, Sands realized, to his great relief, that his tennis partner seemed to be normal. *Surely* most *people are normal*, Sands told himself. He *wanted* very much to believe that he wasn't going to bump into a dead person every time he turned around. Wouldn't Albert have flipped out by now if that were the case? Sure, Sands decided, not knowing when or where he might stumble upon a seemingly normal person who was actually an infernal incarnation might be stressful, but it would be better than finding the things *everywhere*. If he was going to have any hope of living a regular life again, he knew that he was going to have to deal with his newfound anxieties sooner or later. Probably later. He didn't look at anyone until Mike returned to the table.

"So," Grogan said, setting down his tray, "you up for tennis tomorrow, or does your wrist need more time off? This might be my only chance to beat you— to get you while you're crippled."

Sands stared at his hand as he stretched his fingers and rotated his wrist. He hadn't so much as thought about tennis for many days. "Sure. I think it's coming along pretty well."

"You'll just have to ease up on me," Mike said with a mock-serious expression.

"Hmpf. Right. I'll have Sharon reserve a court for us."

"Sharon?"

"My new executive assistant."

"Oh," Mike said, then, "*Oh*," obviously comprehending something of the reason why Sands had a new executive assistant. Grogan seemed slightly embarrassed that he'd asked.

Good God, Sands thought. *Everybody knows that Melanie and I were sleeping together.* Grogan was probably wondering how this all fit with Sands' outburst the last time they'd played tennis, and with their conversation at the Christmas party. *Let him wonder* Sands decided.

"Mike," Sands said, more than ready to change the subject, "I'm curious about a former employee who worked in your plant. Amelia Kilby."

Grogan thought for a moment. "Nope. Doesn't ring a bell." He began sawing into the resistant Swiss steak on his tray.

"Really? She was a worker's comp case a couple years ago. Equipment injury, lost her hand and part of her arm."

"Oh…yeah." Mike waggled his fork in the air. He seemed to be having almost as much trouble chewing his food as he'd had cutting it. "Sorry. I didn't realize you were talking about that long ago. I do remember." He kept chewing. "She died later, didn't she? Unrelated."

"Not completely unrelated," Sands said. Mrs. Kilby's file had a final letter from IRM's insurance company explaining some of the details. "A few weeks after the accident, a blood clot developed. She died in her sleep."

"That's right. What is it that you want to know about her?"

"Well…in her file, there are three reprimands for drinking on the job—the last one about two months before the accident."

"That sounds right."

"But there's no mention of drinking being involved in the accident. Is that correct?" Sands asked.

"I haven't looked at the file or thought about her in two years, Doug, but that sounds right too." Mike poked at his steak, but didn't seem interested in cutting another bite. " Why do you ask?"

"Oh…we're closing out some inactive accounts with the HMO, and I just wanted to make sure that everything had been wrapped up properly. Routine stuff. That's all."

"Oh." Grogan returned his attention to his lunch. "Well, it seems like you've got all your facts straight. I'd say close that one out."

Sands considered that as he watched Mike eat. Douglas wasn't sure what he was hoping to find out. Mr. Kilby—or maybe it had been Mrs. Kilby utilizing her husband's vocal cords—had said that Amelia wasn't a drunkard. The facts, at least in the case of the accident, seemed to bear that out. End of story. Sands thought about Albert going to so much trouble to keep Davis Kilby alive, then again about Albert's story. "Orange or green Jell-O," Sands muttered.

"What?" Mike asked out of the corner of his mouth as he chewed.

"Oh, nothing." Sands said. "Hey, I'm sorry to have wasted your time."

"Wasted? I had to eat lunch anyway. Here's as good a place as any—well, maybe not any. But it's good to see you again. Tomorrow morning? Tennis?"

"Right. I'll have Sharon let you know what time the reservation is for. I'd better get going."

❖   ❖   ❖   ❖   ❖

Sands actually got a little work done that afternoon. His office seemed a safe refuge after the stress of the cafeteria. Caroline stopped by to tell him that Marcus Jubal wanted to meet with him in the morning. She also seemed to take note that he was making an effort to address the bulging in box. Sands suspected that, soon, files would start to disappear, and certain personnel matters would be taken care of on their own, quietly and efficiently. He could have just *told* Caroline to take some of the stuff out of his damn box—*she* was the subordinate, after all—but it seemed safer, less turbulent, for all involved if he played along instead.

It was almost 5:00 PM, and he was about to leave when Sharon buzzed him. "Mr. Sands, Mike Grogan on line two for you."

"Thanks, Sharon." He pressed the button for line two. "Mike, you chickening out of tomorrow morning already?"

"Not on your life, Doug. I'll be there." Grogan paused. "Do you have a minute?"

"Sure. I was just finishing up for the day. What's on your mind?"

There was another pause, then, "Doug…what we were talking about at lunch today, Amelia Kilby…"

Sands' stomach tightened. He'd not thought about Mrs. Kilby since lunch; he'd been *relieved* not to think about her. *Close that one out*, Mike had said, and Sands had been glad to follow that advice. "What about her?"

"This needs to stay off the record…what I'm about to tell you…"

"Okay, Mike."

"Kilby's accident *did* involve alcohol. She'd been drinking. She didn't engage the safety equipment properly. She caught her fingers, got sucked in like somebody with a necktie in a paper shredder." There was a long silence on the line. "Doug?"

"You didn't remember this at lunch?"

"Of course I remembered it," Grogan said. "I knew who you were talking about as soon as you said her name."

"Then why didn't you tell me? Why doesn't her file reflect that?"

"Doug, you work with the insurance company all the time. You know how they would've balked if they'd known that woman was injured through her own negligence."

It was true, Sands knew. Especially on such a large claim: hospitalization, worker's comp, disability. But there was something else as well. "It wouldn't have looked good on your record either, would it, Mike? That you hadn't fired her earlier, or gotten her into a rehab program."

Another pause. "There's that, too. Yes. But she needed the money. She'd worked here for *eighteen years*, Doug. She needed her job. She needed the insurance coverage."

"I see." Sands was caught off guard by this new revelation—not by the fact that Amelia *had* been a drunk, but that Mike had doctored the files and lied to him. But it made sense. Grogan was obviously distraught about the matter; he'd been bothered enough to call and straighten things out. "I don't know what to say. I certainly don't see any need to bring this to the attention of the HMO. I mean, the woman's dead and buried." *For whatever good that's worth*, he thought.

"You can see why this needs to stay off the record, can't you, Doug?" Grogan asked. "It won't do anybody any good to dredge this back up…. Right?"

"You're right. Thanks for calling. I'll see you in the morning."

"See you in the morning."

Sands hung up the phone and sat for a long while trying to figure out what he should do.

CHAPTER 25

Jason tugged at the collar of his dress shirt. How could anybody wear a tie every day? he wondered. He silently thanked God that he didn't have to wear one working at his parents' hardware store. He'd put on a tie today, though, with his only suit. The pants were uncomfortably tight; he was afraid if he had to crouch down for anything that he'd rip the crotch out. He couldn't remember the last time he'd dressed up. Not since before he'd dropped out of high school had he been to church. His parents had noticed the tie and the suit; they'd been relieved that they didn't have to argue with him about it.

"I've always known you're a nice boy, a good boy," his mother had said. Even his father had complimented him: "You look sharp—for a change. Don't forget to comb your hair." That was as good as it got from Pop.

What? Jason wondered. *Did they think I was gonna dress like a slob for my sister's funeral?* Apparently they hadn't been convinced otherwise.

Now, after a couple of hours at the funeral home, the tight collar and the tight pants were bugging the hell out of him. And the sickly sweet smell of all the flowers was about to make him puke. He wished the organist would give it a rest, too. Maybe it was the morbid background music that made Jason want to throw up, and not the flowers. Maybe it was both.

But he was there for Laura. Not that it did a whole helluva lot of good at this point. He wished to God that he could have been there for her sooner, when it would have counted for something. Looking back, he could see that it wasn't his fault, not really, but that didn't make him feel any better. He still thought that he *should* have been able to do something. He'd been there the first night, when his buddy Kyle had introduced them to Lionel Braughton. Jason had let her go off with the other two men. She'd been attacked and raped. Laura had never been the same person again. Since then, Jason had figured out that it wasn't the rape itself that had changed her, at least not the most. It was Lionel.

For a long time after the rape, Jason had thought that his sister had brought all her troubles on herself, that she'd become some kind of sex freak, an S&M junkie, that it was her own fault she'd been raped. That belief was Lionel's doing. He'd made Jason believe it, and Laura too. Lionel had made them think and believe what he wanted them to, just by looking them in the eye and telling them. At the time, Jason and Laura hadn't remembered their encounters with Lionel. Hypnotism, or something like it—that's what Jason thought now that he had a better idea of what Lionel was.

Because now, Jason did remember. All of it. He remembered the night of the rape, and how he, at Lionel's undeniable suggestion, had let Laura go with Kyle and the stranger. He remembered the nights after. She had so often been sick or hysterical then. Jason had taken to watching her while she slept, the only time she'd seemed herself anymore. He remembered the nights that the blue-eyed man, in his expensive suit, had come to Laura's room. Lionel had told Jason to look away, and to forget, and Jason had obeyed.

It wasn't until the most recent visit, the *final* visit, that everything had come together for him. He'd been sitting by Laura's bed that night also. She'd been sleeping, but restlessly. She didn't open her eyes, but she started to talk—except it wasn't her voice; somebody else's voice was coming out of Laura's mouth, and said: "*It drinks my life.*" She said it in that not-her-voice twice: "*It drinks my life.*" Then everything was back to normal. She was sleeping, tossing a little, but normal. Jason was left wondering if he'd imagined it all.

But then Lionel had appeared in the doorway—he was wearing a fancy wool coat and a smug grin—and suddenly everything had made sense, like the whole world had come into focus, and Jason hadn't even realized before that he was seeing it wrong. *It drinks my life.* Lionel wasn't using Laura for sex; he was *drinking her blood—her life.* Jason looked at Lionel and saw blood on the monster's hands, on his face.

"You can't have her," Jason had told him.

Lionel had seemed concerned at first, but just a little. Probably because Jason seemed to know who he was. But Lionel was nothing if not confident; his satisfied smirk returned quickly enough. "Look out the window, Jason. Your sister wants me."

Jason threw his chair at Lionel. *That* had surprised the bastard—but not enough. He was fast and strong. He knocked the chair away easily, but for the first time, there was doubt in his blue eyes. The next thing Jason knew, he was swinging...*something* at Lionel. Some-big-damn-thing was in Jason's hand: a club or a metal rod. Whatever it was, wherever it had come from, it was glowing red and *hot*—but it wasn't burning Jason. He hadn't noticed that until later. At the time, he'd been too intent on busting open Lionel's skull. Almost did it, too. But Lionel ducked out of the way. The fiery rod had slammed into the doorframe—cracked it, scorched it.

Jason wasn't sure exactly what had happened after that. Lionel was simply gone the next instant. As completely as if he'd never been there—except for the smoldering burn on the doorframe, and Laura lying pale in the bed. Thinking back on the brief fight—if you could call it that—and on the raw physical strength that Lionel had demonstrated in the past, Jason had a sinking feeling that maybe he'd gotten off lucky. Chances were that Lionel, if he'd wanted to, could have killed him. Probably Lionel had been too surprised by Jason's resistance, and by what-the-hell-ever that flaming stick was, to fight.

Every night after that, for weeks, Jason had sat with his sleeping sister. He'd sat, and remembered, and hated—hated Lionel for what he'd done to Laura, and hated him for what he'd made Jason think about her. He'd hated himself, too, for failing her.

Lionel hadn't shown up again. He hadn't had to. A few days ago, Laura's heart had just stopped. Cardiac arrest. Nineteen year-olds weren't supposed to die of that. *Especially not my sister, damn it!* Jason smoothed down the lapel of his jacket, which he'd inadvertently crumpled in his fist.

As much as he hated seeing Laura's body lying there in that coffin, the funeral home people had done a good job. *She looks real natural.* Her color was better than it had been for a long time. The doctors didn't know why her heart had been strained beyond its capabilities. Jason knew. And if it was the last thing he did, he was going to set things right.

CHAPTER 26

"How's work going so far?" Albert asked, as he and Sands watched a store-bought lasagna rotate inside the microwave. Tinsley's little house, still comforting despite being the location of several disturbing revelations, was very familiar to Sands now, after more than a week of staying there.

"Pretty well," Sands said. "Lots to catch up on." *Pretty well* was certainly an exaggeration, but not quite an outright lie. By the end of this, his second day back in the office, Douglas had been able to walk among the cubicles without wincing when someone greeted him; he'd gone so far as to have short conversations with a few co-workers, who, he'd been relived to discover, did not seem to be demonic beings in any form. The only reason he left by the stairs, he told himself, was that he needed the exercise.

"Good. Glad to hear it," Albert said. "I know I had what you might call a difficult readjustment. The elevator was especially problematic. I think I used the stairs for months."

"Really? Well, nothing like that for me," Sands said, rapidly spiraling away from the truth. Having survived the office another day, however, wasn't what he wanted to think about at the moment. "Listen, Albert, I need to ask you about something…about Faye and Melanie…and your friends…. I feel like I'm…I don't know, shirking my responsibilities. With Faye, at least, it's my fault that she's in danger, you know? I should be out there. Protecting her. It's not your friends' job. It should be mine."

"Give yourself some time, Douglas. It's *everybody's* job to deal with the…the supernatural. Ghosts. Monsters. Whatever you want to call them."

"But I should be helping," Sands insisted. Because if he allowed that it was other people's responsibility to take care of his problems, then it became *his* responsibility to deal with *their* problems! And he wasn't about to buy into that. Albert could save the world if he wanted, but Douglas just wanted his life back. *Then why the hell did I ask Mike about Amelia Kilby?* he wondered.

"There'll be time for you to help," Albert said. "Believe me, there'll be more than enough time."

"It's not that I *want* to help. I *should* help. What I want is to be done with all this."

"That's a start," Albert said. He didn't say it out of smugness. As always, he was completely sincere. That only made him more infuriating.

✧   ✧   ✧   ✧   ✧

After dinner, Sands surprised himself by offering to go with Albert to the Kilbys' house. That was obviously where Tinsley was going. He had an entire case of nutrition drinks. Since hooking up an IV was out of the question, he thought this was the best way to try to keep the late Mrs. Kilby from starving her husband into joining her in death.

Thinking about the proposition made Sands' head spin. He grew uncomfortable whenever he caught himself thinking about the Kilbys, or Gerry Stafford, or the lurker, in matter-of-fact terms. Sands refused to be drawn into believing that any of this was *normal*. It might be *real*, much to his dismay, but it sure as hell wasn't normal. He thought that would probably be the last hurrah for his sanity, if he began considering dealings with the dead as merely another note on his daily to-do list: Go to the store; pick up the dry cleaning; put gas in the car; feed the old, dead man down the street....

Yet Sands had volunteered to accompany Albert. As the two pulled on their winter gear, Sands thought he knew why he was going. This was payback, recompense to Albert's friends for helping Sands. In a way, it was more like a ransom. Sands would equal their generosity, and the slate would be clean. He would owe them nothing; he was buying his freedom. He already owed Julia. Whatever she'd done, however she'd done it, he was in one piece again. There wasn't even a scar from the 128 stitches in his face. Incredible. But Sands was as resentful as he was grateful. It was just a matter of time, he was sure, until Julia, and maybe Albert too, despite his easy-going ways, demanded something in return. Better to beat them to the punch.

"Is Julia with your other friends?" Sands asked as they stepped out the door, Albert carrying the case of Nutri-Drink.

"She is," Albert said, then, "Oh, that reminds me. Julia left a few odds and ends here a while back. Have you seen a flask anywhere? I think it was silver."

"Flask?" Sands said. They were walking past his car. "No. I haven't seen one. I'll keep an eye out." He cringed inwardly. Here he was lying to Albert after all Tinsley had done for him, but it wasn't like Sands planned on keeping the flask. He could clean it and slip it back into the house easy enough later. His embarrassment at having borrowed the flask without asking outweighed his guilt over lying, so they continued on in silence.

The front door of the Kilby's house was stuck again. Since Albert's hands were full, Sands forced it open. He heard the same crack of what he knew this time was the sheen of ice that had held the door shut. He saw the shimmer of light against an icy interior wall. He smelled the crisp, dry odor of supernal cold, as the insides of his nostrils again froze.

"Does it stay this cold in here during the summer?" Sands asked.

"I don't know. I didn't notice them until this winter."

"But she died two *years* ago," Sands said. "What…did she just get around to coming back and haunting her husband?"

"I don't know what happens after death, Douglas," Albert said. "The spirit world might not work on our timetable."

Spirit world, Sands thought. *What a bunch of hooey. Dead is dead. Or at least it should be.* But he knew he couldn't dismiss what he'd seen in this house. Or the hand he'd felt on his arm in his own home. Adam had died *ten* years ago. "Let's get this over with."

Davis Kilby, dressed in the same sleeveless undershirt and boxer shorts as before, was sitting in one of the kitchen chairs this time. Sands was surprised that the chair had been moved; they'd all looked firmly frozen to the floor last visit. The chair was pulled close to the open refrigerator. Mr. Kilby sat staring intently at the tiny burning bulb that should not have been on. He cast a long shadow across the kitchen. He didn't turn to face Sands and Albert.

But Mrs. Kilby did.

The effect was disconcerting. The old man's face remained directed toward the gaping refrigerator. (It was an outdated model, perhaps an antique, with a curved top and a single door that, open, revealed the interior of both the refrigerator and the freezer. The freezer was years overdue for defrosting; the refrigerator itself, perhaps the only surface in the house, was completely free of ice.) On the side of Mr. Kilby's head, his dead wife's face slid into view, her features rippling the surface of his skull, like a rat crawling beneath a rug.

"She weren't no drunkard," said the overlapping voices of Mr. and Mrs. Kilby. Both mouths moved. The words reverberated from the walls and ceiling of the ice-cave. Davis still did not look at the intruders in his home, but Amelia glared.

"Why so cold, Amelia?" Sands asked.

"Be careful, Douglas," Albert cautioned, but he didn't seem inclined to interfere. Instead, he forced open the basement door. He produced a flashlight from his coat pocket and shined it down the stairs.

"Why so cold?" Sands asked again.

Mrs. Kilby's mouth moved, but neither she nor her husband said anything. As her hateful glare fixed on Sands, she continued working her jaw, as if she were chewing gristly Swiss steak. Then Mr. Kilby slowly turned in his chair. Amelia's face slid along beneath his skin, until the two faces were almost indistinguishable. She never shifted her gaze from Sands. It was Mr. Kilby's voice, prompted or unprompted Sands wasn't sure, that spoke: "It's hot down there."

Sands turned to look at Albert, who was still shining his flashlight down the basement stairs. Somehow, though, Sands felt that the *down there* in question was not the basement.

Albert set the case of Nutri-Drink, except for one can, on the top step and closed the basement door. He set the can on the table. Almost instantly, a thin sheen of ice spread from the table over the drink, enveloping it completely. Albert stared quizzically at the can.

"I don't know that I'd want to sit down and stay for a while," Sands muttered.

"Amelia," Albert said calmly, "Davis needs to eat. I'm trying to help him. I know you love your husband. Do you remember the years you spent with him?"

Mr. Kilby's face—or maybe it was Mrs. Kilby's—contorted suddenly, the jaw still working, but more ferociously now. Mr. Kilby's head slowly turned away, back to the refrigerator, but Amelia's sliding visage twisted and snarled in anguish.

"She weren't no drunkard," said Mr. Kilby, his words even, but with a hint of hostility.

"She *was* a drunk!" Sands said. "She was caught drinking on the job more than once."

Amelia's eyes bulged with rage. Garbled curses filled the air. Mr. Kilby, still calmly facing the refrigerator spoke for them: "The equipment weren't safe."

Albert placed a hand on Sands' shoulder. "Douglas, I don't know if—"

"She *was* a drunk," Sands said again. "She had three reprimands on her record for drinking on her job, and she was drunk the day she lost her hand! Isn't that right, Amelia?"

Mr. Kilby balled his hands into fists. Amelia stretched her mouth in a silent, primal scream—and the world shattered. The ceiling collapsed. Jagged shards of glass—no, *ice*—were raining down upon Sands and Tinsley. Then the full weight struck them. Not the full weight of the ceiling, it turned out. The ceiling had not fallen—just the layers of ice that had covered it. *Just.*

Sands found himself on the floor, blood obscuring his vision. Albert was beside him, equally stunned. Someone might as well have dropped a giant plate glass window on their heads, so solid was the ice. They crawled out of the kitchen, chased relentlessly by Amelia's curses. Mr. Kilby didn't seem to be affected by the cave-in. He sat placidly again, staring into the refrigerator, while his dead wife raged.

Albert and Douglas crawled more quickly, their gloves and the knees of their pants sticking to the ice-encrusted floors. They didn't climb to their feet until they were on the front porch; they did not speak as they staggered back to Tinsley's house. Albert had a few cuts and bruises as well, but he wasn't bleeding as much as Douglas was above his right eye.

"I don't think that was a good idea," Albert said quietly as they approached his home. Sands said nothing.

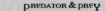

CHAPTER 27

Sands was supposed to meet Mike Grogan at the Iron Rapids Racquet Club at 9:00 AM. At 8:45 AM, Sands pulled into the parking lot at Grogan's plant. Before he'd left Tinsley's house, Sands had called the Racquet Club and left a message that he'd be a few minutes late. "Tell Mr. Grogan that he should go ahead and warm up his serve, because he needs the practice," Sands said to the young man who'd answered the phone. Sands did *not* want Mike to call *his* executive assistant, Melissa, to see if Sands had called to cancel—not while Sands was there in Mike's office.

This is crazy, Sands thought as he climbed out of his car, *but what else is new?*

"Mr. Sands," said Melissa, as Sands walked into her office, "what in the world happened to you?"

"What? Oh." Sands' hand rose and delicately touched the bandage over his right eye. Beneath the outer bandage, two butterfly bandages seemed to have done trick—or at least he hoped they had. The gash had bled, on and off, most of the night, but Sands had checked in the rearview mirror before he got out of his car; the dressing had still been white, not bled through. Albert had urged him to go to the hospital, but Sands had feared that the emergency room—at night—would be much worse, far more anxiety-inducing, than had been the company cafeteria that afternoon. "Long story, Melissa, and you wouldn't believe it."

She smiled, but then her expression became puzzled. "Weren't you and Mike playing tennis this morning?" She flipped a page on her desk calendar.

"Yes. I'm headed that way in just a minute. I called to let him know I'd be late," Sands assured her. "Listen, I realized this morning that I need to pick up some files to corroborate figures with a worker's comp claim. Can you point me toward the right cabinet? It's a former employee. The incident was about two years ago."

"Two years. That should be in Mike's office. I'll show you." She led him into Grogan's office. "This filing cabinet. Let's see, two years ago would be...this drawer. Can I get it for you?"

"No, I'll find it," Sands said. "I don't want to take up your time."

"All right, but let me know if you have trouble." She started back to her desk.

"Will do. Oh...Melissa. I also need to find some OSHA recommendations and safety upgrade records, just to confirm some numbers...?"

"One cabinet over. Same time frame?"

"Right. And predating that a little."

"Second drawer from the bottom."

"Thanks." Sands found what he needed after about fifteen minutes of searching. The phone rang four times during that period. Each time, he was sure that it was Mike, having figured out what he was up to. Sands had no intention of meeting Grogan for tennis; there were the files to scour and the meeting with Marcus Jubal. Luckily, the phone calls all seemed to be routine, and Melissa handled them without any sort of upheaval. She was on the phone as Sands left. He winked and mouthed, "Thank you," on his way out the door.

CHAPTER 28

"Take a look at this," Sands said, dropping the stack of photocopies onto Albert's desk.

"What is it?" Tinsley asked, but as he perused a page or two, he began to suspect. "This is what Davis was talking about last night."

"Right. Davis…or Amelia, whichever."

"It is hard to tell sometime." Albert read over more of the pages. "But this doesn't prove that she wasn't drinking."

"Right again," Sands said, feeling quite pleased with himself by this point. "She may well have been blitzed off her gourd. I wouldn't be surprised if that contributed to the accident. But what this does prove," Sands reached down and tapped the photocopied files, "is that OSHA cited Grogan's facility for safety violations. That's here." He turned back several pages and pointed out the relevant document to Albert. "That was in four years ago. Serious stuff, but it happens. What doesn't happen, though, or *shouldn't*, is this…" Sands flipped ahead a few sheets.

Albert squinted as he read, accentuating his crows feet. He scratched at his beard. "Mike's letter informing OSHA that corrective steps had been taken…including additional safety equipment."

"Right," Sands said, "except…" he rustled through the stack until he found the page he wanted, "…look at this."

"An invoice. I don't understand. It's for…"

Sands impatiently pulled out the previous page, Grogan's letter, and placed it alongside the invoice. "For the safety equipment he mentions in the OSHA letter."

Albert sat back in his chair. "What's the problem, then? I don't see—"

"Look at the date on the invoice, Albert."

Tinsley slowly leaned back up to his desk. "It's more than two years after the letter."

"*After* the letter. *After* Amelia Kilby's accident."

"He lied to OSHA? But all it would have taken was a follow-up visit, and they would have caught that."

"Think Newt Gingrich and the Republican Revolution," Sands said. "They were slashing budgets and federal agencies quicker than you can say 'Contract With America.' OSHA didn't have enough regulators to visit all the factories they needed to inspect once, much less to follow up on something they were assured had been corrected."

"But why?" Albert asked.

"That becomes apparent if you look at this...." Sands spread out several more pages over the invoice and Grogan's letter. "We were having our own budget crunch. Mike was over budget. He couldn't squeeze out the bucks for the safety upgrade, so he put it off and told OSHA what they wanted to hear."

Albert understood. "But Amelia Kilby, possibly snookered, got herself caught up in the machinery before Grogan got around to addressing the problem." He went through all the documents a second time, as Sands watched silently. "It seems like you've got a strong case," Albert said eventually. "What now?"

"What do you mean, 'what now?'"

"I mean," Albert said, "what are you going to do with all this?" He lifted the stack of photocopies from his desk.

"I've already *done* it, Albert. I had a meeting with Marcus Jubal, and I gave him copies of all this."

"You gave it to Marcus?"

"Uh-huh. That's not what we were meeting about originally. He read me the riot act about the whole thing with Melanie, which he had to, I guess. Not that she'd bring a sexual harassment suit, but he's got to cover his butt. So he gave me an official reprimand—which might hurt if I were planning on job-hunting in the next ten or fifteen years, which I'm not. He was pretty pissed, though. I think it's because he knows Faye."

Albert didn't seem to be listening to much of what Sands was saying. Tinsley shook his head urgently. "But you gave a copy of these documents to him?" he asked. "You told him everything you just told me?"

"Well, he doesn't know about Amelia Kilby's *current* whereabouts. I didn't mention the fact that she's…" Sands paused, shifted his voice to a whisper, *"back from the grave."*

"It's not Amelia Kilby I'm worried about at the moment," Albert said, actually beginning to grow angry. "What about *Mike Grogan?"*

"What about him?"

"You just wrecked his career!"

"Oh, no. Don't lay that at my feet. Mike took care of that when he skimped on the safety equipment and lied to OSHA. It just took a while to catch up with him."

"I thought he was your friend," Albert said in disbelief.

"Albert, he broke the law. Somebody *died* because of it. Maybe *two* somebodies, if you aren't able to get Davis Kilby eating." Sands couldn't believe that Albert was attacking him about this. *I try to help him out with this Kilby problem, and this is the thanks I get!* Sands thought.

"I guess I just don't see it so black and white, Douglas."

"I thought...hell, I don't know. I thought maybe if this mess got straightened out that Mrs. Kilby would...you know...go away." Sands shrugged. He hadn't really made that connection before, not even in his own mind—and now that he said it aloud, it sounded stupid. "I mean, wouldn't *you* be pissed if some cheap bastard worried about his budget got you killed?"

"Or maybe I'd be angry about drinking my life away!" Albert shot back. "Can you make *that* go away? Can you change the past?" With the sudden outburst, much of his anger seemed to drain away. He sank back into his padded chair; he looked very tired. "You may be right, but I wouldn't have bet Grogan's career on it."

"What would you have done?" It was an accusation as much as a question. Albert might have exhausted his ire, but Sands was still angry.

"I would have confronted Grogan," Albert said with a sigh. "I suppose I would have tried to gather the proof, like you did, in case he didn't own up to it. But I would have given him that chance. Maybe he could have made amends somehow. At the very least, if *he* had brought it to the company's attention..."

"They still would have fired him, Albert."

"Probably. But he could have retained some of his dignity. Human dignity is important, Douglas."

"He got Amelia Kilby killed," Sands said emphatically. "Where exactly does dignity fit into that? This is justice."

"That's what you've decided? You, Douglas?" Albert asked, growing animated again. "Tell me, what's justice for you having an affair with a twenty-something-year-old girl? Does your *official reprimand* make up for what you've put Faye through? Does that wipe the slate clean?"

"You son of a—!"

"Being able to see what other people can't see doesn't make us any *wiser* than they are. You disavow responsibility for your gift, but now you think it gives you the right to sit as judge over others? You can't run your own life. Why should you run theirs? Why, Douglas? *Why?*"

Sands took a step back, as if Albert had struck him across the face. *Who are you to judge me?* The lurker's words rang in Sands' ears. He heard the scraping of razor teeth. "I'm not going to have this conversation," Sands said. He held his hands up in the air as if he were surrendering. "I'm not. If I need this, I'll go back to Faye."

"You better have this conversation before too long," Albert called after him as Sands left and closed the office door behind him.

CHAPTER 29

Sands didn't go directly back to Tinsley's house after work. Instead, he made a quick detour by the liquor store. Albert's car was already by the curb when Sands did get to the house. Dusk had arrived, brief visitor that it was before deeper darkness fully claimed the cloud-enshrined city. To Sands' mild surprise, Albert wasn't home. *At the store?* Douglas thought. But Tinsley usually did most of his grocery shopping on the weekend. *Maybe he couldn't stand the sight of me.* Sands pondered that thought. He still couldn't comprehend the vehemence of Albert's reaction. Sure, it was tragic that Mike had screwed up, and now he was going to lose his job—but he'd brought in on himself. *He was playing footsie with the budget and got somebody killed, for God's sake!* Sands still felt completely justified in what he'd done—which wasn't to say that he'd returned Mike's angry phone calls. He hadn't.

Sands peeked into Albert's room. Not there. The house was small enough that Douglas couldn't have overlooked his host. Satisfied that he was alone, Sands hurried back out to his car and retrieved the silver flask from beneath the front seat. Back inside, he took a sip of Scotch from the flask—the familiar liquid fire set his esophagus to tingling—then poured the rest into a mostly empty bottle by his bed. The process was simple enough, but he was rushing, trying to finish before Albert got back from wherever he'd gone. Several rivulets of whisky trickled down the side of the bottle, but the flask was the important thing at the moment. Sands rinsed it with hot water until it didn't smell like Scotch, filled it partially with water, like he'd found it, and then stuck it back in the closet of the guest bedroom, under a few odds and ends, so it *conceivably* could have been overlooked by Albert or Julia if they'd indeed been looking for it.

Next, Sands changed out of his work clothes, turned on the television, and waited. As the local news came and went, he wondered if maybe it was time to figure out where he should go next. Not in a larger, existential sense—he *wasn't* ready to tackle that yet—but where he should *live*. Staying with Albert for a week or two had been convenient enough…*Okay, a godsend*, Sands admitted to himself grudgingly. He might well have ended up committed or dead if not for bumping into Albert at the bakery on Christmas morning. *But I've got things under control again*, Sands decided. *More or less.* And Tinsley seemed to have lost his patience—something Sands had never thought that he would witness. It was time to move on. *Or maybe I should try to do something about the lurker first.* Sands had grown accustomed over the years to a life of quiet, lingering frustration, but never before the past few weeks had he ever faced so much uncertainty.

After the local news, Sands flipped the TV to PBS. Thanks to Albert, he'd gotten in the habit of watching the *News Hour, with Jim Lehrer*. Peter Jennings and Tom Brokaw, with their smarmy omniscience, just didn't cut the mustard anymore. Before long, though, Sands was up from the couch and peering out the front window. Albert's car *was* out front; Sands hadn't imagined that. But no Albert. *I bet he's trying to patch things up with Amelia and Davis*, Sands thought. His own confrontation with Mrs. Kilby last night had not been the most productive. "Who'd have guessed that dead people would be so touchy?" he said to himself. *Maybe Albert, if you'd bothered to ask*, Sands thought, but he merely shrugged, not giving voice to that thought.

By the time the *News Hour* was ending, Sands was beginning to worry. He grew increasingly certain that Albert had walked down to the Kilbys'. Anywhere else, he would have taken a car. Just out for a long walk, no destination in particular? Maybe. But Sands' mounting concern wouldn't allow him to relax. So he finished another glass of Scotch, pulled on his boots, and bundled up against the cold.

The Kilbys' house was about a ten-minute walk. Sands was more at ease walking down the street in the Islands now. The general poverty of the area, still stark and pervasive, no longer struck him as being so alien. In just a week or two, the scene had lost its ability to shock him. Familiarity blunted his reaction to the squalid living conditions. In his mind, the people living here were a different strain, but the same species, as Melanie's neighbors at the privatized housing project. *Why in hell would anyone stay here?* he wondered. Especially Albert. At least Melanie had a financial reason for associating with this class of people. *What the hell am I doing here?* Sands wondered next. *I can afford better than this*. Maybe it *was* time to move along. More than maybe. Walking along the snow-muted streets, he decided that he'd press Albert about dealing with the lurker, and then get the hell out.

There was no sign at the Kilby house that Albert had been there. The prints on the narrow, foot-worn path to the porch could have been from tonight, or last night, or last week.... Sands forced the door open and was greeted almost instantly by the colder air inside. Last night's visit, at least initially, hadn't been so bad. Knowing what to expect, Sands had mostly taken in stride the impossible conditions in the house: the ice covering every wall; the glaring light of the powerless bulb in the refrigerator; the dead woman possessing her husband's body. Tonight, however, without Albert—and unlike the increasingly familiar surrounding neighborhood—the house seemed completely *other*. Unnatural, foreboding, wrong.

The intense cold inside blocked the doorway like a solid wall—or perhaps like a vertical surface of water. Sands felt resistance as he stepped across the plane of the threshold. His raised foot seemed to slow as it moved forward; the cold was palpable, substantial, lending buoyancy to his movements. The insidious chill permeated Sands' clothes, his body, leaving no part of him untouched. He imagined himself sinking into the darkness of a calm, bottomless lake. He saw his reflection in an ice-coated wall, and his breath caught in his throat. For an instant, the ice was the frozen surface of the lake, and he was trapped *beneath*.

Sands panicked. He swam to the ice and scrabbled at it, pounded on it, but the force of his blows was dulled by the resistance of the water. He couldn't gain any leverage. Each time he struck the ice, he pushed himself away from it. His lungs *burned*.

And then it was gone. The ice remained, and the cold. But there was no resistance against his body. Gasping, he sucked in the frigid air. It wore his throat raw, but he could breathe. He leaned against the ice wall. Breathing. Gradually, more slowly. His pulse was pounding at his temples.

Breathe. Slowly and deeply. The jagged cold carved the feeling from his lips. Moisture crystallized on his tongue. But he could breathe.

"Albert?" Sands thought for a moment that the lining of his throat would crack and shatter. His tongue was thick and lethargic. The sound of his voice barely penetrated his ears; it did not carry into the house.

He turned down the side hall. To the kitchen. But he found himself walking the wrong direction. The kitchen was the other way. Why was he so disoriented tonight, so hesitant? He stuffed his hands into his pockets and held his arms pressed tightly against his body. It was the cold, he was certain, that was causing him to tremble.

Mr. Kilby, again, was in the kitchen. He sat in the same kitchen chair, staring into the open refrigerator, his back to Sands. "Hello, Davis," Sands said, attempting casualness, but his vocal cords were seared by the cold, and again the ice-cave swallowed almost whole the sound of his voice. Albert was not in the kitchen.

"Hello, Davis," Sands said again, with slightly more success but eliciting no more of a reaction. Mr. Kilby did not turn from the refrigerator, from the dingy white interior and the burning bulb. Mrs. Kilby's visage did not sidle under her husband's skin. Sands looked upon an arctic still-life, of which he was not a part. He stepped closer and to the side of the old man. Mr. Kilby's breath vapor emanated in dual streams from his nostrils, as if he were a gently snoring dragon.

Sands noticed the can of Nutri-Drink on the table, the aluminum cylinder frozen in place, but not upright as Albert had placed it last night. The cave-in could have knocked it over—Sands hadn't paused to notice at the time—but that didn't explain the numerous punctures in the can, the pool of chocolate ice surrounding it on the table.

Sands stepped closer to the old man, closer to the refrigerator. "Davis?" No response. "Amelia?" Then: "The man who's responsible for your accident has been exposed." No response. Now, despite the oppressive cold, Sands noticed a strange scraping sound—and the knife.

Mr. Kilby, in his left hand, held a chef's knife, which he was drawing back and forth, slowly, methodically, across his forearm. The scraping sound that Sands heard was the blade grating against one of the bones in Mr. Kilby's arm. Considering how deeply the old man had sawed, there didn't seem to be enough blood. Every few seconds, a frothy, semi-coagulated ooze of red seeped from the fissure, as if the preternatural cold had already worked its dark magic on Mr. Kilby's blood.

Sands drew back. He sucked in a mouthful of decaying winter and held his breath. Mr. Kilby still seemed to have taken no notice of his visitor. The old man continued drawing the knife back and forth, sawing on his arm, notching the bone, dribbling his lifeblood onto his lap, onto the floor.

Was this the work of Mrs. Kilby? Sands wondered, or had Mr. Kilby gone irretrievably mad? Just then, a brief flash of light caught Sands' attention. Careful not completely to ignore Mr. Kilby, Sands turned toward the light, but it was gone. He couldn't pinpoint where it had come from. There was only the crusty table with its frozen spill of Nutri-Drink—he supposed now that the holes in the can were all stab wounds—and the basement door, open a crack—

There. The light flashed again. From behind the door. In the basement. *Albert?* Sands didn't call out. He felt that any word he uttered might set off the deranged Mr. Kilby. But if it was Albert in the basement, he must be hurt; he must have fallen...or been *stabbed*.

But Sands wasn't about to traipse down the stairs and leave Mr. Kilby with his knife up here. The thought of Albert injured, perhaps bleeding to death, galvanized Sands to action. He stepped deliberately toward Mr. Kilby, not rushing, but carefully watching the knife and moving with deliberate speed. Sands reached down and grasped the old man's left wrist, stopped the sawing motion. With his other hand, Sands reached for the knife.

Mr. Kilby offered no resistance. In fact, he didn't seem to notice when Sands took the knife from him. The old man sat motionless, staring into the refrigerator, hands upon his lap, bleeding a frothy drool every few seconds. Sands quickly found a stiff, frozen dishtowel. He shook it forcefully, showering the kitchen with ice crystals. Then he folded the towel and pressed it onto Mr. Kilby's wound. Sands took Kilby's left hand, which had been holding the knife, and clamped it down over the towel. The old man still did not react. He kept his hand where Sands placed it, but did not exert any noticeable pressure on the towel.

Sands hurried to the basement door and pulled it open. "Albert?"

The flash of light caught him in the eyes but then moved on. The swaying beam of light was coming from the bottom of the steps; it meandered back and forth striking wall, ceiling, Sands, ceiling, wall....

"Albert?"

The case of Nutri-Drink, minus one can, was on the top step and vaguely recognizable beneath a white fur of freezer burn. Sands glanced back at Mr. Kilby; the old man was staring into the refrigerator, unenthusiastically holding the towel on his severely lacerated arm. Sands started down the steps. He was still holding the knife—he wasn't about to leave it where Kilby, *either* of the Kilbys, could get to it—so he was extra careful not to slip on the treacherous, icy stairs.

Near the top, Sands was startled by a drop of water that struck him in the face. He wiped the moisture away, and as he did so, he became aware of the sound of water dripping—the drawn out *blooop...blooop* of water striking water, but there were hundreds of drops falling. The sound of a gentle summer storm greeted him from the basement. As the light swung lazily on it's arc, he saw that water was streaming down the walls alongside the steps. There was still ice—on the walls, on the downward slanting ceiling, on the stairs themselves—but it was melting.

More droplets landed on his head, on his shoulders and back as he hunched forward. *It's hot down there*. Those were the words that had come from Mr. Kilby's mouth last night. It *wasn't* hot, not that Sands could feel, but the ice was melting.

Douglas continued his descent. Closer to the bottom, he realized that the source of the light was a flashlight. "Albert?" he called again. It *was* Albert's flashlight, Sands saw, but not Albert's hand directing the beam; no one's hand directed the beam.

The basement was flooded. The hundreds and thousands of droplets and rivulets were collecting into a pond in the dank, earthen-walled cellar. Sands couldn't tell how deep; he couldn't see the bottom: A foot? Maybe more. The blinding glare of the gently bobbing flashlight didn't allow Sands' eyes to adjust to the otherwise total darkness. The flashlight, Albert's flashlight, was evidently waterproof. Because of its weight distribution, the handle was submerged beneath the more buoyant glass head and bulb. The fetid water, however, seemed too still, too calm, to account for the gyrations of the light beam just a few seconds before.

Sands stopped on the bottom-most step that was not yet submerged. He squatted and set down the knife but couldn't quite reach the flashlight, so he pulled off one glove and, reluctantly, dipped in his hand into the brackish pool. By moving his hand, he tried to create a current and draw the flashlight toward him.

The water sucked from his fingers what little warmth had remained. The flashlight began, slowly, to drift toward him, and in the swaying light, he saw several shapes move away. They startled him as much as the water splashing on his face had, and he had to catch his balance with his other hand. Rats, he saw. Each as large as a small cat. Ducking beneath the surface of the water and fleeing from the flashlight that must have attracted their attention. *That would explain the bobbing*, Sands thought. He watched closely for them as he continued drawing the light toward himself; he didn't *think* that rats would bite his moving fingers, but then again, his expectations of what was and was not possible had not proven particularly dependable over the past weeks.

Finally his fingers brushed against the flashlight. He was careful not to knock it away. There. He had it. He turned it to look for the rats in the murky water—

—And he saw Albert. Floating on his back. His mouth was agape, the basement water flowing in and out as he bobbed gently. A rat, perched on his leg, was chewing at what should have been his right hand, but was nothing more than a mangled stump. His coat lay open on the water, helping keep him afloat. His chest, too, lay open, split by a huge, bloody gash. Albert's eyes stared at the ceiling and were oblivious to the water that constantly dripped into them.

Sands felt himself about to retch, but then he heard the heavy, rapid footsteps thumping down the stairs. Instinctively, he flashed the light in that direction. Mr. Kilby bellowed as the light skipped across his face. Mrs. Kilby was there too, her jaws—superimposed over the husband's gaping mouth—gnawing, rending flesh. The light glittered against the blade of an axe swinging forward. Sands raised his arm to ward off the blow.

The axe handle, just below the blade, struck him across the forearm and snapped—as did his arm. The blade deflected into the wall instead of cleaving his skull. Mr. Kilby was still charging forward. He plowed into Sands and they both tumbled into the water.

The icy blast stole Sands' breath. He was choking on the mixture of water, silt, and blood. He flailed about beneath Mr. Kilby. The old man's hands wrapped around Sands' throat and pushed him deeper, refused him air. The back of his head struck the basement floor—how many feet beneath the surface of the water? A distant light bobbed and jiggled. Through the cold and the roaring pulse in his ears, Sands could hear Mr. Kilby still yelling. Mrs. Kilby's throaty scream struck a crescendo with each renewed throttle of her husband's fingers around Sands' neck.

Beneath his own rising terror, a strangely detached portion of Sands' brain worried about touching a rat, then decided it didn't matter. *I'm going to die*, he thought. *I should be able to snap this old man it two, but I'm going to die.* Sands lungs were burning now. He hadn't been able to take a deep breath before going under. His left arm, which had been struck by the axe handle, didn't seem to respond to his panic, instead floating at his side. *Is the fat bitch going to eat my hand too?* he wondered.

As he thrashed, gradually less and less, and fought the inevitable, this portion of his brain noted how foul the water tasted. His right hand slapped against the floating light—the flashlight! a potential weapon!—but clumsily knocked it away. *Caroline is going to be pissed that I haven't caught up on my work*, Sands' mind thought. He realized wistfully that he would never see Melanie—or any other woman— naked again. He'd never see Faye. Maybe that was for the best; maybe he deserved that.

An air bubble belched forth from his mouth. He felt his hand tearing at the gash in Mr. Kilby's arm, but to no effect. *Faye*, *Melanie*, Douglas thought. *The lurker will see them again. That's for sure.* That struck a chord. Suddenly he smelled not the putrid water that filled his mouth and nose, but the stench of the dumpster, the stench of decay and death. *That thing will kill them. It'll kill Melanie and Faye*, he thought, his calm detachment crumbling even as another feeble air bubble floated to the surface of the water. *And I led it right to Faye!*

Sands tried to thrash wildly, but the water and Mr. Kilby weighed him down. He couldn't budge the frail old man, the sack of skin and bones. Sands' strength, like the oxygen in his lungs, was spent. He reached out with his good hand, splashing madly. He struck something—a leg, Albert's leg. Sands kept thrashing. His hand latched onto something else, something smooth and hard. The broken axe. The handle. The end with the blade? No, that would have sunk to the bottom. This was floating.

He forced himself to concentrate for a moment: The face would be above the arms. The open mouth. Sands could still hear the yelling. As he looked up through the dark water of River Styx, it was the face of the lurker that he saw staring down at him: red, bulging eyes, razor teeth. Sands swung.

His arm cut through the water with the strength and indignation of God Almighty. He felt the blow strike home. With the second blow, the hands released his neck.

Sands shot to the surface, gasping and choking. He sucked in the unnatural air. Mr. Kilby had fallen back against the wall, stunned. His left eye socket and his forehead above were crushed. Amelia's mouth was open wide, straining in an unholy scream that churned the water. Sands realized that he'd let go of the axe handle. Sputtering, trying desperately to catch his breath, he glanced around frantically for the weapon. He tried to stand but stumbled—over Albert's feet, landing face to wide-eyed face on his friend's inert body. Sands recoiled from the cadaver. He launched himself in the other direction, inadvertently pushing off from the gaping wound in Albert's chest. He stumbled in the water again.

The bobbing flashlight was gyrating wildly, creating almost a strobe pattern as the beam whipped this way and that. The water, stoked by Mrs. Kilby's drawn-out, piercing wail, sloshed higher and higher.

Albert's body was submerged for seconds at a time. Sands struggled to his feet lest he be knocked under by the increasingly violent waves. He lunged for the stairs but slipped on the ice and found himself beneath the water again. The intensity of Amelia's scream was compounded many times by the liquid. Both at once, Sands' eardrums burst.

He fought to his feet and lunged at the stairs again, barely managing to keep from sliding back. He clutched his left arm to his body as he climbed upward. Too frantic to take great notice of the terrible pain in his ears, he nonetheless staggered, unable to keep his balance, and slammed into one wall and then the other. He tripped over the case of Nutri-Drink on the top step and tumbled into the kitchen.

That was where Mr. Kilby caught up with him. The man should have been dead, or at the least comatose; a goodly portion of his head was caved in. But Mrs. Kilby *was* dead, had been for years, and she was screaming her lungs—or her husband's lungs—out. So much for *should*.

Sands felt the fingers around his ankle. He was too battered and exhausted to fight back effectively. The room was spinning, his arm was useless, he still couldn't seem to draw more than half a breath. He tried to claw at the floor with his good hand, to drag himself forward—anything to keep from being pulled back down into that watery hell.

It took him a moment to realize that he wasn't being pulled back down—he was being lifted up, off the floor. Mr. Kilby, one hundred ten scrawny pounds of septuagenarian with half his head bashed in, lifted Sands over his head. And threw him.

For an instant Sands was weightless—like when he'd overzealously flung himself at the lurker.

This instant, as had the previous occasion, ended abruptly. He slammed upside down into the open refrigerator. His head cracked against the grillwork near the floor; his foot smashed the impossibly glaring light bulb.

As if everything that had happened until that point was merely a prelude—all hell broke loose.

Sands crumpled to the floor. He clamped his right hand over that ear, and his left ear he tried to press against his shoulder. Mrs. Kilby's ongoing scream, already agonizing, rose to indescribable heights. Sands felt consciousness fleeing. Blood dribbled between his fingers from his ear.

Frail, bloodied Mr. Kilby writhed and danced like he was being electrocuted. He slapped his arms around with such force that his right forearm, sawed partway through, snapped. It remained attached by a few sinews and was slung fiercely with each motion.

Suddenly a great wind was pulling at Sands, trying to suck him into the gaping refrigerator. He pressed himself flat against the floor. At that moment, he would rather have crawled back into the flooded basement than have looked into the icebox. Mrs. Kilby, her screams now shattering sheets of ice, icicles, and windows throughout the house, seemingly felt the same. As her husband's mouth lolled open, her visage was pulled struggling from him. She was a separate entity for two, maybe three seconds—a bloated, one-handed abomination—and then she was gone. Sucked past Sands. He felt the breeze of her passing. Then all was still and quiet.

Sands glanced hesitantly back over his shoulder. There was only a dark, empty refrigerator.

He jumped at a sound from the direction of Mr. Kilby. Sands turned to face him as best he could—

The old man had fallen to his knees. His right eye rolled up into his head; his left was not visible beneath the wreckage of that half of his head. Mr. Kilby toppled forward onto his face and didn't move.

✥   ✥   ✥   ✥   ✥

By the time Sands staggered from the house and down the path that was the front walk, the spasms were beginning in his back. He was drenched from head to toe, bleeding, holding his arm clamped against his body. As he made it to the street, he couldn't continue. He took a few more faltering steps, but then he dropped to one knee. And then the spasms took over in earnest. He lay convulsing on the road.

He felt more than saw the approaching headlights at some point, he wasn't sure how much later. Did the driver see him? Sands was helpless to wave or crawl out of the road.

The car came to a stop at least a dozen yards away. Footsteps, then: "Douglas? *Douglas!*" Hands shaking him. He wanted to open his eyes, but for some reason he couldn't. He'd already seen too much; he could stand no more. "*Douglas.* Where's Albert?"

Squeezing his eyes more tightly closed couldn't save him from the image of what he'd found in the basement. "Dead." His throat was so raw, his voice weak.

"What? *What?*"

"Dead. He's dead."

"Oh, God," said the woman. "I need to stay with him, Clarence. Can you check inside?"

There was darkness. And then voices again. The last thing Sands remembered was being lifted into a car. The door shut, and then…

PART THREE:
The Lurker

CHAPTER 30

Warmth. Sands, when he was aware of anything, noticed warmth. Often it was his arm through which the meliorative sensation spread. But sometimes his back. Or his face. The passage of time was not so much a factor, not a constant one, at least. One instance of warmth stretched out and blended with another; whatever intervening periods did or did not separate them were indistinguishable.

✣   ✣   ✣   ✣   ✣

Scattered haphazardly amidst the instances of warmth were dreams. Nightmares. Flashes of Albert's mutilated body. Limp in the arms of an old man little more than a corpse himself, so skeletal and frail that he shouldn't have been able to hold the body aloft. The flashes were never the same, though. They changed before Sands could see them properly. He would open his mouth to ask a question—and then the scene was different. Sometimes Albert's body was floating in a black pool, and there was no sign of the old man. Or the old man was floating beside Albert instead of holding him. Sometimes the old man was an old woman, not frail but obese. She was a bloated corpse herself, but like a jackal she tore at the flesh of Albert's body. The lurker was not absent; it cracked Albert's bones and sucked the marrow. Or sometimes, the worst times, a small boy, no more than two years old, sat on the bottom-most step leading from the black pool, staring through reproachful tears at the gently bobbing, wide-eyed Albert.

"It's okay, Douglas," said the soft, mothering voice. "Hush, lie still. You're safe here, Douglas. Hush. It's okay. Everything's okay."

Sands associated the voice with the warmth. They didn't always come together—sometimes there was one without the other—but he formed a definite association. The voice often chased the nightmares away, while the warmth soothed his physical pain. That was something else he became aware of: this thing that was his body, and how much it *hurt*. Eventually, as time also reacquired meaning, the worst of the pain as well as the worst of the nightmares receded into the past. The warmth, too, became a thing of the past; the relatively minor discomfort that remained didn't call for it. The voice was constant, however. "Let him sleep. He needs rest more than anything."

There were other voices, Sands came to realize. Sometimes several at once. They would grow louder, more animated, then the softer voice would shush them or shoo them away. Most often they were indistinct, or Sands couldn't remember sentences if he did hear them. At first he noticed the intonations and cadences. Only slowly did recognition of words penetrate his limited world. "So this is the guy," was the first sentence he comprehended, spoken by one of the harsher voices. The words were upsetting; they jarred memories of a larger universe—beyond sound and warmth—memories of people and buildings and cars and changing seasons. There was cruelty in this particular voice, cold and hard; it was a voice Sands wouldn't have wanted to have sneak up behind him in a deserted parking garage. "I'd rather have Tinsley back," the hard-edged voice said.

Sight was one of the last pieces of the puzzle that was Douglas Sands. The first time he remembered opening his eyes, he was unable to focus. Shapes blurred one into the other, contracted and then expanded. For a moment, there was the figure of a man. Sitting in a chair. A black man. There was a face, briefly. He smiled. Then seemed suddenly alarmed. Rushed from the room. There *was* a room, Sands noted. He couldn't make out distinctive features; he didn't think he recognized the room. Exhaustion and darkness quickly called him back.

Sands opened his eyes other times and saw different people in the room. His glimpses were brief; he couldn't keep the various individuals straight: the black man, a white man, an older white man, a woman. Sometimes the person would try to say something to Sands—*would* say something; he *tried* to understand, but the words were almost always a jumble.

One day—it *was* day; the curtains were pulled back, and natural light poured into the room— Sands opened his eyes and was able to keep them open. In fits and starts, his vision settled, and he found himself staring at a longhaired young man sitting in the chair. The man's knee, sticking through a large tear in his jeans, was practically in Sands' face. The young man stared, almost disinterestedly, back at Sands.

"You back to stay this time?" the youth asked. He was the source of the parking-garage voice. Sands disliked him and his sneering bravado immediately, but couldn't gather his faculties quickly enough to respond.

The young man, seeming greatly inconvenienced, got up from the chair, opened the door to the room, and yelled: "Yo, Julia! He's awake!" He stood there with his arms crossed, staring as if Sands were an animal on exhibit in a zoo. The man scowled, then snarled and made a quick move at Sands. Sands drew back, and the man laughed. "You talk, or what?" he asked. "You know what day it is?"

"Of course he doesn't know what day it is," said Julia, stepping into the room. She glanced at her watch. "He's been in and out of consciousness—mostly out—for…ninety hours. Sands recognized Julia. She was at least a foot shorter than the young man, but she brushed past him with an air of authority. "Try to stay out of the way, Jason." She sat and pulled the chair closer to Sands' bed. Before Sands knew what was happening, she was holding his left eye open and shining a small, bright light directly in it. Then the right eye.

"I thought he was a re-tard," Jason said, watching over Julia's shoulder.

Julia lowered the penlight and sighed. She looked back at Jason. "Why don't you…I don't know. Just…go. Go away. Anywhere. Just away." Jason stiffened, and curled his lip behind Julia, but he did as she said and left the room. She waited until his footsteps retreated down the hallway, then turned her full attention back to Sands. "Do you know what state you're in?" she asked.

"Michigan."

"Good. And your name?"

"Douglas Sands."

She seemed impressed. "You're doing better than you have a right to," she said drolly. "I wasn't sure if you were going to be coming back from in there," she tapped him twice on the head, "or not."

Sands remembered her face. And her voice. Though it wasn't as soft, as gentle, as it had been before. He remembered the warmth—and then realized that he could move his arm freely, his left arm, which should have been broken. Broken by the handle of the axe that had… "He's dead?" Sands asked her. "Albert?"

Julia pursed her lips slightly; her brow furrowed. "Yes." That was all she said. She started prodding Sands' forearm, from elbow to wrist, and questioned him in a very neutral tone. "Does that hurt? How about that?" She poked at a spot above his right eye. "That cut you had over your eye was older, wasn't it? You didn't get it the night…" She paused only briefly, not meeting Sands' eyes, not mentioning Albert. "The night you broke your arm."

Sands tried to remember. It all seemed so long ago. "The night before."

"You should've gotten stitches. You're going to have a scar. Don't blame me. What'd you do—throw yourself out another window?"

Sands didn't appreciate her tone of voice, or her unwillingness to say Albert's name, to acknowledge him. Sands remembered the first time he'd met Julia, how she'd looked at him like he was a hurt child. He remembered what he'd said to her then; it still applied: "I don't need your pity," he told her again.

"You're right about that," she said. "You've got more than enough of your own." She pushed the chair back and stood. "Are you hungry? You should be hungry. I'll have somebody bring you some soup. Jason likes playing Florence Nightingale." She moved to the door. "Don't get used to being waited on. If you're well enough to get to the bathroom, you're well enough to get to the kitchen." She stepped out and closed the door.

Sands stared at the door. After the brief whirlwind of people, he felt over-stimulated and exhausted at the same time, as if he'd engaged in hours, instead of minutes, of conversation. He was in a single bed in a small nondescript room: white ceiling and walls with a wallpaper chair rail; bookshelf, bedside table; a second door, also closed, to either a closet or bathroom, he guessed.

This isn't Tinsley's house, Sands knew. That house must be empty, now that Albert… "Jesus," Sands whispered, and lay back onto the bed. Albert was dead. And Julia wouldn't even say his name.

CHAPTER 31

Sands awoke early, before the darkness beyond the beige curtains softened to grey. The second door in the room was to a small bathroom; he'd made it that far during the night, and then back into bed. The house—he assumed it was a house; it *felt* like a house—was very quiet now. During the night, Sands had woken several times and noticed sounds coming from beyond the first door: muffled voices, the droning of a television, footsteps, a creaking floorboard.

In the predawn hush, Sands felt restless. He hadn't slept soundly, not because of the various noises, which weren't particularly intrusive; he'd slept as might a feverish person, turning and rolling, waking up covered in sweat or trembling with damp chill. And the nightmares had not completely relinquished their hold on him.

He noticed at once the slender crack of light that bisected him when the door to the hall opened just an inch. "I'm awake," he said. The door, seemingly indecisive, held its place for a few seconds, then opened farther. A tall man, not Jason, older, closer to Sands' age, stepped into the room. He stood by the door and appeared unsure whether to close it or not. "You can leave it open," Sands said. "I think I've had as much as I can take of being cooped up."

"That's understandable," the man said. His voice was deep, and rough with the early hour. He left the door open as he came in, but didn't turn on the light. "May I?" he gestured toward the chair.

"Sure. Please. It's your house," Sands said.

"Not my house, actually. I'm John. John Hetger." He sat, then reached out to shake hands, which seemed strangely formal to Sands, considering the circumstances. Hetger had a square face, with a pronounced cleft in his chin. His short, parted hair and his eyes were dark brown. He seemed solid—in his grip, his manner, his bearing. "Even if it were my house," he said, as they shook, "you deserve at least a little privacy after what you've been through."

What he'd been through. That was what, at least in part, had been on Sands' mind much of the restless night. "You people are Albert's friends, right? The ones who've been looking out for Faye and Melanie." John nodded. "Are they all right?" Sands asked. "I mean…nothing's happened to them?"

"They're fine."

Sands breathed a sigh of relief. He didn't think he could take it if there had been trouble, not after Albert….

"We've been watching both places, and we've seen the creature you told Albert about," John said calmly, as if he were relating a story out of the newspaper. Never mind that this was a *vampire* he was talking about. "At the apartment complex. Not at your home."

"It's not *my* home anymore," Sands said, more sharply than he'd meant to. "But you've seen it," he rushed on. "The thing, at Melanie's."

John nodded. "It's shown up a few times. Seemed like it just wanted to watch her."

"That's all it wanted to do so *far*." Sands said, suddenly agitated. He remembered—couldn't *forget*—the words from the clock: **IT WAITS. TO KILL**.

John nodded. "You're right. So far. It watched her apartment from a balcony of the adjacent building—"

"The condemned one."

"Yes. And once it climbed onto the balcony of her apartment—"

"*Her* balcony? Good God! You attacked it. You drove it away, right?" Sands couldn't keep the desperation from his voice. John had already said Melanie was okay, but the thought of the lurker watching her, climbing onto her balcony, made him want to rush from the bed and chase down the creature. "Did you kill it?"

"We watched it," John said.

"You *watched* it? And...?"

"We watched it. It watched her. It went away."

"It went away? And you were the people Albert trusted?" Sands couldn't believe his ears. "It went away *this* time. You can be damn sure it'll be back! It's going to kill her if we don't do something!"

"It might try," John said, remaining infuriatingly even-tempered.

"*Might* try? It *will* try. It wants to drink her damn blood! That's what it does!" Sands was tripping over his own words. He was so *sure*, but he couldn't explain. What was he supposed to say? That the *clock* told him?

John started to rise from his seat. "I didn't mean to upset you, Douglas. We should talk later—"

"*No.*" Sands grabbed John's arm. "I mean...you don't have to go.... I'm sorry." Hetger sat back down. "It's just that...I don't know. I..."

"You don't have to explain. It's not easy for anyone." There was a long pause. "Albert thought very highly of you," John offered.

"I doubt Julia would say the same thing."

Hetger restrained a chuckle. "I wouldn't take it personally.... She just doesn't like you."

Sands stared at John and blinked. "She said that?"

He shrugged. "Not in those words." He thought for a second. "Maybe it *was* those words. But I wouldn't worry about—"

"I don't like her either," Sands said, folding his arms. "Not that I'm ungrateful. I mean, this is the second time she's...well, you know."

"Yes. Julia is a tremendous asset for us. It's not necessary for us all to be best friends, but I find a certain amount of transparency in interpersonal relations is helpful," Hetger said. "We have enough challenges without getting under each other's skins."

"Really."

"Yes. That's the kind of thing that can come back and haunt us—if you'll pardon the expression. Albert said that you were very intelligent, a good judge of character, that you could get what you wanted from people."

"He said that? It doesn't necessarily sound like a compliment."

"He meant it as an assessment, not a judgment."

"There's a difference?" Sands asked mockingly, but John took him seriously.

"I think so," he said. "Albert was practiced at making observations about people without attaching value judgments. That can be important."

"So he would say, for example, that Julia is prickly, but he wouldn't mean it as an insult?" Sands suggested.

"I think he said that Julia was intolerant," John said, still straight-faced.

"Intolerant of what? Other people?"

"Of indulgence."

"What the hell does that have to do with me?" Sands asked.

"She thinks that you indulge your self-pity. I think 'wallow in' was the phrase she used," Hetger said. "That's more judgmental language than Albert ever would have used."

Sands' jaw dropped. "So...Albert thought I was..."

"And most people would agree," John continued, "that an extramarital affair is a considerable indulgence. Julia might even say 'unconscionable,' 'unprincipled,' 'slimy'—"

"I think that's enough," Sands said, raising a hand, but then, against his better judgment, asked: "What would *you* say?"

"I would say that it's an indulgence. I think that's fair."

"Fair. And not judgmental?"

"There's a lot of history to any relationship, and I don't think anyone, even the people involved, understand it all."

"Can we talk about something else?" Sands said. "I mean, good God, who the hell are you people to—? Never mind. I know. I asked. Look..." He took a deep breath, sighed, rubbed his face in an effort to wake up more completely; he didn't feel that he'd totally shaken the night's dreams. "I feel terrible about Albert," Sands said at last. He felt this was the time to say it. Hetger didn't seem to have Julia's hang-ups about mentioning Albert.

"Can you tell me what happened?" John asked. "You were there."

"Sort of," Sands said. He paused, then: "I think it was my fault. At least partially." John listened attentively, not interrupting. The curtains were still drawn, but the morning was beginning to creep along outside. "I assume he told you about Davis and Amelia Kilby? What am I saying? Of course he told you—if he told you as much as he seems to have about my situation. Anyway, I think I royally pissed off Amelia, and she...she killed him."

"Why do you think you made her angry?" John asked.

"Believe me, it wasn't that hard to tell."

"But *how* do you think you made her angry? What did you do?"

"Well, the Kilbys," Sands said, "they weren't the world's greatest conversationalists, and..." He stopped suddenly, acutely aware of how completely odd it was to be talking about this, about a ghost, with someone he barely knew. It would be strange to talk about with *anyone*. He still wasn't comfortable merely thinking about the abrupt U-turn his worldview had taken. It was bizarre to talk about. And a miraculous *relief*. He'd confided in Melanie about the voice on the wind when he might otherwise have imploded; he'd told Albert about the lurker. Was it similar desperation that led him to talk to this perfect stranger?

"Douglas?" John asked. "Are you all right?"

"Sorry. Yes. Um...well, it seems Mrs. Kilby's claim to fame was that she wasn't a drunk. I found documents that proved otherwise, and I told her."

"I see. And that didn't go over well."

"Uh...no." Sands took a deep breath. "I also found out that her death wasn't her fault, not altogether, at least. I don't know. I just thought that if that was what she was so angry about, and it got straightened out..."

"Sometimes they're just angry," John said. "Period."

Sands nodded. "I think she'd already killed Albert...." He thought back, trying to connect the dots of everything that had happened those two evenings. "Yeah, she had to have, by the time I told her that it wasn't her fault. I think I'd made her so mad the night before that..." he tossed up his hands, regret and guilt washing over him, making the words difficult to find, "she just snapped. Before that, Albert had mostly been trying to feed Mr. Kilby, to keep him alive despite what Mrs. Kilby was doing to him."

"That sounds like Albert," John said with a wistful smile.

"She hadn't seemed exactly happy *before* that," Sands struggled to continue, "but...but I don't think she would have attacked him. Killed him. Not if I hadn't..."

"Douglas," John said, quietly, firmly, "First of all, as mild and gentle a person as Albert was, he took chances. He took a chance going to that house by himself, many times. He took a chance taking you with him, especially when you didn't know what was going on—not that any of us know precisely what's going on. Second, these creatures seem like people, like human beings, or maybe they used to be. But they're not anymore. They're alien to us. They don't react to situations the way we might think they should. It's quite often impossible to figure out what motivates them. And third, even if something you said or did inadvertently set that thing off—and we can't be sure that it did, or that it wouldn't have happened the next night without you ever having been involved at all—it doesn't do any good to blame yourself. Albert knew enough...he went into that house with his eyes open."

If that was intended to make Sands feel better, it didn't particularly. "Are you saying that Albert's death was *his own* fault?"

This time it was Hetger who sighed. "I'm saying that 'fault' is not a useful criteria in this case. Forget 'fault.' Examine what happened. Learn from it. That's the best way we can give meaning to Albert's death, to his *life*."

"You can be non-judgmental and give meaning if you want," Sands said skeptically, his heart skipping ahead, driving him forward. "Me, I'm trying to own up to the fact that *I got him killed*. Not fired, not hurt. *Killed*." They stared at one another for ten, fifteen, twenty seconds: Sands wide-eyed, trying not to grow any more emotional; Hetger calm but slightly saddened. "At the very least," Sands said finally, "you have to admit that it's not a good idea to piss off these things."

John actually smiled a little at that. "Generally. Although anger can work to our advantage. But generally, yes, I would agree." Hetger slid back the chair and stood. "You'll probably have more questions. I know I do. At some point, when you're up to it, I'd like you to try to write down everything you remember about your friend the vampire, and about the Kilbys. The more we know, the better chance we have. For now, though, there's breakfast if you want any. Julia seemed to think you'd be ready for solid food today."

"You know what Julia would say about whose fault it was, don't you?" Sands asked.

John's eyes narrowed, but he never lost the sincere, slightly amused smile. "I could make an educated guess," he said. "But I don't see any point. Breakfast if you want it." He pulled the door closed behind him. Beyond the beige curtains, morning was in partial, overcast bloom.

CHAPTER 32

In the afternoon, Hetger gave Sands a tour. It didn't take long. The three-bedroom ranch house was nothing extraordinary, and glancing out a few windows, Sands could see that the neighborhood in which it was situated was nothing extraordinary either. The inhabitants of this particular house, however, were not a typical family; they weren't a family at all, not in the strictest sense.

"Of course we're breaking local zoning ordinances about no more than three unrelated persons occupying a single dwelling," John said, and shrugged. It was a characteristic, noncommittal gesture, and every time Sands saw it, it reminded him of what Hetger had suggested about Albert's common practice: observation without attaching value judgments. John was merely citing the zoning restriction, not denouncing it, not expressing regret at violating it; the zoning laws existed, as did the necessity of ignoring them.

As John had mentioned earlier, the owner of the house was Nathan James. Nathan, a slender, very dark-skinned black man, probably under thirty, Douglas guessed, was at his computer when Sands met him. One of the bedrooms, the largest, was a makeshift computer lab and was crammed with tables and shelves full of electronic and computer equipment. An extensive series of wires and cables ran in every direction, the nervous system of an advanced technological being.

"Douglas, good to meet you," Nathan said, extending a hand. He had an infectious smile, and penetrating, intelligent eyes.

"We unhook Nathan from the computer every few days," said Jason, who was sitting by a terminal at a different table. "He's got a jack stuffed up his—"

"You've already met Jason, I believe," Hetger broke in.

"I handle most of the technology side of the business," Nathan said, "but if you have a question about first-person shooters or internet porn, then Jason is your man."

"Up yours, man."

"Or," Nathan added, to Sands, "he also sells witty retorts, three for a dollar. But you have to give him a couple months' advance warning."

"Screw you, man."

"That's sixty-six cents," Nathan said. He took a dollar bill from his pocket, wadded it into a ball, and threw it at Jason. "Keep the change, man."

One of the other bedrooms, Hetger told Sands as he continued showing him around, was Nathan's room. The smallest bedroom was usually reserved for Julia, but she'd given it up to Sands for the time being. The dining room was jammed with several single beds and a couch, and served as a sort of barracks for whoever else needed a place to sleep, usually Hetger and Jason. Albert had crashed there on occasion; Julia was asleep when Sands and John poked their heads in.

"Helping people like she does, helping them heal, wears her out," John said. "I think it might be the toughest job any of us has."

Sands waited until they were out of earshot of the dining room before asking about Julia. "How does she…? I mean, she's done that to me twice, now," he said, fumbling for the right question. "What exactly…?"

"Different ones of us have different gifts, Douglas," John said. "You'll get as many different explanations as people you ask."

"You say 'different ones of us.' Hunters, you mean."

"Right. That's the most common name we give ourselves. It seems to fit."

"Albert said that some people take that name too seriously," Sands said.

John shrugged. "You'll get a lot of opinions on that too."

"What do you think?"

"I think there are a lot of different situations."

That didn't satisfy Sands, but he let it go. Perhaps the answer was more than equivocation; Hetger had seemed willing enough to speak frankly on other subjects. "You said something about different gifts…." Sands prompted him.

"The more hunters we come into contact with," John said, "we begin to see patterns, similarities. Julia is able to aid a person's natural healing process to a certain extent, as you know. That seems to be a fairly limited gift, although it does show up occasionally. All of us seem to be able to *see* things— things that most people don't see."

"Things that *normal* people don't see," Sands said. John smiled, but said nothing. "I know. I know," Sands said. "That's a value judgment."

Hetger laughed. "I think it's safe to say that we don't fit the norm." He grew more serious. "But neither do the things we see. Every hunter I've spoken to or heard from, even Albert, said that these things we see are *wrong* somehow."

The two men were walking through the kitchen and toward the small utility room beyond when Hetger said that. Sands suddenly felt that his legs couldn't support him; his knees buckled, and he steadied himself with a hand on the back of one of the kitchen chairs.

John noticed his distress and came back to him. "Are you all right? This may be too much too soon."

"I'll be okay. Give me a second." Sands pulled the chair back from the table and sat. He *was* okay, physically, despite the passing weakness in his legs. Sands recognized the sensation that struck him lame, but the overwhelming intensity of this new wave of relief caught him off guard. He'd been moved close to tears the morning in Albert's kitchen, with the smell of coffee and bacon, when Albert had let him know that he wasn't alone. This very morning, Sands had felt the relief of being able to talk to someone, a stranger, for God's sake, about what he'd been through. And now, to hear the words, to hear Hetger confirm that he and others had experienced an insanity so very much like Sands' own... He was overcome. To the point that he literally had to sit down or fall.

Sands, aside from his occasionally volatile temper, was not normally an emotional person. He was not the tearful type, and he was not comfortable in the least retreating before upwelling feelings. So the wave of relief that battered him was also tinged with self-consciousness. He didn't meet Hetger's eyes as John stood by him, wondering if he was all right. *It must have something to do with what Julia has done to me,* Sands decided of these sudden bursts of delicate emotions. *She's got my physiology all out of whack—my hormones or electrolytes or something.*

"Guess I'm still more tired than I thought," he said, climbing unsteadily to his feet, unable—or unwilling—to bear John's scrutiny any longer. "What's next?"

"Nothing too exciting," Hetger said, still watching him closely. He led Sands back to the utility room. "Washer and dryer here, if you need to do laundry at some point." He opened one of the other two doors leading from that room and showed Sands the garage. "This car and the van are Nathan's, but we all use them as necessary. Some of us have other cars parked elsewhere. We don't want a parade of vehicles coming in and out, especially all through the night, which is when we're out a lot, so we ferry each other as possible. You'll notice both the car and van have tinted windows; we try to maintain the impression that it's Nathan coming and going as much as possible. The pretense wouldn't hold up under close scrutiny, but we hope if we don't draw attention, no one will have reason to watch closely. We don't need complaints to the city aldermen about the number of people staying here."

"Zoning ordinances," Sands said, a bit facetiously.

"Right." John closed that door and led Sands out the other, into the backyard.

Even with overcast skies, glare from the piled snow was nearly blinding. Sands squinted and shielded his eyes. A tall privacy fence enclosed the entire back yard. A wide, shoveled path led to an aluminum storage shed.

"This is really the last thing to see," John said.

"Let me guess: This is your ice-fishing shack, and we need it because the Loch Ness Monster has migrated to Lake Michigan."

"Actually," Hetger said, "the one in Lake Michigan is a descendent of Nessie." Sands stopped in his tracks. John turned back to face him, straight-faced. "Just kidding. *Actually*," he turned back toward the shed and opened the door, "this is our bomb shelter."

"Good God."

The shed, incredibly dark in contrast to outside, was practically empty, aside from a few shelves lining the walls—and a cylindrical steel hatch that rose nearly a foot from the earthen floor. The hatch was equipped with a wheel lock, like a bank vault or an old submarine. "Original technology circa 1955," John said, as he turned the wheel, "with a few upgrades of our own, thanks to Nathan and others. Ventilation and electricity are currently hooked to the local power grid. There's a generator, or course, should we need to go self-sufficient."

Sands couldn't help laughing. He'd thought that *he* was crazy carrying around a baseball bat and freezing half to death in his car. "If I meet a ghost with nuclear capability, I think I'll just shoot myself."

"If you do meet one," John said, "you probably won't *need* to shoot yourself." Sands couldn't tell if he was joking.

The hatch was well-oiled—no strained creak as Hetger lifted it open. A rhythmic, metal clanking reached them from within and grew louder as they climbed down the ladder. The first room was full of crates and packed shelves. Sands saw bottled water that seemed to be relatively fresh—as opposed to some of the freeze-dried and canned food, which was coated with dust. In the second, smaller room—which, along with the first and a minuscule lavatory, was the extent of the shelter—was a cot, a footlocker, and a tightly muscled black man on a weight bench. The bar he was pressing was loaded. Each time he raised or lowered his arms, the weights rattled.

"Clarence," John said, "this is Douglas Sands."

Clarence, Sands thought. The name was familiar from somewhere, but he couldn't place it at first.

Clarence was lighter-skinned than Nathan. The stuffy room smelled strongly of his sweat, which darkened his shirt and glistened on his remarkably defined muscles. He ignored John and Douglas, finished five more reps, and only then let the bar slam into its holder. He sat up slowly, taking deep breaths that made his chest swell beneath his wet shirt. "Sands, huh?"

"*Clarence*," Sands said, taking a step back as he suddenly remembered where he'd heard the name. Albert had mentioned him, when he'd called and told his friends, these friends, about needing to keep Faye and Melanie safe: *Maybe it'll keep Clarence busy.* But Sands, now that he saw Clarence, recognized the man's face too. "You killed Gerry Stafford," he said, his words part surprise, part accusation.

Clarence's expression never changed; he didn't seem bothered by the charge Sands leveled at him. "He was already dead," Clarence said. "I just sent him back to hell. Seems folks don't come back from heaven. They must like it there."

"Gerry never hurt *anyone*," Sands said.

"Maybe he hadn't yet," Clarence shrugged, but unlike Hetger, he managed to make the gesture dismissive, scornful. "Not that we know about. Tinsley thought those old folks wouldn't ever hurt nobody either. But you know more about that than I do."

Sands took a step toward Clarence but stopped when he felt John's hand on his shoulder. Clarence, sitting unconcerned on the edge of the weight bench, didn't seem to feel particularly threatened. "That's a nice little gut you got there, Sands. How long you been sitting behind a desk?"

Sands bristled and instinctively sucked in his stomach—as much as he could.

"You're gonna want to get in shape if you plan to stick around long—live long, that is," Clarence said.

"I'm not in such bad shape," Sands said, with more ire than conviction.

"What? You play golf once a week?"

Sands hesitated. He tried not to look at the beaded sweat on Clarence's shoulders and biceps. "Tennis," Sands said.

Clarence's eyes grew wide. "Ohhh...*tennis*. If I'd only known..."

"Well," said Hetger, squeezing Sands' shoulder, "now that you've met everybody..."

Clarence had already lost interest in them. He was pulling clean clothes from a duffel bag under the cot. Hetger and Sands left him. They climbed back up the ladder into the dark shed, then confronted again the relatively bright outdoors. A scattering of lazy snowflakes was drifting to the ground from the grey heavens.

"*Seems folks don't come back from heaven,*" Sands muttered mockingly. "And that guy does what you tell him?"

"Hm?" John cocked his head. "Oh. No, not really. As communal as we are about a lot of things, we're fairly democratic—small 'd'—in many ways too."

"You mean," Sands was trying to sort out what he'd seen so far, "everybody just does what they want?"

"Within reason. You didn't come here to have people tell you what to do, did you?" John asked.

"I was *brought* here," Sands said. "*Unconscious.*"

"That's true, but you wouldn't stay if you were expected to take orders, would you?"

Sands didn't know what to say. Hetger evidently expected that Sands *was* going to stay, and Sands didn't know if he was ready to walk away from a group of people who would understand what he'd been going through. But he wasn't sure he wanted to stay, either. "I won't stay if *that guy*," he pointed back toward the shed, "is running around killing people indiscriminately—"

"Clarence doesn't do anything indiscriminately," John said. "None of us do. We discuss what should be done. We argue. Sometimes we come to an agreement; sometimes we don't."

"Killing Gerry was *murder*," Douglas insisted.

"Murder? If he was already dead?"

"He didn't *look* dead. Not to me, not then. Not to *most* people. Not to a court of law."

"Courts of law aren't equipped to deal with the things we see, Douglas," Hetger said very solemnly. "Why didn't you call the police when Melanie was in danger?"

Sands glared at Hetger, but didn't answer, then stalked off toward the house. The snow was beginning to fall more determinedly.

❖   ❖   ❖   ❖   ❖

John knocked on the door to the small bedroom a couple of hours and two inches of snow later. The darkness was again asserting itself beyond the beige curtains. "If it makes any difference," he said after he'd come in, "I think Albert was right about Stafford. I don't think he posed an immediate threat to anyone. But we've seen that change so quickly. *You've* seen it change."

Sands wasn't buying it. "And since he *might eventually, possibly* have been a danger, he deserved to have his skull split open."

"The vampire," John said, "that you think is stalking your wife—"

"It threatened her!" Sands snapped. "And Melanie!"

"Okay. A verbal threat. Have you ever seen it drinking blood? Anyone's?"

"Completely different."

"Did you chase it with a broken bottle, with a baseball bat, because you wanted to discuss the matter?" John asked. "Did you throw yourself out a window at it because you wanted to *talk*?"

"I *know* it wants to kill her!"

"Do you know what Clarence might have known about Stafford? There's very little that's black and white in our world, Douglas." Sands lay back down on his bed; he locked his fingers under his head and stared at the ceiling. "I'm not saying that what you did was wrong," John continued after a moment. "And although I don't agree with what Clarence did, I can't be positive that I'm right and he's wrong, not when each of us is following the dictates of his own conscience, of personal revelation." Another strained silence fell between them.

"What's important," Hetger said eventually, "is that we move forward, that we help each other learn and survive. You don't have to decide right now how long you're going to stick around, but I do need to know if you're willing to help us with this vampire, because standing guard over your wife and that other woman has been keeping all of us busy for a couple of weeks now."

"Of course I'll help," Sands grumbled, still not looking at John.

"Good. Be ready to go in ten minutes."

CHAPTER 33

Sands climbed into the van with the others: he and Julia in the back, Clarence driving, and Jason in the passenger's seat. There were two seats in the back, and an old, dirty carpet on the floor, but most of the space was taken up by various storage compartments, several of them locked.

Clarence turned around and called to Sands: "Yo, Pete Sampras, shut the door."

"Isn't John coming?" Sands asked Julia.

She shook her head. "He's staying here with Nathan tonight."

Sands pulled closed the heavy, sliding door, and within seconds the van pulled out of the garage and into the burgeoning night. Julia had brought a half-full duffel bag, similar to the sort Clarence had under the cot in the bomb shelter, probably military surplus. All that Sands had with him was his Louisville Slugger; Julia had handed it to him before they'd left. "I got this out of your car," she'd said.

"Is my car still at Albert's?" he'd wanted to know.

"It's safe," Julia had said. "Parked on the south side."

The Southside street where his car was parked was, in fact, where Clarence dropped them off fifteen minutes after they'd left the house. Sands' car was parked behind Julia's. Otherwise, the street was deserted. Southside was the old business district, a collection of large, square buildings, former banks and department stores that were now empty shells or used only for storage. The police station was also in Southside, so the area had not suffered extensively at the hands of vandals and was a reasonable place to leave an unattended car for brief periods of time—brief enough that the vehicle wasn't buried by the ever-vigilant snowplows.

In this portion of the city, the north wind reveled in the long, straight avenues, achieving unbroken momentum and scouring the narrow canyons of glass and steel. Sands hunched his shoulders against the probing, penetrating cold and tried to keep him mind on the task at hand. The wind here was merely an inconvenience, a discomfort, not something to fear. There was no voice, only a mindless, uneven whistling.

After Clarence and Jason drove away, Sands waited impatiently while Julia opened the trunk of her car and began methodically unpacking the contents of her duffel. The proximity of the police station rapidly became a matter of concern rather than comfort when Julia opened a large plastic case revealing a crossbow.

Sands glanced around nervously. "Good God!" Julia ignored his alarm as she gave the weapon a quick visual inspection. The next, smaller plastic case contained at least a dozen quarrels. "You pick up all that at Wal-Mart?" Sands asked sarcastically.

"No. We only get the guns at Wal-Mart," she said. "God bless America. And for this," she said, re-closing the two cases, "God bless the internet." She took a few other items from the duffel bag, stuffed them into a smaller knapsack, and left the duffel and plastic cases in the trunk, which she closed. "Let's go. We'll move your car in the morning."

Sands watched as the diminutive woman opened the driver's door; he crossed his arms and jutted out his jaw defiantly. "I don't mind acknowledging that you know more about what's going on than I do," he said. "But part of the reason for that is that nobody's told me what we're doing."

"There hasn't been a lot of time," Julia said. "John didn't know if you were going to come with us. You spent so long moping in your room." Sands opened his mouth, but she wasn't done: "If you want to get in the car, we'll have plenty of time to talk about whatever you want to. If not, fine. Either way, I'm going."

Sands opened his mouth again, but Julia was already in the car and starting the engine. Grudgingly, he climbed into the passenger's seat. They pulled away from the snow pile, somewhere beneath which lay a curb.

"Why the *hell* do you have a crossbow?" Sands asked, almost as soon as they were underway.

"How do *you* kill a vampire?" Julia asked. "Hammer a stake through its heart? From what I hear, they don't often hold still for that."

"Then we're going after it?"

"No," Julia said, not taking her eyes off the road. "Just a stakeout, but self-defense is never a bad idea."

"Then why'd you leave it in the trunk?"

"The back seat folds forward. There's an opening to the trunk. But if I don't need it, a crossbow on the dash tends to make people suspicious."

"Oh." That made sense to Sands. He tested the comforting weight of his Louisville Slugger. At least he had two good hands now. "Should I have a gun or something?" he asked.

"Do you have any training with firearms? Have you ever practiced?"

"Uh…no."

"Then I don't want to be around if you have a gun." They drove in silence for several minutes, heading west. Southside's empty, hulking buildings gave way to smaller shops, then to residential neighborhoods. "Clarence would be happy to teach you," Julia said eventually.

"What?"

"To shoot. About guns. He'd be happy to teach you if you want."

"I wouldn't think he'd be happy to do anything," Sands said. Julia smiled. It was the first time he could remember seeing that. "Did Albert tell you about Gerry Stafford?" he asked her.

Julia's smile faded. "Disagreeing with Clarence isn't reason not to take advantage of his expertise."

"So he knows about guns."

"He knows about lots of things."

Sands didn't appreciate the pedantic tone of voice that Julia adopted in talking with him, talking *at* him. She had to be ten years younger than he was. John Hetger, at least, had been fairly forthright in their conversations that day, but Sands still had so many questions, with more popping into his mind every minute. How was he supposed to understand anything if he didn't ask? And yet Julia treated him like an imposition. *I don't have to put up with that*, he thought, willing to return hostility for hostility. He couldn't, however, completely discount (or explain) the way Julia had helped him overcome his various injuries. Her strange abilities were a definite asset, as was what she knew about this disturbing world, knowledge that she dangled over him like a carrot, while at the same time beating him with a stick for some unspoken transgression. Infuriatingly enough, she was valuable to him, even if she wasn't particularly attractive. Sands was glad of that; the situation would have been that much more intolerable had lust been added to the already contentious dynamic of their interactions. He would have resented her that much more.

As it was, he thought of her as almost toadlike, with her slightly bulbous, too-bright eyes. Sitting on a cushion to see over the steering wheel, she possessed neither Faye's grace nor Melanie's raw vibrancy, yet Julia seemed endowed with a supreme confidence, a sense of purpose and direction, that both of the other women lacked.

Before long, as they drove, the streets and landmarks grew increasingly familiar to Sands. He knew which way Julia was about to turn and what was around each next corner. "We're going to my house," he said.

"You should be glad," Julia said. "This is the cushy job."

"Why's that?"

"We can sit in the car, walk around the block every hour or two, and keep a good eye on your place. Clarence and Jason are watching the girl's place. There's no good spot to watch from in the parking lot there. They have to sit out in the woods, in the cold, behind the buildings."

"You all have been doing this since that first night that Albert called?" Sands asked.

Julia nodded. "Two people at the girl's. Usually two at your house; sometimes John would do it alone. We've only ever seen the...your vampire at the apartment."

"So you're breaking me in easy."

"Pretty much."

She parked across the street and diagonal from Sands' house, roughly at the property line of two neighbors. "So each can think we're visiting the other, and nobody gets worried about a strange car out front," she explained.

Staring at his own home as might a stranger, as might a burglar casing the property, made Sands uneasy. He hadn't been back or spoken with Faye since New Year's Eve. Though it wasn't her fault, he found himself resenting the fact that Faye was sitting comfortably inside—reading, watching television, whatever—while he was in a cold car with a contrary, unattractive woman who despised him. His wife, like Melanie, had no idea, *really* no idea, what he'd gone through trying to safeguard her. Instead of being grateful, she'd kicked him out of the house. He could be dead for all she cared.

"Here," Julia said, interrupting his morose reverie. She shoved a bundle from her knapsack into his hands. "Try this on."

After a moment of fumbling, he saw that it was a thin, plastic headset with a small microphone and a receiver that hooked over his ear. Julia slipped on an identical set. Sands struggled with his briefly but got it on. "I feel like the host for a workout video."

"*I prefer to think of myself as an air traffic controller,*" Nathan's voice buzzed in his right ear. Sands jumped.

"They're voice activated," Julia said. He heard her in stereo, normally in his left ear, and through the earphone in his right. She reached over and adjusted the fit of his headset. "Lower the headphone to this position," she demonstrated, "and it's off." He no longer heard her through the earphone. "You don't transmit or receive. Back up," she returned the microphone to its earlier position, and Sands picked up her voice electronically again, "and you're on. Home One and Home Two in position."

"*Read you loud and clear, Home One*," Nathan said.

"*This is Rental One*," Clarence said. "*You read me, Sugar Daddy?*"

"*Loud and clear, Rental One. How 'bout Rental Two?*"

"*I'm here, freezin' my butt off*," Jason said.

"*Loud and clear, Rental Two. Better you than me.*"

"Where's Hetger?" Sands asked Julia.

"*He's here with me*," Nathan answered, "*and that would be Base One to you, Home Two.*"

Julia clicked her microphone to the off position. "If you're talking to me, then turn off first, or it gets too confusing. And no names on the wire—"

"But there's no wire."

"*Less chatter, Home Two*," Nathan said.

Julia reached over and clicked off Sands' set again. "You're very observant. There's no wire. Figure of speech. But like I said, no names. We might bleed onto cell phones. Probably nobody could follow anything unless they were really trying hard, but better safe than sorry."

Sands nodded.

"You can talk now. It's off."

"Right."

"Look," Julia said slightly exasperated. "You can leave it turned on and put it on the seat next to you. You'll hear if anybody calls. I'm going to make a quick circuit around the house. Remember, the windows are tinted pretty dark. If you don't move around a lot, nobody will notice you're in the car. I'll be right back." Sands, clicking his headset back on, heard her after she'd gotten out of the car. *"Home One, here. I'm making a quick loop."*

"Gotcha, Home One," Nathan said.

Sands sat alone in the car and looked at his own neighborhood for the first time as an outsider. He was hiding from his neighbors: the Donners, the Murrays, old Mrs. Lannister. *And what the hell for?* he wondered. *I'm just trying to protect my own wife, for God's sake.* But he knew the answer as soon as the question formed in his mind: Yes, he was trying to protect his wife. And from what? A vampire. Would his neighbors *ever* understand that? Would Faye? How long had it taken *him* to believe the lurker actually existed, even after seeing it with his own eyes? There was no rational way to explain it to someone. No sane way.

Well, screw them, he decided. *We'll take care of the problem, and they can go on living their safe little lives.* Never knowing that their safety was little more than a paper-thin illusion.

Sands stared at his home, knowing that he couldn't go back. He wondered how things had ever gotten this far—not the insane things that he'd begun to see and hear, but the creeping, progressive destruction of his contentment. Had it really been that slow in coming, or had he simply not noticed until it was too late? His frustration mounted as he sat there; his home of two decades was across the street but inaccessible, everything he saw familiar yet foreign. Through the living room windows and stained glass transom over the front door, he could see warm light emanating.

That would be the lamp on the table in the foyer. Faye's mother had given them that lamp as a house-warming gift. It was hideous. Douglas had gone so far as to "accidentally" break it once, but Faye had insisted on gluing it back together. Now the bulb didn't fit tightly, and the finial was slightly askew. A second accident, however, had always seemed too risky. *I should have smashed it when I got my stuff on New Year's Eve,* he thought. But that was not the kind of fight that he and Faye had; their arguments were not tumultuous affairs of shouting and breaking things. They favored innuendo and feints within feints. Their marriage had long been a battle of misdirection.

By the time Julia returned to the car, the interior was noticeably cooler, and Sands' mood was as sour as it could be. "Home One, here. All clear so far," she said.

"*Gotcha, Home One,*" Nathan promptly responded.

Julia took off her headset and placed it in her lap. She motioned for Sands to turn his off, which he did. "Tomorrow you should call in to work," she told him. "That, or go in. You missed last Thursday and Friday. They'll be wondering—"

"Stop telling me what to do," he snapped at her—despite the fact that he knew she was right. He hadn't even thought about work, or the fact that tomorrow would be Monday. The old parameters of his life had ceased to hold meaning for him: his marriage, his job, something as basic as the days of the week.

Julia stiffened. "All right," she said, obviously forcing herself to keep her voice down. Still, her words came fast and furious: "That's about all I'm going to take. We've been trying to take care of people who are important to you, and I personally have saved you *two* trips to the hospital. If you don't want to so much as say thank you, that's fine. I can live with that. I can accept the fact that you're a self-absorbed, skirt-chasing, jerk mired in permanent adolescence, but if you're going to be part of this operation, you damn well better be ready to listen and learn, because as you've seen, when things go wrong, they can go incredibly, *deadly* wrong. I am sorry that your marriage isn't working out, or didn't work out, or whatever, but I've been through a failed marriage too. I've lost a husband and a son, my little Timothy. So you can blame the world and hate everyone else for your problems if you want, but I can do without your attitude."

"I'm sorry you lost a son," Sands said in a voice equally as angry as Julia's. His words shocked him as much as they did her, and somehow sucked the hostility from the environment almost completely. Sands continued in a more reasonable, almost sheepish tone: "I lost a son. We...we lost a son. Faye and I."

Julia looked away from him. He could see her swallow. "I'm sorry," she said.

"You're right," Sands said. "I need to call work tomorrow."

They sat in silence for quite a while. Sands turned his headset back on, but there was no talk from the others to distract him. The earlier flurries had ended, but the wind was starting to pick up. Sands tried to ignore the trees and shrubs bending and gyrating; he tried not to listen to the intermittent moaning. He didn't hear the bone-chilling sound, the small innocent voice. He closed his eyes, well aware that he shouldn't, that he and Julia were there to watch. But he couldn't bring himself to look at his own home again. He was too terrified that he would see a small figure walking across the street in the dead of night, a small hand reaching for him.

Sands forced his eyes to open. He wondered if Julia still saw her little boy—the way that he did Adam. She didn't sound as if she'd lost him to divorce. Sands looked at her, but she was intent on the house. He wanted to ask her, but he didn't dare. The question was too personal, and what the asking revealed about him too uncomfortable. He finally managed to look again at his home. There was no little boy in the street, no voice on the wind. But for how long would that remain true? How many hours could he sit here, so close to the place he'd already fled more than once?

He grasped for any distraction—and seized on one, despite renewed pain it might cause Julia. "What happened to Albert's body?" he asked her.

Julia, lost to her own somber thoughts until he spoke, was not cheered by the question. "We cremated him," she said.

"Did the police—?"

"The police don't know. No one else knows."

Sands was taken aback by that. "What do you mean no one else knows? He's dead. How can no one else know? I would think the people at the crematorium would have noticed."

"John has friends," Julia said, frowning at Sands' sarcasm. "It's taken care of. People will figure out he's missing eventually, but no one will know what happened. If the police ever start asking around, you'll have to be among those who know only that he's missing, since you were staying with him."

"Good God," Sands said under his breath. "So he'll just vanish. Doesn't he have family…?"

"He doesn't, but even if he did, it'd have to be the same way, Douglas. The hunt takes precedence over everything else: family, friends, work. It has to," she stressed.

"But I need to call about work." The skepticism was slowly creeping back into his tone of voice.

"If you plan on keeping your job, you have to cover yourself. Alibis, good reasons for missing work." Julia shrugged. Everyone, it seemed to Sands, had appropriated Hetger's gesture. "You don't *have* to keep your job, but it might be a good idea. It's not easy living on nothing. Some of us have investments. I just sold a house. I'm living off that. For now."

"Doesn't sound like a great retirement plan."

"None of us is planning on retirement."

Sands didn't like the way Julia said that. Did she mean that the battle would never be over, or something more ominous, more in keeping with Albert's fate? Before Sands had an opportunity to pursue that question—or to decide if he wanted to pursue it—the headset in Julia's lap crackled to life.

"*Rental One here. We see him. Repeat. We see him.*"

Sands reached to turn his headset on, but Julia stopped him. She stared at her own as if it were a snake poised to strike. "Just listen," she whispered. "If there's talk on the line, it might hear."

Sands didn't understand how that might happen, unless the lurker were standing right next to

Clarence and Jason. The voice from the headset was clear enough to Sands and Julia, but they were in a small, enclosed space. But he took Julia's word for it and just listened.

There was nothing to listen *to* for several minutes. Six, to be exact. But they seemed to stretch out forever and ever. In the middle of this intense silence, Sands suddenly had to go to the bathroom very badly.

Julia hardly moved the whole time. She didn't take her eyes from the headset. "If it were just watching from the abandoned building," she whispered, "they would've said that. It must have been moving, passing near them. Probably approaching the building to climb the wall. If it does what it did before."

"Then what are we waiting for?" Sands whispered urgently in return. He wasn't sure how sensitive the microphone was, what volume of speech would activate it. The last thing he wanted was to say something stupid and get someone—even Clarence or Jason—killed. The next to the last thing he wanted was to stay there knowing that the lurker was climbing Melanie's building, working its way toward her window. "Let's *go*. It's there. Faye's safe. She doesn't need us." Julia shushed him, but Sands wasn't about to give up. "*They* might need us!" He made sure to keep his voice lower than Julia's. She was closer to the mike than he was—but what if his deeper voice carried further or resonated more? He tried to keep silent, but it was a losing battle. "*Let's go*."

"They're only going to watch," Julia whispered. "That's all *it's* done so far. It hasn't shown any signs of—"

"*Oh, hell! It's gone in!*" came Clarence's voice, followed by confused rustling sounds.

"*It broke the glass door, the sliding door!*" Jason said, much more loudly. "*We're going in!*"

Julia quickly put on her headset. Sands clicked his on. He heard more rustling sounds, Clarence and Jason in motion, snow crunching underfoot, breathing.

"Julia," Sands said through clenched teeth, "let's go! Now!"

"*No time, Home Two,*" Hetger's voice buzzed. "*No names either,*" he said curtly.

Julia put her hand over her mike. "It would be over before we got there," she said, but she was far from taking this in stride. Her left hand was white-knuckled on the steering wheel, just as both of Sands' hands were wrapped around his baseball bat.

He could picture the lurker with its hands around Melanie's throat. He couldn't listen to this; he wanted to rip the headset off but couldn't make himself. "We've got to get there!"

Footsteps through the earpiece, but not the sound of feet crunching through snow. A more solid impact. The steps. And then the tenor changed as Clarence and Jason reached the breezeway.

"Oh, hell!" Sands reached for the keys in the ignition. Julia knocked his hand away.

A loud thud. Then a gunshot! Sands and Julia started as one. Screaming. A woman screaming. *Melanie.* One of the men was shouting too, but the words were garbled. More screams. Another explosion of gunfire. Glass shattering.

"*Come on!*" one of them shouted. Sands wasn't sure if it was Clarence or Jason.

Douglas was trying to listen beyond the male voice, to hear if Melanie was still screaming. He thought he heard her. Was she hurt? If she was screaming, then she was still alive. But was it really her? Was it what he *wanted* to hear?

Footsteps in the breezeway again. And heavy breathing. Stairs. "*It went out there! Look! That way!*" It was Clarence, excited but in control, giving Jason instructions: "*You see that? Fourth floor. With the tarp.*"

"*I see it.*"

"*Let's go. Stick with me.*"

"What about Melanie?" Sands said urgently, trying not to yell into the mike.

There was only the heavy breathing and the sounds of hurried movement at first, then: "*She's okay. I think.*" It was Jason.

"He *thinks?*" This time Sands did yell. "What do you mean you *think?*"

"*Home Two, quiet or off the line. Your choice,*" Hetger said.

"*Rental One and Two, clear the area as quickly as possible,*" said Nathan. "*I've got 9-1-1 on the way.*"

"She could be bleeding to death!" Sands shouted. "She needs help now!"

Julia ripped the headset off of him. They were ready to argue, but another crash over the headsets caught their attention. "*We're in,*" Jason said. Sands knew exactly where they were. The abandoned building, the fourth-floor apartment with the blue tarp covering the hole where the sliding door and a balcony should be. "*We see the trail. It goes...hell, it goes down the hole in the crawl space, behind the water heater.*"

"*S and D?*" came Clarence's voice.

"Yes," Hetger said immediately, no hesitancy or indecisiveness now. "*Rental One and Two, proceed from your end. Home One and Two, move to site thirty-three. Do you copy?"*

"Home One and Two, copy," Julia said.

"Rental One and Two, copy."

"Rentals, hurry it up," Nathan added. *"I'm on the scanner. Cops there in less than two."*

"Loud and clear, Sugar Daddy."

"What the hell are they talking about?" Sands asked Julia. "What's site thirty-three? What's S and D?"

Julia tossed his headset back to him and cranked the engine. "Site thirty-three is where we're going right now. S and D is 'Search and Destroy.'" She seemed worried but determined as they roared away from the snow-covered curb.

CHAPTER 34

Julia drove back toward Southside as fast as she could without attracting police attention. At this point, a mere speeding ticket could prove disastrous in more ways than one: she and Sands could end up in jail, and the other hunters could end up dead.

"Pull down the backseat and get the cases up from the trunk," Julia told him. "There's a crowbar too. Get that."

Sands grumbled as he climbed over the seat and was tossed around by the unexpected careening of the car over icy roads.

"*Scanner report,*" Nathan's voice crackled over the headset, which Sands had left on the front seat. "*Officer Friendly has arrived. The girl is fine. Repeat: fine. No ambulance called. She probably didn't even see our fang.*"

"Which means Officer Friendly will be looking for our boys," Julia added.

"*We're at site six,*" Jason said. "*Friendly ain't gonna follow us down here.*"

"*Don't be too sure,*" Hetger cautioned. "*Sugar Daddy, keep an ear out for any talk of K-9. Could be trouble.*"

"*Will do.*"

As he fumbled with the seat and the plastic cases from the trunk, Sands told himself over and over again: *She's okay. Melanie's okay. Thank God. She's okay.* Knowing that she was safe almost made up for those agonizing moments of visualizing the fanged creature making its way toward Melanie's apartment, climbing the wall, of picturing the razor teeth slicing her throat. The gunshots had stopped his heart cold. His own encounters with the lurker had been horrible enough, but listening, helpless, not knowing, was far worse. Adrenaline was coursing through his body; he fought to control the pronounced trembling of his hands.

As Sands finally maneuvered the crossbow case through the opening from the trunk, Julia made a hard right, costing him his balance and sending him crashing against the window.

"Sorry," Julia said. "We're almost there."

Site thirty-three, Sands learned shortly and to his considerable dismay, was a manhole leading into the municipal sewer system. "Which building?" he'd asked when the car came to a stop.

"No building." Julia pointed at the manhole cover.

"We're going *down there?*"

Julia had parked half a block away, but of course *now* there were a few other cars driving along the street, so she and Sands had to wait. After slipping several of the quarrels into a side pouch, Julia slipped on her knapsack and tried, with little success, to tuck the crossbow under her coat; she was simply too small a person to conceal the bulky weapon convincingly.

"Here," Sands said, handing her the Louisville Slugger and taking the crossbow. "Let me carry that until we get out of sight."

"Thanks. Give me the crowbar too."

Considering how fast people usually drove, Sands couldn't believe the *ages* it seemed to take for the other cars to pass by, turn a corner, drive out of sight. Then, just as Sands opened his door, another car came into view, and they had to wait longer.

"Um…" Sands began, determined to take advantage of the maddening delay. "What exactly are we going to do once we get down there?" He was wearing the headset but turned it off before he spoke.

Julia took a deep breath. She covered her microphone, rather than turning off the set. "We're going to try to box it in: Clarence and Jason from the north, us closing in from the southwest, John from the southeast. Over the last two weeks, we've been watching your friends *and* doing a little scouting, in case it came to this. We were willing to observe as long as it didn't take aggressive actions. It was hard enough convincing Clarence to go along with that. But after tonight…"

"Search and Destroy," Sands said. Julia nodded. "You couldn't have mapped out all the sewers," he added.

"Didn't have to. Nathan found schematics. We pinpointed a series of choke points where tunnel series converge, scouted out those spots. But if this thing can squeeze itself into lines smaller than a human should be able to fit in, we're screwed."

"It'll get away," Sands said remembering how quickly the lurker had moved when he'd seen it. "They'll lose it down there. It's too fast."

"They don't have to keep it in sight," Julia said. "Clarence must have touched it. They're following a visible trail."

"What do you…? What kind of visible trail?"

"You'll know if you see it," Julia assured him. "Kind of looks like smoke, but it's not. You'll know. It's something Clarence can do…like when we see those things and just *know*."

"And like you helping me recover. That's Clarence's gift?"

"Right. One of them. Gift, edge, whatever you want to call it."

Sands nodded. He tried to absorb all that. *I'm following a smoky trail, that's not really smoke, tracking a vampire through the sewers so I can kill it with a crossbow and a baseball bat.* On second thought, he decided not to examine the details too closely at the moment.

"The headsets have GPS locators built in," Julia continued. "Nathan will direct us and coordinate our movements."

"And John is going down by himself?" Sands asked, at the same time thinking that nobody could pay him enough to do that. Then he realized that he *had* done that—not in the sewers, but he'd faced the lurker alone and survived. Barely.

Julia didn't answer this time. She was scanning the street. The last traffic was clearing. "Let's go."

Sands didn't have an easy time concealing the crossbow either. He was sure that, had anyone seen him, they would have thought that he looked incredibly like someone trying to hide a lethal weapon under his coat. Thankfully, Julia knew precisely what she wanted to do. She attacked the edges of the manhole with the crowbar. In less than thirty seconds, she'd broken through the ice and packed snow and pried the cover open. "We've been clearing a few of these off every few nights," she told Sands as she flicked on a flashlight from her knapsack and began to climb down the ladder. "We never would have gotten through all winter's worth of ice and snow in time."

"Should I pull the cover back on?" Sands called down after her as he began his descent.

"Unless you want John Q. Public and Officer Friendly following us down."

"I was thinking more about us getting out if we need to." He handed down the crossbow and struggled with the manhole cover, all the while precariously keeping his balance on the ladder and picturing the next car ready to turn the corner any second. Finally, the cover clanked into place.

At the bottom of the ladder, Sands tried to catch his breath, but he quickly found that breathing deeply almost made him gag. In the enclosed darkness, the stench of decay was overpowering.

"You'll get used to it," Julia said, covering her mike. "A little bit." She gave Sands the bat.

He followed her lead, covering his mike when he wanted to speak to her; he didn't want to miss something coming from Nathan or the others. Sands tapped the edge of the crossbow. "How have you hidden that thing before? I could barely fit it under my jacket."

"I haven't used it before," Julia said.

"What do you mean?"

"I mean that I haven't used it before, except for target practice. This is our first vampire."

"Our first vampire," Sands repeated. The words seemed to echo down the tunnel. "*Our*, meaning…?"

"Meaning everybody. Jason has seen one before, even found out its name, but we haven't come across one otherwise."

All of Sands' reservations, which he'd been holding down with relative success, came flooding to the surface. He suddenly wondered if Julia, if *any* of them, knew what the hell they were doing.

✤   ✤   ✤   ✤   ✤

"*Rental Two here. We're approaching choke point A.*"

"*I'm picking you up, Rental Two,*" Nathan said. "*Target status?*"

"*It's still running south,*" Clarence responded.

Sands and Julia were moving north and east. The major sewer lines were laid out in a grid pattern, one line for every few blocks above, with smaller, inaccessible pipes servicing many areas. Every so often, Sugar Daddy directed Homes One and Two a few blocks east, but their primary heading was north. The city stretched farther north and south along the axis of the Iron River than it did east and west. Hetger, conversely, was edging west as he moved north. The plan was for the hunters to converge on the lurker and then take it five on one.

But what if somebody dies before we converge? Sands wondered.

The sewers were cold, but not so much as the streets above. The constant burbling of water belied the foul nature of the polluted stream that ran under—and over—foot. During the spring, these tunnels would be rushing torrents, filled by runoff from the melting snow. Sands' boots were not waterproof enough to keep his feet dry, and in places the putrid water rose to ankle-deep. As one by one his toes lost their feeling, the black water reminded him of Albert's floating, lifeless body, while the stench evoked memories of the lurker and a dumpster overflowing with festering garbage.

Julia had given Sands a spare flashlight from her knapsack. As he shined the light down each side tunnel, he expected suddenly to see the fiendish sneer of the lurker; he kept thinking that he heard the scraping of the razor teeth. All that any of them knew about the creature's location was what they could glean from Clarence and Jason's brief reports and Nathan's subsequent triangulation.

"*Rental Two here. We're approaching choke point B. Bloodsucker still heading south.*"

"*We're gonna close down B.*" Clarence said.

"*Understood,*" Nathan answered. "*Homes One and Two, Base One, hold your positions. You're each about…half a mile from B, southwest and southeast. A little less than that from each other.*"

"*Home One. We're holding position.*"

"*Base One here. Holding position. Everybody stay on your toes. If bloodsucker didn't already know it has company, it will after this.*"

After this? Sands wondered. *After what?* Then he felt the tremor.

The tunnel rumbled beneath his feet. The soundwave, too, barreled through the tunnels like a locomotive. For a moment, Sands expected to see the single light of an engine coming straight for him. But the sound and the vibrations faded away.

"What the hell was that?" Sands exclaimed—just as a second tremor rocked the tunnel.

"That," Julia said, "*was* choke point B."

Sands couldn't believe what he was hearing; he couldn't believe how matter-of-factly Julia was telling him. "They *blew it up?*" he asked. "With what—dynamite?"

"Grenades."

"Oh. My. God."

"*Homes One and Two, Base One, on your toes,*" Nathan reiterated. "*It's getting close.*"

Sands wasn't sure which frightened him more: the prospect of running headlong into the lurker, or the idea of Clarence and Jason lobbing grenades in the sewers. Douglas' hands had mostly stopped trembling now, but his heart was racing; he didn't know how it could work that hard and not explode.

As intimidating as making their way through the tunnels was, holding their position was worse. Sands and Julia shone their lights along passages to the north and east. And waited. The cold seeped into their bones from the ground up, and the stench of the sewers permeated their every breath.

"*Listen up, everybody,*" Clarence said after a few minutes. "*I think we got its attention. It's turned east. Coming your way, Base One.*"

East. Toward Hetger. Sands' breath caught in his throat. "If they have a trail to follow," he asked Julia, irritated by his own intense worry, "why the hell didn't we just stay together and track the damn thing down?"

"We don't know how long the trail will last. Could be days. Might be hours, or not that long. This way, if it disappears, we still have a chance."

A chance to all get killed, he thought.

"*Base One,*" Nathan came on, "*reverse direction. I don't want that thing getting around to the north, behind you.*"

"*Will do,*" Hetger said.

Sands felt again the helplessness he'd suffered in the car, as he'd listened to Clarence and Jason. His mind had been full of images of the lurker and what it was doing to Melanie. Now he saw the beast creeping through the black tunnels, stalking John. And all that the rest of them would hear would be a few screams, maybe cursing—and then nothing, except each other grunting and breathing hard as they rushed to the scene, too late.

Still, he and Julia were holding their position. It was driving him crazy. He experimented worriedly, holding the flashlight and the bat. He'd be forced to swing one-handed again; at least he'd be able to use his right hand this time. *We should have gone to Wal-Mart*, he thought suddenly. *I should've bought a gun. Lots of guns. Big guns.* Standing by Julia, with their pathetic beams of light, Sands felt incredibly small, and the darkness was immense.

"*Uh-oh*," someone's voice crackled over the headset. That got Sands' attention in a hurry. "*Rental Two here. We've got a, uh…crack. A hole in the tunnel wall.*"

"*To the north*," Clarence added. "*That show up on your map, Sugar Daddy?*"

"*Are you standing in front of it?*"

"*Right.*"

"*No. It's not on the schematics. Is that where the trail—?*"

"*Yes*," Clarence said. "*It went in. Looks like it's time to crawl. Rental Two, no point in you crawling up my ass. Wait here till I see where this is going.*"

"*What if you come up on it?*" Jason asked, worried.

"*Then I blow its head off*," Clarence said without hesitation.

"*I copy that*," Nathan said. "*Home One and Two, move east two, maybe three, intersections, so you can support Base One.*"

"Loud and clear," Sands said, relieved not to need to sit still any longer. He and Julia hurried on toward Hetger.

"*Hell*," came Clarence's voice, "*this thing turns back on itself. Goes straight up then does a one-eighty.*"

"*If it goes back above ground, we've lost it*," Jason said.

"*Nah*," Clarence said. "*Depends on how long the trail's good. We can track it up top, just more people to watch out for.*"

"*Rental One*," Nathan broke in, "*have you crawled back out?*"

"*Nope. Still going forward.*"

"Okay. You must be directly over Rental Two. Still see the trail?"

"Yep. I still got it."

The tunnel Sands and Julia were following dog-legged to the south and then east again. At the next intersection, Sands, before he realized what he was seeing, stepped through a stream of smoke hanging in the air and running along the north-south passage—but the smoke did not dissipate or react at all to his passing. "What the hell...?"

"We've got the trail right here!" Julia said into her headset. "In the north-south tunnel. This has to be more recent than Rental's." She shined her light anxiously first one direction and then the other. Sands, realizing now what she was saying, did the same.

"Which way is it going?" Jason asked.

"I said north-south," Julia responded.

"But which way?"

"How the hell should I know?" she snapped.

She knew soon enough. In the space of a few seconds, as she and Sands scanned the four expanses of tunnel—empty tunnel, darkness, empty tunnel, darkness—the beast was on them.

Suddenly Sands was stumbling backwards. He managed to shield himself with the Louisville Slugger, but it was knocked from his grasp. The bat clattered off a concrete wall, landed in the water.

A voice was buzzing in his ear: "Rentals, one intersection west, then south! Base One, due west! Now! Now!" Sands didn't have time to absorb the meaning of the words. He intuited that they weren't for him. Both his and Julia's flashlights were now lying in the muck, casting long, threatening shadows.

The lurker was throttling Julia. Its claws were digging into her throat, cutting off her air. It would kill her quickly—unless Sands stopped it. He grabbed the creature by the shoulders and pulled it from her—actually flung it against the far wall! For only a split second, Sands stood frozen, astounded at what he'd just done—it was all the time the lurker needed.

It leapt at him, lashed out and raked him across the face with a clawed hand. Sands crumpled and fell headlong into the fetid water. The lurker pounced again. It lifted Sands by his hair and drew back its claws. The beast's red eyes glared from merely inches away. Its nose twitched at the scent of the blood running down his face.

Poised to strike, a sudden impact jarred the creature's body. It turned, and Sands saw the crossbow bolt embedded in the back of the lurker's shoulder. It shoved him to the ground and turned back toward Julia.

Shoot it again! Sands wanted to shout as he tried to catch himself, but his jaw was numb and his mouth filling with blood. *Reload! Shoot it again!*

But instead of reloading the crossbow, Julia pointed at the fanged beast. "Get away!" she shouted at it.

A magnificent spark ignited in the air between them as the lurker advanced. The monster stopped suddenly, as if momentarily stunned. It stepped toward her again. Another spark, and the beast stumbled back. It opened its razor-toothed maw and hissed—then it sneered, a chilling, mocking expression on that grotesque face. It whirled and grabbed again at Sands. He was just climbing to his feet and had no hope of eluding the beast—

An explosion erupted behind Sands' head. A portion of the lurker's chest ripped open, spraying Sands with blood and bits of flesh. The gunshot rang in his ears.

The lurker staggered back from the force of the shot, but kept its feet. It recovered incredibly quickly and leapt at Sands—

—Over his head. And landed on Jason. Two more shots rang out. Sands saw at least one tear through the back of the lurker, but the beast seemed unfazed. It had Jason. It was tearing meaty chunks from his face with its razor teeth. Sands could hear Jason's muffled and frantic screams for help.

Then another was voice shouting: "Get out of the way!" Sands spun and saw Julia pointing the crossbow at him—past him, but he was in the way. "Move!" He sloshed to the side of the tunnel, but as he did, something caught in his back. The spasms were beginning, the muscles in his lower back seizing up.

No! Damn it! Sands staggered out of Julia's line of fire, but the lurker had turned and was using Jason as a shield. His chewed and bloody face was barely recognizable—except for his eyes, wide with pain. The lurker held him upright, now facing them, with one gangly arm wrapped around him, claws jabbed knuckle-deep into Jason's chest.

Julia tried to take aim, but it was no use, and as she hesitated, the lurker rooted around with his claws inside Jason. Jason thrashed and screamed but couldn't get free. His mouth seemed to be stretched impossibly wide—then Sands realized that much of Jason's cheek was ripped away.

Giving up on getting a clear shot, Julia rushed forward. She thrust the crossbow at Sands rather than dropping it in the water, and then reached for something else in her knapsack. Sands tried to charge forward with her—they *had* to save Jason!—but each step jerked the muscles in his back into a tighter knot. He tried to ignore the pain but found himself almost doubled over in just a few steps as Julia rushed ahead.

"Get away from him!" she shouted. Another burst of sparks from nowhere filled the air as she approached the lurker. The beast cringed—but seemed unhurt this time, and when it realized that, the bloodthirsty sneer again contorted its features.

By now, Julia had what she wanted from her knapsack—the silver flask. She yanked open the stopper and doused both Jason and the lurker with liquid—*water*, Sands knew, unless she'd changed it.

The lurker didn't flinch this time, nor did it seem affected in the least. Jason was still wide-eyed but silent now, his ragged mouth hanging agape. Julia was shocked at the impotence of the water—and more shocked as the lurker slipped its hand deeper into Jason's churned torso, snapped loose a bone, and jabbed the rib's jagged edge into her chest. She collapsed to her knees.

What had begun as a knot of muscles in Sands back was changing, growing, spreading like a ravenous tumor, sending shoots to wrap around his spine, his stomach, his lungs. A burning like he'd never felt rose from the pit of his gut. The miraculous strength with which he'd flung the lurker across the tunnel withered away to nothing. His legs could barely hold him. He watched helplessly as Julia slumped to the ground, as if she were sinking into the foul waters. Sands couldn't breathe. His lungs were crushed from within and the stench of decay assaulted him from without. He felt powerless against the encroaching darkness of these sewers, of the lurker, of the creatures that would claim his world. Lights danced before his eyes.

He thought at first that the lights were of his own creation, carrion-feeders of pain and nausea, but other lights were shining in the tunnel—other flashlights. "You're not going *anywhere*," he heard John Hetger say—to the lurker, Sands realized after a moment. John had the beast fixed with a withering glare, and amazingly enough the lurker seemed unable to disobey. It neither attacked nor fled, but it did still hold Jason, wide-eyed and limp. Clarence, too, was by Hetger. They must have arrived at nearly the same instant. Clarence held the second light and a sawed-off shotgun, but like Julia, he didn't have a clear shot: Sands, Julia, and Jason were all three in his way.

Sands staggered closer to the lurker. He couldn't stand by and watch Jason and Julia killed. But with each step, the pain in his belly grew more intense. He could no longer feel his legs. The spasms in his lower back had spread the length of his spine, and the burning in his lungs made him dizzy. Somewhere in the depths of his soul, the world that he had known gave its final death knells. Nothing that had been true for him was true anymore. The life he had known no longer existed. But if life, all life, was to flee him, Sands was determined that his broken body and spirit would drag the lurker with him.

Staggering unsteadily toward the beast, a violent convulsion wracked his body. The pain and the fire rushed up from his soul, which was torn asunder. Sands reeled toward the lurker, cursing his own weakness as his legs failed him. He felt his hands and knees submerged in the cold wastes. The primordial sludge threatened to overwhelm him, to pull him down and drown him. The fire within him was a great churning he could no longer contain. Sands' body heaved, and he vomited forth from his mouth and nose a gaseous stream—a vapor that was the final vestige of his dying world.

He felt like a distant observer as the vapor, a blood-red cloud, engulfed Jason and the lurker. The creature bellowed in agony and tossed Jason like a rag doll to the side. It thrashed and screeched as its skin began to cook, simmering and steaming. The hiss and the stink of burning flesh filled the tunnel. Still, the lurker never looked away from John. Its red eyes glared hatred and pain and fear, but never turned away.

Then Sands' body was heaving again. This time bile and clumped matter burned his throat and spewed into the water, splashing his face. The lurker danced like a man on fire, burning away to nothing. Sands felt the concussion of a shotgun blast, and then another. The uppermost portion of the lurker was no longer. The creature had ceased to exist from the shoulders up. An arm splashed into the water, hissing, sputtering. The lurker's torso and legs continued their macabre dance.

Then the darkness crowded away all else—the darkness and the foul, fetid waters of decay.

CHAPTER 35

The rhythmic *ta-tump*, *ta-tump*, *ta-tump* of tires on cracked pavement eased Sands back to consciousness. From the sound and the vibration, he came to notice his face propped against a window. Next he was confronted by the dull but deep throbbing in his face; he touched his fingers to his cheek and felt a damp bandage. He was less worried about his face a moment later, when the expansive ache in his chest and stomach asserted itself. Sands grunted.

"Welcome back."

Sands looked to his left, toward the driver's seat, and recognized Hetger's profile. Douglas quickly became more fully cognizant of his surroundings: They were in an unfamiliar car, driving somewhere, on a large road, an interstate. He twisted around in his seat and tried to ignore the pain in his back. Clarence was in the seat behind Hetger, staring silently out the window into darkness. Julia was behind Sands. The shoulder-strap seatbelt held her upright as she slept—Sands hoped she was sleeping. Her coat covered what he assumed was a bulky bandage on her chest.

"You're going to need to take some vacation time from work," John said to Sands. "If you plan on trying to keep your job."

"Where's Jason?" Sands asked. He wasn't ready to look to the future, not with the present in such stark doubt.

"He's dead," Clarence said flatly. His breath fogged the window he was looking out, but he didn't seem to notice.

"Is Julia all right?" Sands asked more quietly, afraid he might wake her.

"She will be," John said.

Sands sighed with relief, but not deeply; the breath shot pain through his chest. "Did we leave Jason…his body?"

Hetger nodded. "We had two of you to carry, and not a lot of time. It's not easy climbing out of the sewers with bodies over your shoulders and not being noticed. Everybody was out: fire crews, paramedics, police."

"Then those *were* grenades," Sands said.

"Choke point ain't much good if you don't close it," Clarence said.

"And the…thing, the vampire?"

"Dead," Hetger said. He was silent for perhaps half a mile, then added: "Jason would have been glad of that. He thinks it was a vampire that killed his sister. *Thought* that. And I have some questions about the death of a friend. So this one's for George, too."

They lapsed into silence again. Sands gave himself back to the *ta-tump, ta-tump* of the tires and the drone of the car on the highway, but now that he was conscious, there was no escape from the various physical pains, and from the mental fatigue of post-adrenaline rush. He felt like he'd been wrung out and left in a wrinkled heap. He knew that there was little reason other than dumb luck that he was still alive; he felt in Jason's absence the enormity of what he and these other hunters were up against. "We never should've gone down there," he said.

Hetger glanced at him in the dark. "That monster is dead. Your wife and the girl are safe."

"And Jason's dead."

John nodded. "We all know the chance we're taking. I thought you did too."

Sands didn't say anything. He had known. More than once, he'd willingly put his well-being, his life, on the line for the sake of Faye's and Melanie's safety. He had known. He'd abandoned much of his hubris after his first face-to-face encounter with the lurker. It was the confidence of Albert and Julia and Hetger and the others, with their computers and headsets and can-do attitudes, that had led Sands to believe that the unnatural creatures could be dealt with. *And look where that got Albert*, he thought. *And Jason, now.* He almost said it aloud, almost told John how stupid they'd all been. But on this rare occasion, Sands held his tongue—less for desire to spare Hetger's feelings than for the lingering suspicion that Clarence would pull out the sawed-off shotgun and blow Sands' head off.

Why risk it? he decided. The lurker was dead. Sands was done with these people. But what did he have to look ahead to? A life with Faye seemed doubtful, and he wasn't sure that he wanted that, regardless. He suspected his ties with Melanie were severed, and that was probably for the best. He'd be carrying around the memories of Albert and of Jason—even if Jason *had* been a jerk, he'd tried to save Sands' life, and died in the attempt. Did it have to have happened that way? Sands wondered. He remembered suddenly Julia pouring water over the lurker. What the hell was that supposed to accomplish? He had a sinking feeling that his having borrowed the silver flask might have taken on tragic overtones. But he couldn't be sure. Would he ever again, Sands wondered, be sure of anything?

The road of the future appeared singularly unappealing at the moment, so he shifted his attention instead to the more immediate, the more literal road. Interstate 75, a sign proclaimed. *We're going to Flint?* he wondered. *Who the hell wants to go to Flint?*

"Where are we headed?" he asked.

"Away," was all Clarence said.

"There was an awful lot of police activity," John said. "We thought it'd be best to get away for a little while, let the hubbub die down. They're going to find Jason's body, too. That won't help."

"But where are we *going?*"

"Clarence has a cousin. We can stay with her for a few days. Hopefully she'll be willing to be our alibi, say we've been there the past few days, if there turns out to be a need for that."

"You mean if the police come looking for us," Sands said.

"Yes. If anything ties Jason or Melanie or any of that to us."

"What about Nathan?"

"Nathan has software that will provide definitive proof that he was online in a chatroom all night."

That all sounded fairly reasonable to Sands—but then again, chasing a vampire through the sewers had seemed fairly reasonable a few hours ago. As they drove north, the wind whistled through the seal around one of the windows. The sound was high-pitched, a literal whistle, not like the moaning the wind made when it whipped around the back corner of Douglas' house and over the snow-covered swimming pool. He was still dubious about spending more time with these people, especially Clarence, who seemed to have lapsed deeper into his mostly unresponsive silence, but listening to the wind, Sands was far from in a hurry to return to Iron Rapids.

Other World of Darkness novels
by Gherbod Fleming

In the Clan Novel Series
Clan Novel: Gangrel
Clan Novel: Ventrue
Clan Novel: Assamite
Clan Novel: Brujah
Clan Novel: Nosferatu

Trilogy of the Blood Curse
The Devil's Advocate
The Winnowing
Dark Prophecy

THE RAGE RISES...

Garou — the werewolves of legend. Once they fostered humankind, once they hunted it. Now the Garou must choose their battles and their allies wisely, for the Red Star burns in the Umbral sky. Can the Apocalypse itself be far behind?

Will the tribes set aside their differences to confront an ancient enemy in Eastern Europe, or be consumed by their own Rage?

The seven-book Tribe Novel Series begins with:

Tribe Novels:
Shadow Lords
& Get of Fenris

February 2001.

WEREWOLF
THE APOCALYPSE

White Wolf
PUBLISHING

The Vampire
Clan Novel Series ....

Clan Novel: Toreador
These artists are the most sophisticated of the Kindred.

Clan Novel: Tzimisce
Fleshcrafters, experts of the arcane, and the most cruel of Sabbat vampires.

Clan Novel: Gangrel
Feral shapeshifters distanced from the society of the Kindred.

Clan Novel: Setite
The much-loathed serpentine masters of moral and spiritual corruption.

Clan Novel: Ventrue
The most political of vampires, they lead the Camarilla.

Clan Novel: Lasombra
The leaders of the Sabbat and the most Machiavellian of all Kindred.

Clan Novel: Assamite
The most feared clan, for they are assassins of both vampires and mortals.

Clan Novel: Ravnos
These devilish gypsies are not welcomed by the Camarilla, nor tolerated by the Sabbat.

Clan Novel: Malkavian
Thought insane by other Kindred, they know that within madness lies wisdom.

Clan Novel: Giovanni
Still a respected part of the mortal world, this mercantile clan is also home to necromancers.

Clan Novel: Brujah
Street-punks and rebels, they are aggressive and vengeful in defense of their beliefs.

Clan Novel: Tremere
The most magical of the clans and the most tightly organized.

Clan Novel: Nosferatu
Horrific to behold, these sneaks know more secrets than the other clans—secrets that will only be revealed in this, the last of the Vampire Clan Novels.